David Ambrose

The Discrete Charm of
Charlie Monk

POCKET
BOOKS

LONDON • SYDNEY • NEW YORK • TOKYO • SINGAPORE • TORONTO

First published in Great Britain by Macmillan, 2000
This edition published by Pocket Books, 2002
An imprint of Simon & Schuster UK Ltd
A Viacom Company

3 5 7 9 10 8 6 4 2

Simon & Schuster UK Ltd
Africa House
64–78 Kingsway
London WC2B 6AH

www.simonsays.co.uk

A CIP catalogue record for this book
is available from the British Library

ISBN 0–7434–1613–9

Printed and bound in Great Britain by
Bookmarque Ltd, Croydon

To Dorthea and Peter Hay – treasured friends,
critics and collaborators

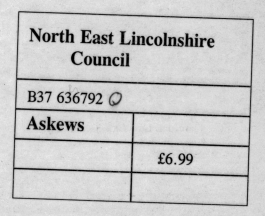

I dreamt I was a butterfly, and didn't know when I awoke if I was a man who had dreamt he was a butterfly, or a butterfly who now dreamt he was a man.

Chuang Tzu's dream
500 years BC

I had to start playing Bond from scratch – not even Ian Fleming knew much about Bond at this time. He has no mother. He has no father. He doesn't come from anywhere and he hadn't been anywhere when he became 007. He was born – kerplump – thirty-three years old.

Sean Connery
Observer,
1 March 1998

PROLOGUE

The middle-aged man seated opposite Susan nodded emphatically, anxious to convince her that he was paying attention and taking in everything she said.

'Of course I understand,' he repeated. 'I'm not stupid. All I'm asking is that somebody tells me what's going on. What am I doing here?'

Susan was careful to maintain eye contact with him as she spoke. 'You've had a viral infection of a very rare kind. It's all cleared up now, and physically you're perfectly well. However, it has damaged a part of your brain which has affected your memory.'

'That's ridiculous. There's nothing wrong with my memory. I know who I am, I know where I live, what I do . . .'

'You remember everything that happened before you were attacked by the virus.'

'But I haven't been sick. I lead a perfectly normal life with my wife and family, and now suddenly I wake up in this place. It's obvious what's happened. I've been kidnapped!'

He was becoming agitated, shifting on his chair, waving his hands and slapping the table to emphasize a point.

'You haven't been kidnapped, Brian. This is a hospital. You're being looked after.'

1

'Why am I wearing these clothes? Where did these clothes come from?' He got to his feet, disdainfully brushing the white cotton smock and trousers he had on.

'They're hospital issue. They're what you always wear in here.'

'How long have I been here? Where's my wife?'

'Your wife's waiting to see you.'

'Well, bring her in, for heaven's sake! Where is she?'

'If you'll wait here, I'll go and get her.' Susan stood up. 'There's just one thing, Brian. You'll find she's changed.'

'Changed? Changed how? What d'you mean?'

'She looks older than you remember her.'

His brow creased with a puzzled frown. 'Why? Why should she look older? Is this some kind of trick? Are you playing a trick on me?'

'It's not a trick, Brian. It's just that you remember her as she was a long time ago, before your illness. The last time you saw her was only three days ago, but the way you remember her is the way she looked twenty years ago.'

He blinked rapidly several times as he stared at her, still frowning. 'I don't understand. Why are you saying all this? You're trying to confuse me.'

She shook her head gently. 'No, just trying to prepare you, Brian. I'll go and bring your wife in now, if you're ready.'

'I wish you would. I have no idea what you're talking about, I don't know what's going on here. I want to see my wife, and I'd be glad if you'd get her.'

There was panic in his voice, as well as the indignant tone of someone who feels he has been badly treated and to whom an apology is overdue. It was the way this conversation between them always ended. The moment she was through the door and out of sight, he wouldn't remember a thing: not a word that had been spoken, nor even the fact that she had been there. Even if she came back after five seconds, it would be as though he had never seen her before.

Susan closed the door behind her and entered an adjoining room where a male nurse sat watching a TV monitor. On it she could see the room she'd just left, with Brian Kay standing with his arms folded defiantly, gazing at the door she'd closed behind her. In a few moments, she knew, a puzzled look would come over his face, rather like someone who'd walked into some room in his house, the kitchen, perhaps, or a bedroom, and suddenly couldn't remember what he'd wanted there. After a moment, he would give up trying and let the mystery drop, then he would go and stare out of the window (which did not open and was unbreakable) until something else happened to distract his attention.

Susan waited, and sure enough, as though he was following the scenario she'd just written in her head, he went over to the window and remained there. Susan went through another door and into a corridor.

As she walked, she caught a glimpse of herself in a glass door, moving with that stately grace that being almost seven months pregnant brought to a woman. At least it did to her. Or, to be precise, she thought of it as a stately grace. To others it may have resembled more a duck-like waddle. She may even have thought such a thing herself in the past. But now, pregnant for the first time, and more thrilled about it than by anything she'd ever done, she decided that 'stately grace' was the only possible description of her progress.

3

In a small, bare side room to the right at the end of the corridor, sitting on a plain, square sofa, was a woman of about fifty with greying hair and a face that must have once been very pretty, but was now lined and drawn with worry. She looked up anxiously as Susan approached her.

'All right, Dorothy,' she said to the older woman, 'if you're ready . . .'

The woman nodded and got to her feet, clutching the purse that had been resting on her lap as though it gave her some measure of confidence for these painful twice-weekly confrontations. The two women started back up the corridor.

'How's it going?' the older woman asked, glancing at the bulge around Susan's midriff.

'You know – good days and bad, the way it's supposed to. At least so the books say.'

Dorothy smiled. 'D'you know if it's a boy or a girl?'

'Boy.'

'Have you picked a name?'

'Christopher. After my husband's father who died last year. Then Amery, after my father. It's an old German name – Almeric originally – used in English since the Norman conquest. Eventually it got over to France and became Amery. But we'll call him Christopher.'

'Nice name. I always liked Christopher.'

They entered the room where the male nurse still sat before his TV monitor. He had been joined by a colleague whom Susan knew slightly. They exchanged a nod of acknowledgement. On the screen Brian Kay could still be seen, gazing out of the window, motionless.

Susan opened the door in the far wall and stood aside to let Dorothy enter. Brian turned to see who had come in, and for some moments gazed at the woman who stood

4

before him without so much as a flicker of recognition in his face.

Eventually she said softly, 'Brian?'

It was usually the voice that made the connection for him. Recognition dawned, and with it came the appalling shock, the realization that something was terribly and inexplicably wrong.

'Dorothy . . .?'

His voice trembled with disbelief, his breath taken away by the completeness of his inability to grasp the moment.

'My God, what's happened? Are you ill? Your face . . .!'

They began again the process of calming and explaining that Dorothy had to endure each time she came to see the man she loved. 'This is Dr Flemyng. She's trying to help you, darling. You have to be patient.'

Brian looked at Susan, as though somehow offended by her presence. 'I've never seen this woman in my life. What d'you mean she's trying to help me? Help me how? What's going on?'

Susan looked back at him with a gentle smile and prepared to go through the tortuous ritual yet again. But at the back of her mind was a nagging thought that she hadn't yet allowed herself to speak about to anyone. She barely even allowed herself to think that maybe, just maybe, the idea that had been playing in her imagination these past few weeks could work.

It would take time, and a good deal of refinement and research, but maybe she had spotted an opening that would provide a way through the cruel armour of his amnesia.

Part One

Part One

1

The sea was a slab of cold grey steel beneath a moonless sky. Only as they descended almost to its surface did it come alive, its ceaseless motion growing more visible with every foot of altitude they lost.

A few yards above the rolling swell, a door was hauled back in the helicopter's side and a blast of cold air hit the four occupants – two pilots, the operator of the winch, and the man in wetsuit and helmet who was to be lowered to the black waters beneath.

Charlie Monk watched as the torpedo-shaped object on which his life would depend for the next few hours descended before him and lay bobbing on the waves, attached to the hovering chopper by a single line. Then he hitched himself into a body-harness and prepared to be swung out into space.

As he descended, he used the line to pull the floating object into position directly beneath him. He dropped on to it like a man astride a motorbike, his legs in the water up to his thighs. Before releasing his harness, he pressed a switch and started up the battery-operated motor. Satisfied that it was running smoothly, he released his harness, detached the line from the dinghy and waved all clear to the chopper. Moments later, it had disappeared into the night, the clatter of its engine replaced by the lazy, timeless sound of wind and waves.

Charlie stretched out on his stomach and fixed his feet into the cavity provided. Then, lying flat along the craft, he began travelling over the water at a little over five knots. The electric motor was virtually silent, and the only proof of its surprising power was the hard slap of water as the tiny craft skimmed and bounced its way across the choppy sea. When he really opened up the throttle it would do far more – up to fifty knots in the right conditions, though out here the ocean was too rough for top speed; the craft would merely bounce and capsize. But if he dipped the nose and ploughed beneath the waves, it would become a supercharged submersible, fast enough to catch, invisibly and silently, just about anything at sea.

A control panel set into the smooth surface of the machine gave him its speed and exact position according to satellite. He calculated that, in ten minutes at most, the lights of the luxury private yacht with which he was to rendezvous should become visible.

He opened up the throttle a fraction. The little craft bucked and slapped the water harder than before. It was an uncomfortable ride, even painful after a while. The trick of enduring it was more than simply to ignore it; what Charlie had been trained to do was empty his mind of everything except the task ahead. His reflexes would take care of the rest. One of his instructors had called it a state of active meditation. Charlie had never been sure what that meant; all he cared was that it worked, helping him curb his impatience despite the adrenalin that was pulsing through his veins.

Another glance at the panel under his chin told him

that the boat he was looking for should be in sight by now. He lifted his gaze to the horizon, but could see nothing. He slipped his night goggles over his eyes – and immediately saw a cluster of lights in the distance, no more than pinpricks in the darkness. The *Lady Alexandra* was exactly where she was supposed to be. He set course to intercept.

The standard manoeuvre was to submerge and approach from behind. On a night like this he could stay on the surface until he was almost level with the vessel; there was little chance of being seen. However, he could save time by diving now and opening up the throttle underwater. He reached down to the side of the craft and pressed a catch to open a panel. From the cavity behind it he pulled out an airline with a mask which he attached to his face.

Moments later his world was transformed into a silent, inky blackness which he cut through with exhilarating speed. The computer kept him on course and would slow him automatically when he drew close to the yacht. It would also negotiate any invisible obstacles picked up by his sensors: sleeping whales, for example, were best avoided.

But tonight his trajectory was swift and direct. When he felt himself decelerate, he looked up through his goggles and saw the hull just ahead, its twin screws, each powered by a thirteen-thousand-horsepower diesel engine, churning through the water. He knew the vessel had set sail from the Canaries and was heading for New York, planning to make landfall at the Ambrose Lighthouse. Although she would be capable of twenty-eight or thirty knots full speed, she could only cover such a distance by keeping her speed to something between

11

twelve and fifteen knots. As he tracked her, he found she was doing thirteen.

Staying beneath the waterline, he brought himself alongside towards the stern. As he closed in, he pressed another switch to inflate an air bag that would cushion his contact with the aluminium hull. From the nose of his craft he extended a steel arm with a suction pad on the end that would hold it in place alongside the yacht until he needed it again. Only then did he kill the motor.

His head broke the surface of the water and he peered cautiously up. He saw that only a handful of cabin windows were lit; it was three a.m. and some of the eight-strong crew would most likely be asleep. The yacht's owner, he knew, had a reputation for working and making phone calls late into the night, so he expected to find him awake, along with anyone he might consider necessary to his comfort and convenience.

So far as he could see, there was no sign of any movement on deck. The yacht's engines had taken on a different note now that he listened to them from above the waterline: a distant, muted hum had replaced the throbbing growl of sheer brute power.

Using two suction pads like the one he had fixed under water to hold his torpedo scooter in place, he began to haul himself up the hull. Each pad was fixed and released by the operation of a tiny valve; the rest was muscle power, each arm and shoulder in turn taking the full weight of his whole body.

When he reached the rail he paused to check again that there was nobody in sight, then left the pads where they were and swung himself over and on to the deck. He had been briefed on the precise layout of the vessel, even studying copies of the builder's plans. He had committed every detail to memory, so that he knew precisely where he was and what to look out for.

He moved swiftly, the blackness of his clothing making him all but invisible. Only the wet footprints he left behind showed that anyone had been there, and in a moment they would disappear. When he reached the double doors that he was looking for, he dropped one hand to his hip and slipped the silenced automatic from its holster. His other hand pushed one of the doors open, and he slipped through, scanning the space inside for signs of movement. There were none.

A staircase appeared ahead of him, reaching a landing ten steps down which then forked into two more flights that doubled back beneath the first one. He took the right fork, then headed down a corridor towards the prow. The concealed lighting provided a soft, luxurious glow. Ahead was a corner, and he could see that the light beyond it was brighter. This meant that there was probably a bodyguard, maybe two, outside the stateroom of the man he was looking for.

He stopped, pressing his back to the wall, listening. The distant vibration of the engines travelled through every surface in the ship – almost imperceptibly, but enough to mask the faint sounds of movement or even breathing that he was straining to catch.

Then he heard it – the unmistakable crack of a joint as a leg was stretched or crossed, plus the heavy yawn of somebody bored and making an effort to stay awake. There was no other sound, no spoken exchange, no grunted acknowledgement by one man of another's presence. He concluded there was only one of them.

Charlie turned the corner with a movement so swift and balanced that it was almost balletic. The big man who had just rearranged himself on his tubular steel and leather chair had barely time to realize what was happening before the edge of Charlie's hand slashed against his throat – so hard that his windpipe was snapped, the shock causing an instantaneous cardiac arrest.

The moment had been almost soundless, nothing but a dull gasp of air escaping the dead man's lips. Charlie grabbed him so that he didn't fall sideways and hit the floor with a warning thud; there was an ante-room between the corridor and the boss-man's stateroom, and Charlie knew there was a chance that some other goon might be on guard in there.

He lowered the dead man gently to the floor, and was still bending when the door behind him opened. The man who emerged opened his mouth to shout a warning as he reached for the weapon under his arm. But Charlie sprang, covering the space between them before the big gun was out of its holster. By the time the two men connected there was a thin-blade knife in Charlie's hand which plunged, as part of an unbroken movement, into the man's heart. Charlie's other hand was over the man's mouth to stifle the cry that had not yet reached his lips.

Before doing anything else, he pulled both bodies into the ante-room and locked the outer door. Then he approached the second door and listened. Music played softly, a piano concerto – Mozart perhaps. Charlie thought he recognized it, but wasn't sure.

He grasped the doorknob, turned and pushed a fraction of an inch. It was unlocked. He waited, but there was no reaction from the other side. He pushed the door further open, gun in hand, its miraculously compact silencer adding no more than a slight bulge to the barrel.

The man in bed looked up from the papers he was

studying. He was obese but solid-looking, with thick dark hair and hooded eyes. There was an expression of annoyance on his face; he was unaccustomed to having people enter his presence except on his orders. But when he saw the black-clad figure standing there, annoyance turned abruptly to alarm. His hand shot out for the panic button at his side, but it was barely halfway there before a bullet split his skull between the eyes.

Charlie moved closer to make absolutely sure that the man was dead. Part of his job was to make sure, to leave no room for doubt. There was none. All he had to do now was finish up. It wouldn't take long.

Five minutes later he was back on the water, slowly circling the *Lady Alexandra* until he heard the muffled detonation of the explosives he had planted in the hull. He waited until she sank, turning in the water like a wounded turtle before spiralling out of sight, then pressed the signalling device that would bring the chopper to collect him.

Flying back to base, he looked down at the sea and remembered the phrase he'd thought of earlier to describe it. 'Like a slab of cold grey steel beneath a moonless sky.' Where had he got that from? That wasn't the kind of thing that usually came into his head.

Still, he thought, wherever it came from, it was true.

2

Virgil Fry was an ingratiating little man whom Charlie would have despised if he'd bothered to have an opinion of him at all. His rat-like features and pencil-thin moustache were forever composed into an artificial smile. In his cheap and flashy clothes, he seemed about to break into some awful song and dance routine.

'So what's this one, Charlie?' he asked, picking up one of the canvases propped against the wall. 'Got a name, has it?'

Fry's accent, which Charlie had been unable to place when they first met, was, he now knew, Australian.

'It's a river scene,' Charlie said. 'Mountains in the background – there, you see. Wild.'

'Oh, yes . . . yes, I see. Very nice.'

The little man scribbled 'River scene' on his pad, then tore the leaf off and stuck it on a corner of the painting.

'And this one?' he said, moving on to the next.

'Clouds,' Charlie said. 'Clouds and sky, and the play of light over the sea. You can't see the sea, but it's the kind of sky you get over the sea.'

Virgil Fry nodded, made another note, and stuck it on a corner of the canvas. In all, there were fourteen paintings, all done since Fry's last visit one month earlier. For the last couple of years he'd come by every month and bought the whole of Charlie's output. That was a lot of paintings. Charlie didn't care what Fry did with them, just that he took them away. Otherwise Charlie would have thrown them out with the trash. That was how he and the little man had met. He'd come knocking at Charlie's door one day, saying he'd seen these paintings in a pile of junk outside, and he'd asked about them. Eventually he'd found out that Charlie was the artist.

'It's a business proposition, Mr Monk,' he'd said. 'I don't pretend to be a connoisseur, but I'm a dealer and I know what sells. Your work will find a niche in a popular market. You see, you're partly abstract, but only partly, not quite entirely, if you see what I mean.'

Charlie didn't see what he meant, and didn't care, so he didn't interrupt as Fry droned on.

'There are definitely people, not collectors, ordinary buyers, out there looking for just this calibre of product. At the right price, you could do very nicely. I take forty per cent. Naturally all my accounts will be open to your inspection. You can, if you so wish, initiate your own audit at any time . . .'

Charlie had agreed in order to shut the little man up as much as anything else. The idea that people would pay money to hang his paintings on their walls struck him as so improbable that he didn't give it much thought. But Fry had been as good as his word, and a regular trickle of money had been appearing in Charlie's bank account since that day. Not that he needed the money; his needs were more than adequately taken care of by the people he worked for. Painting for him was a diversion, a way, though not the only one, of killing time between jobs.

He couldn't remember how it had all started. He remembered drawing and scribbling when he was a kid,

17

the way all kids do. There had been art classes when he got older, but he'd only attended because they were compulsory and, more importantly, they didn't involve any real work. Beyond that he'd shown no interest in painting – until the Farm, which was what they called the place he'd eventually been sent to when everybody else had given up on him. But he still couldn't recall what had got him started, though he remembered how much, to his surprise, he found he enjoyed it.

From the outset he'd painted landscapes mostly, but with, as Fry had pointed out, a strangely abstract quality to them. He didn't analyse the process, though he was vaguely conscious of painting not what he saw so much as his response to what he saw, something from within; though what the hell that meant was anybody's guess.

If he had to define what painting meant for him, he'd have to say it calmed him and at the same time kept boredom at bay. Restlessness and boredom were his twin demons. They'd got him into a lot of trouble in his life, especially his early life. But that was a period he tried not to think about any more.

'Till next time then, Mr Monk.'

Charlie waved a perfunctory farewell as the door closed behind the departing dealer. Glad to be alone again, he turned back to the easel on his terrace and the painting he'd been working on before Fry's arrival. He sat on the low wooden stool and picked up his palette of paints and a brush. Although he looked out over the anchored ranks of some of the most expensive private yachts and motor cruisers on the West Coast, the land-scape on his canvas was a desert, the image plucked partly from memory, partly from imagination. At least,

18

to him it was a desert. To others it might be just a pattern of line and colour, an abstract design; or *partly* abstract, not quite entirely, as Fry would say. Whatever that meant.

He switched on the radio he'd been listening to earlier. Sometimes in the afternoons when he was home he tuned in to the various talk shows. He was fascinated by the things some people were willing to discuss in public. Much of the time it was just background chatter, but occasionally a story so extraordinary came up that he found himself pausing in his work to listen more closely, aghast at the lives some people led. Today, for example, they had an ex-soldier in the studio. He was obviously deeply disturbed and claimed to have been the victim of mind-control experiments in the army. Charlie found himself fascinated by his story, although he didn't really believe that such things happened. But there was a patent sincerity in the way the man spoke which made his story strangely compelling. When the show ended, Charlie found to his surprise that he had been doing nothing but listen for the best part of an hour. His brush lay on his palette, the paint dried hard on its bristles.

3

It was a Saturday afternoon and Christopher, Susan's six-year-old son, was playing noisily with Buzz, his spaniel puppy, outside in the garden. Susan was in the bedroom, getting out of her old jeans and into something a little more fetching before picking John up at the airport. She always made an effort to look good for him, and he always told her she'd look good no matter what she wore. They were, in other words, still as romantically in love after eight years of marriage as they'd ever been. The separations that their different careers imposed on them were borne reluctantly, and with a sense that such things only made their time together more precious.

On that particular afternoon John was returning from a trip to Russia. Like her, he was a doctor, though he'd never gone into research and spent only a couple of years in regular practice. He'd been told in medical school that he had the makings of a fine surgeon; it was as much a matter of temperament as cutting-edge knowledge, and John qualified for success in both departments. He had shown a particular curiosity about disorders of the pancreas, and his professor had assured him that, as a specialist in a relatively small and complex field, fame and fortune could be his for the asking.

But fame and fortune had never been part of John

Flemyng's plans for the future. Even before college he had known that self-interest was not a priority for him. He wasn't any kind of radical or even very politically aware; he didn't criticize others who dedicated their lives to success and the pursuit of money; nor was he religious in the sense of embracing any particular faith, dogma or even philosophical view. He just believed that the difference between right and wrong was usually self-evident, and that a failure to observe it was unnatural and as harmful to oneself as it was to others.

Some of his college friends, when Susan first knew him, used to laugh and call him Dudley Do-Right behind his back. But those friendships had lasted, and over the years the respect in which John was held had grown into admiration. Nobody had been surprised when he had forsaken private medicine and taken his skills to an international aid organization, volunteering to work for a subsistence wage in some of the most troubled spots on earth. He'd been through famine, natural disasters and epidemics of every imaginable kind. Now, after ten years, he was number two in the agency, although he didn't let this stop him going out in the field and being a hands-on boss whenever possible. He was a remarkable man. From the first day she had met him, Susan had known that this was the person she wanted to spend the rest of her life with.

The trip to Russia had come up unexpectedly ten days ago. A mysterious strain of flu, or what seemed to be flu, had broken out in a small town called Ostyakhon in the upper-central part of Sibera, about ninety miles south of Noril'sk. It attacked only the very young and the very old, causing twenty-five deaths in the space of a few days. The risk that it might spread and become an epidemic was something that could not be ignored. John had responded at once to the Russian call for help and had flown out with a team of four assistants.

Susan knew he was pleased with how the trip had gone. They'd spoken on the phone almost every day, and although he'd been depressed by much of what he'd found, he told her they had traced the problem to a bacterium frozen in the permafrost but released after an unusually warm summer, whereupon it had mutated after contact with industrial waste from a fish cannery on the shore of Lake Khantayskoye.

The last time they'd spoken had been late the previous afternoon. He'd sounded dog-tired and a little distracted. He told her that he couldn't say much on the phone, but something interesting had come up that he would discuss with her when he got back. She'd put Christopher on for a few minutes. He loved talking long-distance to his father while finding on a globe of the world exactly where his father was speaking from, and roughly where the satellite would be that was connecting them.

She wasn't taking Christopher with her to collect John; a crowded airport, with its waits and delays and general confusion, was no place for a six-year-old. He would be tired and cranky before his father even stepped off the plane. Much better to save their reunion for home. Besides, his friend Ben was having a birthday party, so she planned to drop him off on the way. She was about to go downstairs and call Christopher in from the garden when the phone rang. It was Frank Henty, one of the people who worked for John at the agency.

'Susan,' he said, 'I was afraid you might have left. It's good I caught you.'

There was something in his voice that she sensed at once, something she didn't like.

'I was just leaving,' she said. 'What is it? Something about John?'

He hesitated. 'I think it's better if you wait there until I come over.'

She felt herself go cold.

'Tell me now,' she said. 'Tell me what's happened.'

He remained evasive. 'Look,' he said, 'I think you should have someone with you. D'you have anyone there?'

'For pity's sake, Frank, just tell me what you have to say.' She'd meant to sound authoritative and firm, but her voice was trembling. She seemed suddenly to have no air in her lungs. She realized, too, that she was sitting on the edge of the bed, although she'd been standing when she reached for the phone and didn't remember changing position.

'There's been an accident,' he said. He sounded as though his mouth was dry and he was having trouble getting the words out. 'Not the flight from Noril'sk – they never got on it. The connecting flight. It was a small plane, single-engined. John and the other four in his team were on it, along with a pilot. It seems it disappeared somewhere between Ostyakhon and Noril'sk. They have people out looking for it now. We only discovered something was wrong an hour ago. Our travel people called me at home.'

He stopped. She could hear only silence. Or, rather, she could hear Christopher and the barking of the dog outside, and traffic and people in the distance. She could hear her own heart beating. But beyond these things was a silence she had never heard until now. It sounded like the underlying silence of a universe that was both infinite and empty. Empty, that is, of anything that made sense of loving or caring for people, or maybe just any kind of feelings at all. None of it meant anything if things like this could happen. None of it meant anything; so what she was feeling couldn't be real.

'Susan?'

'Yes, I'm here.'

'I'm in the office. I can be over in ten minutes.'

'No, I . . . I'm all right, I . . . When will you have more information?'

It was a stupid question to which she realized he could not have an answer. But at least she had said something. It was important to say something.

'That's difficult to say,' he said. 'That's why I'm here. It's the best way to stay in touch.'

'Yes, it's best . . . I'll wait here . . . You'll call me as soon as you have any news?'

'Of course.'

She had learned the symptoms of shock in first-year medical school: withdrawal of blood supply from outer tissue, creating a cold, clammy feel to the skin; an abrupt drop in blood pressure; a weak but rapid pulse rate. They had also told her that emotional shock was as potent a cause of this condition as the loss of a limb. Now she understood how it was that the mind could deliver such a body blow. The most important thing, she knew, was not to give way to panic and the paralysis that came with it. That was cowardly, and she had to think about Christopher.

When he saw her coming from the house, he called Buzz, ready to put him in the glassed-in patio where he didn't mind staying alone with his playthings for a while. But Susan told him to leave the little dog where he was. Buzz could stay in the garden for the few minutes it would take for her to run Christopher over to Ben's house. She would be coming right back and not going to the airport.

'Isn't Daddy coming home?' he asked, disappointed.

She dropped down to bring her eyes on a level with his. 'Daddy isn't coming home today,' she said. 'Something's happened and he's been delayed.'

'When is he coming?'

'I can't say right now. But I want you to go over to Ben's house like we planned, then I have to come back here and do some things – for Daddy. Come on, now, let's go.'

The ten-minute drive with Christopher at her side was one of the hardest things she'd ever done. She knew that he sensed something was wrong, but he couldn't define it. Luckily he was distracted by the excitement of the party. She left him with a kiss and a promise that either she'd pick him up around seven, or call and arrange something with Ben's mom. As she drove home, her hands began to shake. She hit the steering wheel to steady them. She wasn't going to lose control. That was a self-indulgence she would not permit.

Back home she checked her machine. No calls. That meant Frank had no further news. She thought about calling him or going to the office, but there was no point.

All the same, she felt the need to talk to somebody. But who could she draw with her into this limbo of horrible uncertainty? It was an unfair thing to do to anybody. It couldn't achieve anything but make them feel bad.

There was only her father.

Amery Hyde had never been a demonstrative man. Even in words he was careful what he said and how he said it. It was a temperament which had served him well through a glittering career in the diplomatic service. Retired now, he divided his time between sitting on commissions and advisory bodies and a couple of visiting professorships. He was a good-hearted man, and, as a little girl and an only child, she had loved him with something bordering on folly. There had been a special closeness between them since her mother's death from a stroke ten years ago.

She let his phone in Washington DC ring for a long time. She was about to hang up when finally he answered. As always he was happy to hear her voice, but immediately realized that something was wrong. He listened in silence, and said he would get the first plane.

Susan heard herself assuring him it wasn't necessary, saying automatically the things she felt she ought to say, not wanting to put others, even him, to any inconvenience or change of plan. He didn't argue, just repeated that he'd be there as soon as he could. He told her to stay at home and keep in touch with Frank at the office. He would get a cab from the airport. She thanked him in a whisper.

Half an hour later Frank called to say that the wreckage of the light plane had been found, scattered over a wide area. The cause of the crash was so far unknown.

There had been no survivors.

4

Charlie's opponent circled him with a wide-blade knife that glinted almost hypnotically as it moved. Charlie was unarmed, facing a man who was clearly adept at hand-to-hand fighting. He could tell that from the way the man moved, the way he kept you guessing where that razor-edge would be a second from now.

The best thing, Charlie knew, was to force him to make the first move. Or carry on with this dance till he left an opening wide enough for Charlie to get through. And he would, in time. It was just a question of out-waiting him. Charlie turned slowly, following the other man's movements.

When the lunge came, it was from an unexpected angle. It was clever. All the same, Charlie got there. His speed, as always, gave him all the edge he needed. Then he was past the blade long enough to grab the man who was holding it. Disarming him was easy, accomplished with no unnecessary force. Charlie never went beyond what was necessary in these things. That was part of his training.

The instructor blew his whistle. Charlie fell back into line and the next man stepped forward. He and the man with the knife went through the same circling routine while the rest looked on. They all knew they weren't playing games. The man before Charlie had been taken out to have his badly slashed hands attended to, and another man earlier had been knocked senseless by a blow to the side of his head. They were facing a formidable and highly trained killer. They were all trained killers themselves, but this man was the one to beat. And Charlie was the only one who'd done it.

But then, all through his training, Charlie had always been the best. He remembered somebody once saying that he was wired differently. He knew what that meant: it meant they thought he was a psychopath. It didn't offend him. He didn't pick a fight about it. On the contrary, he thought it was probably true, and the best thing he could do was take advantage of the fact. Think positive.

A cry of pain and the latest 'volunteer' fell awkwardly on the mat and had to be helped up. He was a German, but it was an Englishman who took his place. They routinely had international participants in their various counter-terrorist exercises – chiefly British, French or German, sometimes others. They called it cross-training. The SAS, GSG-9, GIGN and GIS had things to learn from as well as things to offer Delta Force (the US Army's counter-terrorist group) and Devgroup (formerly the Navy SEALS). The world's counter-terrorist forces were now coordinated in a way that the West's intelligence services had never achieved in the old cold war days.

Charlie himself was a member of neither Delta Force nor Devgroup, though he had trained and served with both. The group he was in now had no name, no visible structure and no known commander. All he knew about it were the orders he received. He didn't even know anyone else who belonged to it, except for the man he called Control. And Control came to Charlie, never

Charlie to Control. Whatever his outfit's name was, and wherever its headquarters, if any, they were unknown to Charlie.

The instructor's whistle blew twice to announce that the session was over. In the locker room the men from different groups and nations didn't mix. Members of one group arrived together and left together. Fraternization was discouraged.

Charlie pulled on his tracksuit and left, exchanging only a flicker of acknowledgement with the other men around him. Outside he walked to where his Porsche was parked beneath an overhang, protected from the baking California sun. He showed his pass and was saluted through the heavily guarded compound gates. He headed north and an hour later was back in Los Angeles.

He parked his car in its numbered space beneath the building and took the elevator to his apartment. As he entered, he was hit by the golden glow of sunset over the ocean. He looked at his watch. Carol would arrive in an hour. His face cracked into a grin of anticipation. He crossed to his wet bar in the corner, took a beer from the fridge and flipped the top.

Carol. Was that Carole with an 'e' or without? And what the hell was her second name? Wagradsky? Waginsky? No. Wazinsky? Goddamnit, that could be embarrassing, forgetting a girl's name like that. Not that she would mind. Carol was an easygoing, down-to-earth girl. Direct. They'd met in a bar ten days ago, and after a couple of drinks it was she who'd proposed they go somewhere and fuck. She had a body to dream about. Just the thought of it made him start to get hard. If he didn't start thinking about something else, he was going to have to jerk off before she arrived, and he didn't want to do that.

Not that it would inhibit his performance if he did. They'd still be all over each other the moment she came through the door, the way they had been every time so far. Later they'd get dressed, go out and eat, probably that little Italian place downstairs, then return to the apartment.

He decided to take his beer out on the terrace and watch the sun disappear. He sat with his feet up on the wall and watched the sea turn molten, like a great vat of burning gold. Charlie was sensitive to colour. He used it boldly in his painting. Yet, strangely enough, he couldn't recall a single colour from his childhood. It was as though all his earliest memories existed only in monochrome. It was only after they'd sent him to the Farm when he was about sixteen that colour had entered his life. It was like a film he'd seen on television once. The first part had been all in black and white, then suddenly it burst into colour. That was how he felt.

All the best things that had ever happened to him had started at the Farm. They'd taught him how to make something of himself, get the most out of life that he could, which had turned out to be more than he could have ever imagined. Now here he was with a place of his own, all the essentials provided and enough money for all the fun he could handle. Not bad for a guy of . . . what age was he now? Thirty? Thirty-one? Two? He'd never known for sure when he was born. Not that it made any difference. Birth, like childhood, was in the past, and best left there. The more of the past he could forget, he told himself, the better off he'd be.

The sun had gone down. Suddenly it was dusk. Glancing at his watch, he pushed himself to his feet and went back inside to take a shower before Carol arrived.

In the morning his phone rang early. He reached out a soapy hand from his bath and answered. He recognized the voice at once. It was Control.

'Hi, Charlie. You got time for a chat?'

'Sure.'

'Let's say around three.'

It was a code which had nothing to do with the time of day. The number three referred to a prearranged dead-drop location – this one a left luggage locker in the downtown Greyhound station.

Charlie respected the speed limit on the freeways. For one thing, the cops loved to bust any good-looking young guy in an expensive car like his Porsche, and the hassle was something he could do without. Of course, if it was an emergency and he was on a job, he'd take his chances. He could out-drive them if he had to. It was something he'd been trained for. But so far it hadn't been necessary.

A little over half an hour after getting out of his bath, he was opening the left luggage locker in the Greyhound station and taking out the standard white envelope he found there. Sometimes it contained instructions, which could be detailed or just a few words. Sometimes, as on this occasion, it contained only an air ticket: a return, to Boston's Logan airport. He got back into his car and headed for LAX.

Moments before take-off, someone eased himself into the empty first-class seat alongside Charlie. He turned to his right and saw the familiar patrician profile of Control – steel-grey hair, impeccable suit, pale blue questioning eyes and thin, ironic mouth.

'How are you, Charlie?'

'Never better, sir.'

They made small talk for a while. Then, over mineral water and a salad, Control outlined the job ahead.

5

They broke the news to Christopher together. She didn't know whether her father had had to break much bad news in his life; she supposed he had. At any rate, she couldn't have got through the ordeal without him. Somehow they managed to tell the child the truth – that Daddy wasn't coming back. At all. Ever.

Throughout those dreadful few days she never had to ask her father for a thing. He anticipated every need of hers and almost all of Christopher's. He took care of practical matters – lawyers, insurance and, most importantly, the funeral arrangements. John's body was flown back with the other victims and delivered to a local funeral parlour. They removed him from the sealed plastic bag in which he'd been transported and prepared him to be viewed by relatives and friends. Susan went with her father, leaning heavily on his arm. She had already been told that John had not been facially disfigured in any way. There was a terrible injury to the back of his head and considerable bodily damage, but lying there in his coffin he could have been asleep. Hesitantly, as though her hand was being willed by some agency that was not part of her, she reached out to touch his face. Its coldness, even though she had been prepared for it, shocked her. Only much later, when Christopher was safely tucked up in bed, did she allow herself to break down in her father's arms.

It was ten days before Susan insisted that her father should go home now and resume his life. She would manage because she had to. Christopher was back in school, in no way forgetting his father, but already adapting to a universe in which death had become a presence far sooner than it should.

She drove him to the airport. As they hugged each other at the barrier, she told him that she'd never quite known how much she loved him until then.

Amery Hyde blinked back a tear and his distinguished features twisted into a smile – as though somehow apologizing for making her say what she'd just said, but touched beyond words by it all the same. He kissed her on the forehead, before starting down the tunnel to the plane. He paused once to wave, then disappeared.

The packed lecture theatre fell silent as Susan stepped up to the podium. Everybody knew about her recent tragedy. Many had sent notes of sympathy and attended the funeral. As she entered there was a ripple of applause, and one or two started getting uncertainly to their feet, unsure what the proper etiquette might be in such a situation.

Susan held up her hands for silence, thanked them for their concern and the warmth of the many messages she'd received, then said that if they didn't mind she would like to get right into her lecture. She asked for the lights to be dimmed.

'First,' she began, 'we're going to look at a video of Brian Kay greeting his wife shortly after he was admitted into full-time care almost twenty years ago.'

The large screen behind her flickered into life. It showed an anonymous white-painted room in which a young-looking Brian Kay sat staring vacantly into space. A door opened and Dorothy entered. She was young and pretty with dark hair cut short to frame her face attractively. The moment he saw her, Brian came to life, springing to his feet and throwing open his arms to embrace her as though they'd been separated for months.

'Darling,' he said, his voice breaking with emotion, 'I was so worried. I didn't know where you were. I thought something had happened to you. I thought you were dead.'

Dorothy calmed him, reassured him that everything was all right. She said he didn't remember, but he'd seen her yesterday.

'Yesterday?' he echoed in disbelief. 'When yesterday? Where did I see you yesterday?'

'Here, yesterday morning, the same time.'

'What is this place? What am I doing here? What's happening?'

Patiently she explained that he'd been sick, but he was recovering now and would return home soon.

'Sick? I haven't been sick. What's supposed to be wrong with me?'

'You caught a virus. It affected your memory.'

'There's nothing wrong with my memory.'

Susan pressed the clicker in her hand and the tape stopped.

'Of course, we know that Brian never did get well enough to return home. In fact his condition has remained essentially unchanged from that day until now. I think you're all familiar with the details of the virus and the nature of the physical damage caused by it. It attacked that part of Brian Kay's brain that processed sense perceptions into short- and long-term memory. Consequently he became trapped in an eternal present, with no way of translating his moment-by-moment perceptions into any kind of meaningful narrative which he could then store in the way that normal memory is stored. The only things he remembered were the things he'd learned before the disease attacked him. His whole past remained intact – childhood, college, marriage, followed by a career teaching English in high school. But with the onset of his illness, an unbridgeable gulf had opened up between that past and the present moment – and each successive present moment. At the same time, his intelligence has remained undiminished in terms of his capacity to understand things. For example, he never has any problem grasping the nature of his condition when it's explained to him. The problem is that the moment the explanation is over, he forgets it. He cannot learn, because he cannot transfer anything from perception into memory.'

She paused a moment. Despite all her experience in teaching and lecturing, speaking in public was not something that came naturally to her. She felt somehow depersonalized before an audience, as though in a strange way she ceased to be herself before all those attentive faces and became instead simply a conduit for the ideas she was attempting to communicate. At least, she told herself, this implied a loss of self-consciousness which helped her over a certain innate shyness. She took a sip from the glass of water on the table before her and continued.

'When I first became involved in this case a little over seven years ago, Brian's condition had remained unchanged since the onset of his illness. I'm going to show you now a video of Brian greeting his wife about that time – that is some thirteen years into his illness.'

The image on the screen was of Brian once again sitting vacantly in an anonymous though different room. A different nurse opened the door and his wife entered. Dorothy had changed – not greatly, but enough for the change to be startling if you were told that it had taken place from one day to the next. That, as Susan pointed out to her audience, was the impression Brian was getting when he looked at her. His only memory of her was the way she had looked thirteen years earlier. Now he was seeing a woman with hair already turning grey and with lines around her eyes and mouth. He froze as he saw her and stepped back in alarm.

'My God, darling! What's happened to you? Are you ill?'

The audience watched in silence as Dorothy explained his condition to him yet again, in the same words she had used countless times already. He nodded, taking it all in, then reacted with anger and frustration that nothing had been done to help him, and demanded to know why he had not been told all this before.

Susan pressed her clicker to stop the tape. 'Now let me show you how Brian greets his wife now when she visits him.'

The tape she played showed Brian and Dorothy as they were now, but his behaviour when she entered was exactly as it had been twenty years ago: delighted, confused and full of angry questions about himself and his situation, but without any of his previous alarm at Dorothy's 'overnight' change in appearance.

'The procedure we developed,' Susan continued as the

lights came up, 'was non-invasive but allowed us to send a visual image directly into the brain, bypassing the eye in the way that sound can bypass the ear in certain kinds of hearing aid. It allowed us also to bypass that part of the brain which would normally process visual stimuli into memory. Sadly, it remains a long way from a full cure, but it is a start. Next time we'll take a look down some of the avenues that may yet lead to such a cure.'

The gathering broke up, most of the audience filing quietly out while a handful of friends gathered around Susan.

One man stood alone near the door, unremarked by anyone. He was short, thin-faced and nervous-looking, with straggly grey hair pulled back in a ponytail. He wore jeans and an old corduroy jacket, and looked as though he hadn't shaved for a couple of days. When Susan stepped out of the room and started down the corridor, still accompanied by two or three people, he followed her. Only when she had passed through the main doors and was crossing the quadrangle alone did he fall in step alongside her.

'Excuse me, Dr Flemyng,' he began, 'I'm sorry to approach you without warning like this, but it's important that I talk to you privately – as soon as possible.'

She stopped and turned to look at him. His accent was English, but elided and flattened in the manner of someone who had spent much of his life in the United States.

'What about?' she asked. 'Who are you?'

'My name's Dan Samples. I'm a journalist. I want to talk to you about your husband.'

She felt a chill of unease. She didn't much like the look

38

of this man, and she was far from sure she wanted to talk to him about anything, and especially not about John.

'What about my husband?' she asked, not hiding the distrust in her voice.

He glanced furtively around, as though afraid they were being watched. 'D'you mind if we get out of the open, go somewhere private?'

She stayed firmly where she was. 'If you have anything to say to me about my husband, I'd prefer you said it right here.'

He looked uneasy, but didn't argue.

'I can tell you who killed him,' he said.

'You're crazy,' she said, once she was over the initial shock his words had dealt her. 'Nobody killed my husband. He died in a plane crash.'

The man in front of her shook his head almost imperceptibly. 'I was with him the night before. He knew something might happen. He didn't know what, but believe me, Dr Flemyng, he was scared.'

She passed a hand over her eyes, suddenly feeling alarmingly unsteady. Her instinct was to reach out for support, but there was no one to reach out to except this stranger towards whom she felt a sudden burning anger.

'Mr . . . Samples, did you say your name was . . .?

'Dan. Dan Samples.'

'Mr Samples, I hope this isn't your idea of . . . of some kind of joke.'

She was aware of how idiotic this sounded, but the words seemed to leave her mouth without even passing through her brain.

'I was supposed to be on that plane with him,' he said quietly, holding her gaze with his own, 'but I stayed behind to file something for one of the publications I write for. We planned to meet up again in Boston in a few days. He wanted me to meet you.'

'He never mentioned your name. How do I even know you knew him?'

Samples reached into his jacket and withdrew a polaroid photograph which he held out to her. She took it, and saw a picture of John and Dan Samples sitting with a couple of drinks in what looked like the lobby of some not very luxurious hotel. John was talking, Samples listening attentively.

'Okay,' she said, 'this picture says you met my husband. It doesn't tell me any more than that.'

She offered to give back the polaroid, but he waved her hand away. 'Keep it,' he said, 'it's probably the last picture taken of him.'

She hesitated, then slipped the photograph into her coat pocket. 'Just tell me what you know, Mr Samples – or think you know.'

He looked around nervously again, as though afraid they were being watched. 'Dr Flemyng,' he said, 'I'm putting my own life in considerable danger just by talking to you. Could we go somewhere private?'

Going anywhere alone with this man was the last thing she intended doing. All the same, she knew she had to hear whatever it was he had to say.

'There's a cafeteria just around the corner,' she said. 'Nobody will pay us any attention if we talk there.'

6

The man watching the rear of the tall and run-down-looking hotel saw a laundry van pull up. He watched as the driver got out and went around to the back of the van. His hand tightened on the phone in his pocket, ready to give the alarm if anything suspicious happened; a van that size could carry an assault team. But he relaxed as he saw nothing more suspicious than racks of dry-cleaning in plastic covers and piles of laundry boxes.

With an ease that looked as though it came from years of practice, the delivery man leaned into a rack of hanging coats and dresses and tossed them over his shoulder. In addition, before stepping down into the road, he picked up a big square cardboard box that appeared to be almost weightless, and carried the whole lot through a door marked 'Deliveries'.

The man over the road glanced at his watch. There didn't seem on the surface to be anything suspicious in all this, but if the van driver wasn't out again within a few minutes he was going to start wondering.

Inside the building, the pile of dry cleaning on Charlie's shoulder came to life as he tipped it forward. The man concealed in the clothes landed lightly on his feet. He was about Charlie's height and a similar build; carrying him as though he weighed nothing had taken considerable muscle control.

The same was true of the cardboard box, which hit the floor with a solid thud when Charlie dropped it. He handed the cap he was wearing to the man who stood waiting for it, then took off his windjammer and handed that over too. The man slipped it on, then went back out the door through which Charlie had just carried him in. Across the street the man who was watching relaxed as the delivery van drove off. The area was quiet now. No sign of anything unusual. No sign of anything much at all.

Charlie, meanwhile, was working fast. Inside the cardboard box were ropes, hooks and rappelling gear. There was also a Heckler and Koch 10mm sub-machine gun, a .45 Glock handgun and a belt of sting and stun grenades. He dragged the whole lot into the elevator just behind him, and pressed the top floor. By the time he got there he was ready for action. He knew where to find the final short flight of stairs that would lead him to the roof. There hadn't been time to get him a key, so he just shouldered open the barred and reinforced skylight and crawled out on to the flat rooftop.

Another lookout was positioned opposite the front of the building. The first thing he saw was a figure leaping crazily out into space, apparently a suicide jumping from the roof of the building. It was a moment before he realized that the man was attached to a rope that arced out behind him, and then tightened. By the time the lookout had snatched the mobile phone from his pocket and started punching buttons, the figure he was watching had swung into the wall with a force that should have broken every bone in his body, even though he balanced himself to absorb the impact with his legs. But he just pushed out again and fell another six floors almost faster than the eye could follow him. He pushed off the wall again and this time swung sideways, by which time a weapon had appeared in his hand.

The man over the road didn't have time to utter a word into his mobile phone before the din of breaking glass and gunfire filled the air. Seconds later an unreal silence descended. The man knew that his comrades were dead and their mission defeated. His only consolation was that he himself, along with all the six other members of the back-up team, would live to fight another day.

It was only when the wail of sirens and clatter of helicopters broke the vacuum of silence that he realized he was mistaken. He heard shouts from his comrades. One of them ran out of a corner building two blocks along. There was a shot, and he fell.

The man turned, heading for the stairs that he knew led to a back alley and his best chance of escape. But he was barely halfway down when booted feet came thundering up. He glimpsed the silhouetted SWAT team, and then the universe exploded as air ripped through his brain.

Charlie heard the shots dimly in the distance. His thoughts were on other things as he stood guard, as he had been trained to do, over the three bloody corpses and the device the size of a hatbox that they had been preparing to detonate when he had killed them.

The device, he knew, was an atomic bomb. A crude, home-made affair, but with twice the killing power of the one dropped on Hiroshima. He did not think that they'd had time to arm it, and there was nothing he could see that suggested it was about to go off.

But he could not be sure until the experts arrived, which he knew they would any moment now. Meanwhile he had to keep his nerve and just do the job he was paid for.

7

Susan and the man who called himself Dan Samples sat facing each other across the small formica-topped cafeteria table. He had immediately accepted her suggestion that they come here, glad of any opportunity to get away from the open space they had been standing in. Neither had spoken until they'd bought two cappuccinos and taken them to the furthest corner table.

As they sat down she said, 'I don't think you told me what newspaper you write for.'

'I don't write for any newspaper, Dr Flemyng. I'm freelance. I write for a number of specialist publications, mostly with a subscription readership. I also have my own site on the Internet. Just type in my name on any search engine, you'll see the kind of stories I cover.'

Susan sat back in her chair, putting more distance between them and narrowing her eyes with scepticism. She suddenly had a distinct and not very flattering picture of the kind of journalist Dan Samples was. A specialist, no doubt, in conspiracy theories of every kind, at least half of which probably involved UFO sightings and messages from other worlds.

He seemed to read the thought in her eyes, and for the first time smiled faintly.

'I don't know if you ever spend much time surfing the

Net. It's full of every crank theory you can imagine, and then some. But in most things, no matter how exaggerated they become, you'll usually find a kernel of truth somewhere. Sometimes quite a big one.'

'And you have a theory about my husband's death, Mr Samples?'

The smile had gone from his lips, and there was a steadiness in his gaze that surprised her slightly. It wasn't the fixed stare of obsession, just a man trying to convince her to take him seriously.

'I've been following up a number of related stories for over two years now. Gradually they all led me towards the same point of origin. That point, Dr Flemyng, appears to be you.'

She felt a jolt of surprise. 'Me? What kind of stories are you talking about?'

He seemed to debate briefly how to go on, then avoided answering her question directly.

'Dr Flemyng, your research is funded by something called the Pilgrim Foundation, isn't it?'

'Yes, but what does that have to do with—?'

He cut in before she finished.

'The Pilgrim Foundation killed your husband.'

She felt her heart miss a beat. At the same time she wanted to hit him, throw something, express in physical violence the rage and confusion she felt.

'That's absurd! What in God's name are you talking about? What conceivable reason would they have to kill my husband?'

'Dr Flemyng, what you did with Brian Kay – and other patients like him – was access a part of the brain that can no longer be accessed in the normal way. The procedure amounted to a major improvement in the treatment of certain conditions, and in our knowledge of brain function generally. You created a memory, in this case a visual memory, by artificial means.'

'So?' she said tersely. 'What does all that have to do with this absurd story of yours?'

'As I understand it, anything you develop as a result of your funding by the Pilgrim Foundation is partly owned by the Foundation – correct? And patented by their lawyers?'

'Yes.'

'And you always knew that.'

'It's perfectly normal practice in funded research.'

'But I'm sure you don't need me to tell you about the implications of your research for such things as mind control, brainwashing and much more.'

As she looked at him, she felt her anger being replaced by sheer disbelief.

'Is that what all this is supposed to be about? Mind control?'

'That is what it's all about, Dr Flemyng.'

She continued to look at him. A curious urge to laugh out loud began to build in her.

'Why does this somehow not surprise me?' she said.

He didn't seem disturbed by her response. On the contrary, he seemed to have expected it.

'Please just hear me out. Then decide whether you believe me or not.'

'I think your imagination is getting a little overheated, Mr Samples. My research is a long way from the kind of science fiction you're talking about.'

'Are you sure?'

His voice was as calm as his gaze, accepting the challenge of her disbelief.

'There was some remarkably advanced work under way in Russia before the collapse of the Soviet Union,' he continued. 'When the Iron Curtain came down, it was no surprise that the old enemies decided to join forces. Which was very convenient for the West, because it turned out the old enemy was ahead of us – mainly because they had always enjoyed a certain advantage in hushing up their failed experiments. There are still things you can get away with in the East more easily than in the West. As your husband found out last week. That's why they chose to kill him there.'

'You're saying they killed him because of what you told him?'

'Yes.'

'For heaven's sake, what *did* you tell him?'

'I told him about the story I was working on, which was how I came to be there.'

'Which happened to coincide with this outbreak of flu, to which my husband happened to get called.'

'That's right.'

'I always find coincidences hard to believe, Mr Samples.'

He shrugged as if to say he couldn't help that.

She turned in her chair, as though this thing was beyond a joke now, beyond even personal insult, beyond anything she any longer had a name for. She felt restless and anxious to get away from him.

'Mr Samples, you're talking paranoid nonsense.'

She was on her feet, ready to leave. He remained seated, looking up at her.

'Your husband believed me.'

She looked down at him coldly. 'You have a photograph, but no record of this conversation? No tape? Notes even?'

He shook his head. 'The thing is, Dr Flemyng, that neither your husband nor I together could prove anything – without you. Only you can unravel the truth. He said he'd talk to you when he got back, and he was sure that you'd cooperate.'

She thought back to their last phone conversation. John had said that he had 'things to tell her', but that could have meant anything. And yet, she remembered, he'd sounded strange. Tired, yes. But something more?

A door banged. Samples flinched and his eyes shot fearfully in the direction of the noise. When he saw it was just a couple of students coming in, he turned back to her.

Slowly she sat down again.

'You have no tape of this conversation, no notes. You must at least have some evidence of what you're asking me to believe.'

'I have extensive documentation. To an outsider, frankly, it wouldn't mean a great deal – otherwise I would already have made very public use of it. But to you, Dr Flemyng, it will be a shocking revelation of how your work has been abused.'

'Why don't we just cut to the chase? Show me this "documentation".'

'I'm not foolish enough to carry it around with me. But if you'll come with me . . .'

'I'm not going anywhere with you, Mr Samples. I don't know you, and you don't exactly inspire me with confidence.'

He shrugged as though he regretted her attitude but found it reasonable, and got to his feet.

'I'll get it to you, Dr Flemyng. Depend on it. When you've had time to study it, I'll get in touch with you again.'

'What if I want to get in touch with you – for whatever reason?'

He shook his head. 'The fewer people know how to find me, the better. I know you still suspect I'm crazy, or paranoid, or maybe up to some scam – but you'll change your mind. I'll be in touch.'

Before she realized it, she was looking across the restaurant at the door swinging shut behind him. That was pretty good, she thought to herself: he'd managed to walk out on her before she could walk out on him. A neat piece of gamesmanship.

For a moment she thought of going after him, but sensed it would be a mistake. If he was as crazy as she feared, she'd never get rid of him after handing him a victory like that. A moment more and it was too late to do anything; she'd never find him out there now.

'Is everything all right, Dr Flemyng?'

The heavy Czech accent came from so close to her ear that she was startled. It was George, who ran the cafeteria. She looked at him blankly.

'Yes,' she said, 'fine.'

Then she followed his gaze and understood why he was asking. When Samples left she must have got to her feet again without realizing it. The suddenness of her movement had jarred the table, but she hadn't even heard the crash of their coffee cups hitting the floor.

8

Charlie stared at the ceiling. It was almost dawn. Debbie slept peacefully at his side. They had fallen asleep around two-thirty, but he had woken just after four as abruptly as if someone had fired a shot in the room.

He looked at her: chestnut-coloured hair spread out in long, thick tresses on the pillow, framing a face that was both delicate and sensuous. He thought of waking her, but decided against it. Instead he slipped out of bed, pulled on a robe, and went through to his living room.

His mouth was dry, so he opened a small bottle of mineral water, then lowered himself into a deep, square, comfortable armchair. He let his head fall back and closed his eyes. Thoughts and images flowed through his brain in a chaotic stream of consciousness. Why a 'stream', he wondered idly. More like a river in full flood, dams and bridges swept away. You had to make an effort to impose order. You put yourself together, he reflected, out of the pieces you could salvage, assembling them like a child's construction set.

But who chose the pattern? Who decided what you built?

Odd thought. Where had that come from?

He opened his eyes. It was almost morning. He got up and walked over to the long glass wall dividing his apartment from the terrace. A thin grey mist was drifting in from the sea, just visible now in the first light.

Charlie stared into it and felt that he was staring into his own head. Thoughts and memories arose, half formed, out of the swirling mists of time, but disappeared before he could seize on them and give them names. Though he knew that, if he waited, one memory would emerge. He knew what it would be. It was the memory that always came back to him in this frame of mind and about this time in the morning.

Kathy Ryan was the first girl he'd ever loved, and the first girl who had loved him. She had taught him what love meant when he most needed it. Looking back he knew it had been real, not just some adolescent crush. It must have been in the sixth or was it seventh school they'd sent him to? (Out of how many? Who cared? Too many, and not enough. He hadn't learned a damn thing that whole time. Just an endless round of fights and punishment and truancy and more fights.)

They'd just been kids, he and Kathy. It had never been a sexual thing, though it would have become one if they hadn't got picked up that time they ran off together. They'd just lammed out one morning. Without a word spoken, just a look between them, they'd known what they wanted. They took off with just the clothes they wore and the change in their pockets.

He remembered it still as the best day of his life. In a sense it was the first day of his life. He'd broken out and found freedom with someone he cared for and who cared for him. Someone who, by the time they'd walked hand in hand through the city and reached the rail yards on the far side, he knew he wanted to be with and protect and make love to for the rest of his life. She told him she felt the same way. All they both wanted was somewhere private, some place they could be alone.

They were caught trying to jump a freight train. He'd fought like a tiger against two cops bigger than himself, but in the end they'd got the cuffs on him. Instead of spending the night of his dreams with Kathy, he'd spent it alone in a police cell. Next day he'd been driven back to the orphanage in the kind of armoured van that was used for carrying prisoners to jail. Then he'd been left alone in a room with the three gorillas who were responsible for 'security' in the place, who told him they were going to teach him a lesson he'd never forget. Except it didn't all go their way. He'd hurt one of them pretty badly before the other two got hold of baseball bats and laid him out with a brutal beating. After that they'd thrown him in the 'hole'. He'd been there more times than he could remember, but never this badly hurt. He knew he'd get nothing to eat or drink for twenty-four hours, sometimes longer. For all they knew or cared he could die in there. In fact he thought he was going to. As the numbness wore off, the pain got worse. Later he must have passed out. When he came to, the pain started again. He tried to think of Kathy. That helped some. But the pain was still bad.

When they finally dragged him out and had him checked over by a doctor, he was told he was being moved – right then, that morning. He was put in another prison van and taken on a long drive, way out into the country. They went in through the gates of some place that looked like a big park or private ranch. He could see groups of young men working out and playing sports and scrambling over obstacle courses. It looked like some kind of training camp. That was his first sight of the Farm, and the first day of his new life.

His only regret was that he didn't know how to get in touch with Kathy. All he'd known was that when she wasn't in school she'd lived in the girls' orphanage a couple of miles away. He didn't have the name or address of it or anything. Even if he had, he didn't know if he'd be able to write to her – or, for that matter, what he'd say. And anyway, maybe they'd moved her on the way they had him. Maybe her life was better now. Certainly his was getting better, no question about that; but he'd have liked her to be a part of it. Maybe one day, he told himself, she would be. That was his dream.

Meanwhile he had his memories. But memory, he had come to realize, played strange tricks. Like the way he couldn't remember colour from before the Farm. Or Kathy's face. Even though he remembered everything about her better than he remembered anything in his life, he still couldn't conjure up an image of her face. Maybe he'd thought of her too often and too hard, and somehow worn out his mental picture of her. Or perhaps, he told himself, we only think we remember people clearly, whereas in fact all we retain is a kind of general impression, enough to know them when we see them again, but not enough to conjure them up like a picture on a TV screen.

Yet he could remember other people. He could remember Debbie in the next room, just the way he'd seen her a few minutes ago. If he closed his eyes he could picture almost anybody he chose, male or female. So why did Kathy's face escape him? Obviously there was some kind of self-censorship going on. Before the Farm was a rotten part of his life that he wanted to forget. It was as though he'd scooped out that part of his memory, leaving only fragments and echoes that no longer formed a coherent whole. Kathy had been the only good thing in that life, and it saddened him that he seemed to have blocked her out with the rest of it. He wondered if he'd know her if he saw her again. Then he wondered, as he often wondered, what had become of her.

'Charlie . . .? Where are you . . .?'

Debbie was calling his name from the bedroom, her voice drowsy and thickened by sleep. Normally he would have found it sexually arousing, but now his thoughts remained stubbornly elsewhere.

But where exactly? If not here, then where were his thoughts?

'Charlie, come on back to bed, sweetie . . . I want some more of what you gave me earlier . . .'

That sounded good. Wasn't that what he wanted, too?

And yet . . . and yet . . . what was he struggling to remember? And why did it matter? After all, it was only in these moments when he had nothing more urgent to occupy his mind that he found himself turning to the past and trying to make sense of it. Mostly he had better things to do.

'Charlie . . .?'

Like now.

'Right here, honey. I'm coming.'

He turned from the window and retraced his footsteps to the bedroom, shedding his robe along with his fragmented memories as he went, preparing to bury himself in something more substantial than the past.

9

Amery Hyde was a tall man with the lean frame of the athlete he once was, and the agility of a man much younger than his sixty-four years. Susan knew that he was attractive to women. She also knew he'd had affairs since her mother's death, and in a way she was surprised he hadn't remarried. But she'd never asked any questions, and he hadn't volunteered any details – until these last few weeks while he'd been seeing her through John's death.

She didn't learn anything particularly new about him. What was interesting was hearing him tell her things himself. It was, she felt, the way they would have talked if they'd spent more time together in the past. It was a sad irony that they were spending it together now only because of John's death.

Logically, that made it tragic that she should have grown so close to her father. Yet that was absurd. Would things ever, she wondered, go back to making sense?

She and Christopher had come to Washington for a long weekend. He was in bed now. They were leaving him with Mrs Collier, her father's housekeeper, and were having a drink before going to a dinner party around the corner. It would be only the second time she'd left him since John's death. He hadn't been disturbed the first time, nor did he object when she asked if he minded her doing it again. It was good, she thought, that he should feel relaxed about it rather than clinging fearfully to her.

Her father poured her a glass of Chablis, then added an exquisitely measured fraction of water to his whisky. He took a sip and savoured it as though its taste might give him an answer to the question his daughter had just put to him.

'I don't think,' he said eventually, 'that you should do anything about this man Samples unless he contacts you again.'

'Then what? Have him arrested? Questioned?'

'I'm afraid you'd have insufficient grounds. After all, he didn't threaten you in any way.'

'But if there's anything in what he said . . .'

'Let's take it a step at a time.'

Their eyes connected. That was what he'd said when he was getting her through the first shock of bereavement. A step at a time.

'Yes,' she said, 'you're right. I'll wait until he contacts me.'

They fell silent. He stared into the flickering fire in the grate.

'Do you think it's possible that your work could be used in the way this man was suggesting?' he asked, without looking at her.

'I've thought about it. In theory, of course it is. But then, that's true of every advance in medicine or science in general. You have to balance that risk against the positive things you can achieve. But in the end a scientist's job is to find out how the world works, not pronounce on it morally. And a doctor's is to give the sick any help you can, not withhold treatment in case you're blamed for some misuse of it later.'

'Nobody's talking about blame here. Human beings do what they're capable of – on every level, unfortunately, good and bad.'

Again they sat in thoughtful silence for some moments.

'You'd have to solve a few problems before you could use what I did the way Samples was claiming.'

'But could those problems be solved?'

'Yes, in principle. I can think of ways, experiments you might try.' She paused and looked at her father. 'But they're not the kind of experiments that a civilized society would condone.'

Amery Hyde frowned, drawing out a white-spotted blue handkerchief that he ran across the base of his nose several times, sniffing softly. Then he glanced at his watch.

'We'd better be going,' he said.

They were dining with a former Secretary of State, the chairman of the House foreign relations committee, a member of the Joint Chiefs and a couple of editors. Even by Washington standards it was a pretty high-powered group, and the conversation would be as entertaining as it would be interesting. She had been looking forward to the evening, as she knew her father had. Now she felt she'd almost spoilt it.

'I'm sorry,' she said, 'I shouldn't have brought this up now. But I couldn't earlier with Christopher around, and I didn't want to on the phone . . .'

He waved his hand to stop her. 'You're right to tell me. I'm only sorry I can't be more helpful. I'll make some enquiries – discreetly. But there was no hint of anything wrong when I checked them out last time.'

At her request, her father had 'asked around' about the Pilgrim Foundation after they had first approached her. A man named Latimer West had called her out of the blue one day and made an appointment to see her. He'd spent an hour telling her about the Pilgrim Foundation and what it was doing for scientists like her. At the end of their conversation he'd given her his card and invited her to get in touch if she was interested in going further. She needed research funding, but she was trying to avoid sources like the big drug companies because they tied you up for life. That was when she had turned to her father for advice.

'As you might guess from the name,' he had told her, 'quite a number of the trustees trace their families back to the Pilgrim Fathers. There seems to be no religious or political bias in what they do, or any kind of bias so far as I can see. They're not a pressure group, their funding is real and its source isn't suspect. They seem genuinely to want to back worthwhile independent research.'

That was how it had started. Without them, she would never have been able to help Brian Kay, or any of the others she had helped and would go on helping in the future.

A clock struck in the next room. Her father looked at her, concerned. 'We don't have to go,' he said, 'if you're not feeling up to it.'

'No, I'm fine. I want to go. I feel better now I've talked about it.'

He gave her a quick smile and squeezed her hand briefly. Then they walked through to the hall, where he helped her on with her coat.

10

One of the first things that Susan had done after her conversation with Dan Samples had been to check him out on the Net. On the first search engine she tried, his name brought up over thirty references; on the second and third even more – mostly articles written by him about the usual grab bag of paranoid conspiracy theories.

In a way, she felt, the sources carefully indexed at the end of his various pieces said it all. Titles like: 'OPERATION MIND CONTROL'; 'THE ZAPPING OF AMERICA'; 'THE MIND MANIPULATORS'; 'WERE WE CONTROLLED?'

To be honest, one among them gave her pause for thought: 'INDIVIDUAL RIGHTS AND THE FEDERAL ROLE IN BEHAVIOR MODIFICATION' – Prepared by the Staff of the Sub-committee on Constitutional Rights of the Committee of the Judiciary, United States Senate (Washington: Government Printing Office, 1974).

However, that impressive effect was diminished by the acknowledgement that followed it: 'BEEPERS IN KIDS' HEADS COULD STOP ABDUCTORS', *Las Vegas Sun*, Oct. 7, 1987.

And she thought that before making up her mind she would have to know more about 'THE CONTROL OF CANDY JONES' (Playboy Press, 1976).

The obsessions of Samples and those like him centred on the idea that some amorphous and shadowy group of power-brokers were intent on establishing control of what George Orwell called 'the space between our ears'. Samples differed from some of his peers in that he believed these would-be controllers to be entirely human, whereas others remained convinced they were at least partially made up of visitors from space.

Susan found it hard to believe (despite pictures) in people being radio-controlled by implants in the head. Or radiation discs hidden (though seldom found) under the dash of victims' cars to give them cancer. Or the idea of bombardment by high-frequency waves from helicopters, or from some truck next to your car in a traffic jam.

She sat back with a sigh, as she had earlier in the restaurant, putting a distance between herself and the world Dan Samples lived in. She didn't want any part of it. The worst thing about it, and perhaps the hardest part to believe, was the degree of institutionalized evil it implied within not just dictatorships and fanatical cults, but equally in so-called democracies.

She was going to need powerful proof.

As the days went by and no call came from Samples, her conviction grew that he was just a harmless crank with insufficient evidence to back up his fantasies. With this came a growing sense of outrage that he should have intruded into her private tragedy to gratify his taste for paranoid invention. She decided she wasn't just going to let the matter drop. Genuine science had enough prejudice and ignorance to overcome without neurotics and charl-atans like Dan Sample obscuring the real issues with crude superstition. She decided to go after the man.

In one of his articles he listed a number of organizations which he accused of being fronts for the channelling of money, public and private, into illegal experiments. Many of them were august and widely respected bodies. One of them was the Pilgrim Foundation. She didn't know whether this reference had ever come to the knowledge of anybody in the foundation, but she decided to make sure that it did. Their lawyers would doubtless take over from there.

Latimer West, who ran the Pilgrim Foundation – officially he was its General Administrator, with a seat on the board of trustees but no voting powers – received the news of Samples' libel with equanimity. 'It's something that happens from time to time,' he told her. 'Eruptions of confabulatory nonsense like pimples on the face of an adolescent. Most people grow out of it. It's rarely worth suing – for one thing they don't have any money. And if you use the law to close them down, you just make yourself look like the kind of bogeyman they say you are. But you're right, I'll have this looked into. Sometimes, when they go too far, you have to fire a warning shot across their bows.'

Susan had never been sure if she liked Latimer West. There was an unappealing plump sleekness about the man. He managed somehow to be both unctuous and condescending at the same time, and he wore an eternally hovering smile behind which she was sure lurked a killer instinct. He had degrees in medicine and business administration, and clearly relished the entrée into the higher levels of both social and intellectual chic that his position afforded him. Nonetheless, the idea of his being in any way an evil man struck her as patently absurd. Samples' charges against the Pilgrim Foundation just didn't make sense on any level. The people behind it as well as the people supported by it included some of the country's elite. Only paranoid fools – and embittered losers – could convince themselves that there was a rottenness at the heart of such a thing.

Aside from whatever the foundation might do, she felt an urge to confront Samples himself and demand an apology for involving John's death in his infantile games. He wasn't going to get away with his hit-and-run treatment of her. However, one of his claims that proved true was his boast of being a hard man to find. There was no e-mail or any other kind of address for him on the Net. As she didn't even know where he lived, she didn't know where to begin searching for the possibility of a phone number, though the likelihood of his being listed anywhere was remote.

When she spoke with her father on the phone, his advice was to let the whole thing drop. No real harm had been done, and provided the man didn't harass her further she should just forget about him.

Yet she couldn't. She went back through the stuff on the Net. This time she found a publisher's name listed at the end of one of Samples' articles, along with an address – in Baltimore – to which you could write for further material or for copies of some of the books quoted. It was probably, she imagined, a desktop operation working out of somebody's apartment over a Chinese take-out. She checked, and discovered they had a phone number. She dialled it, and after several rings a youngish male voice answered.

'I wonder if you can help me,' she said, having established she was talking to the right place. 'I'm trying to get in touch with a man called Dan Samples. I know he writes for you sometimes.'

There was a silence at the other end of the line. She could hear the man breathing, so she knew he hadn't hung up. But the space between them was charged with mistrust.

'What d'you want with him?' the voice asked eventually.

'He came to see me a few days ago. I'd like to talk some more with him about something we discussed.'

There was another brief silence, then the man said, 'I'm afraid that's not going to be possible. Dan Samples died yesterday.'

11

As always, surprise was essential. For that reason, Control had said, Charlie would have to jump at ten thousand feet. That way his plane would be mistaken for a routine night flight out of the city's main airport.

Charlie launched himself into the black void. After a few moments he became aware of a thin scattering of lights on the ground below, like pale reflections of the glittering stars overhead. He spread his arms and legs and began the tricky slalom through the air that he had to accomplish with absolute precision before pulling his parachute rip-cord.

After several seconds of intense concentration, he saw from the satellite-generated figures on the inside of his visor that he was where he needed to be. He pulled his rip-cord, bracing himself for the jolt as his chute opened. For a moment he hung like a marionette, swaying from side to side on its strings. The flickering data on his visor slowed almost to a standstill. Then he began to manoeuvre himself down with the clinical precision he had been taught in a special training session just that morning.

When his visor told him he was at a thousand feet, he touched a point on the side of his helmet. The words 'Night Vision On' flashed over a crystal-clear view of the embassy compound beneath him. He could see the straight lines of paths and buildings and the outer wall, softened here and there by foliage. On one rooftop he could see the massive radio antennae that he had been warned to avoid.

What he couldn't see, and this slightly worried him, was any evidence of the military back-up he had been told would be waiting outside the compound. Perhaps, he told himself, it was camouflaged, or hidden by trees and the surrounding buildings; he hoped, at any rate, that it was there.

Beyond that he had no time for reflection. The ground was coming up at him swiftly, and the patch of it on which he had to land in the south-east corner seemed impossibly small. All he could do was head for it and hope to miss the trees.

He felt a jab in the ribs and heard the sharp snap of a branch. It couldn't have made too much noise, he told himself, because a moment later the thud of his feet hitting the ground sounded far louder in his ears. He rolled forward, pulled in his chute and hid it, wedged by a stone, under a bush.

From where he crouched he had a clear view across the compound and could see the lighted windows of the room he had to take. It was, he knew, the banqueting hall. A reception had been in progress when the terrorists struck. Diplomats and politicians from all over the world were being held hostage. The terms demanded for their release were unacceptable, and it was known that the terrorists were fanatics and ready to die for their cause. A full-scale military assault would be impossible without massive loss of life. That was when Charlie had been called in.

Charlie's orders were very clear, a fact which didn't make them any easier to carry out. There was one hostage above all whom he was to identify and pay special attention to. This was a senator, young and popular, who was being groomed by his party for high office. Charlie didn't know it but, all things being equal, this young senator would be running for Vice-President in three years' time. The plan then was that he would move on into the White House – all things remaining equal. That was why Charlie had received very special orders concerning this man.

He glanced at the device on his wrist. Among other things, it operated as a watch. The local time, he saw, was 23:05. He pressed a point on one side of the device, and immediately a voice responded from the speaker in his helmet.

'Bravo-one, we read you. Fortunes favour.'

It meant that the back-up he had been promised was there and ready, even though he hadn't seen them from the air. He didn't respond. The signal he'd just sent them was all they needed. Now they would wait until they heard the first explosion.

He unstrapped the light machine-gun from his back, checked the stun and sting grenades at his waist, and started to move forward. There were a couple of electronic tripwires that he'd been warned about and which he skirted carefully. Finally he stood right alongside one of the tall, lighted windows. Roller blinds had been drawn inside so he couldn't see in, which was fine by him because it meant they couldn't see out as he attached an explosive device to the bulletproof glass. It took only a moment, then he pressed himself against the wall and waited.

When the charge blew, and before anyone inside even started shooting, he lobbed in two stun grenades. They exploded with deafening and blinding force, and Charlie pitched into the room with a forward roll, firing as he moved.

The hostages, trained as most of them routinely were for this sort of eventuality, had already hit the floor. The terrorists, disoriented and completely taken by surprise, were firing wildly in all directions. He mowed three of them down before the other five could turn their guns on him. Still moving, he got them all with two short bursts of rapid fire, but not before something punched him in the shoulder like a fist. He knew it was a bullet that had found an opening in his body armour. But it didn't stop him or even slow him down. The adrenalin was pumping; he was immortal.

On the periphery of his vision he sensed fresh movement. Two more terrorists had entered the room, their guns blazing. He rolled again, still firing, and saw them both fall. He came to a stop on one knee, poised and ready to spring in any direction.

Then he saw the senator, whose photograph he had been shown in his briefing by Control. The pathetic image he saw now was barely recognizable as the same man. The confident smile and clear-eyed gaze had been replaced by abject terror and confusion. When Charlie gestured for him to move towards him, he didn't respond. Charlie gestured again, more emphatically. The senator cowered away in the opposite direction, terrified of any movement near him. His lips quivered and he was whimpering like a child.

Charlie reached out and grabbed him and pushed him to the ground, then looked around for further signs of danger. He sensed more than saw the movement behind him: a warning look of fear in the eyes of another of the hostages was all it took. He swung around, firing, and rolled a couple more times. Something ripped through his neck, snapping his head as though he'd been rabbit punched.

He saw now that the terrorist who had fired was a young woman. Thick, dark hair flew out around her head, like a glamour model whirling for the camera. Except she was already dead, ripped almost in two by the savage hail of Charlie's bullets. Her own weapon fell from her fingers as she slid down the wall she had been slammed against, leaving a thick crimson smear behind her.

An unreal silence fell. Only a few seconds, but it felt like an eternity, a shift into a whole new dimension. With it came several white-hot knives of pain that his adrenalin had so far anaesthetized. He knew he was badly hurt, but he could breathe. When he put a hand to his neck he could feel blood, but not the gusher there would have been if the carotid artery had been hit. He was going to be able to hang on, though his head was beginning to swim.

Then, in the distance, he heard shouts and more shooting as the waiting soldiers stormed the compound. It would soon be over. There wasn't much time.

Dragging the helpless young senator with him, he shouldered open a door and headed towards the sound of shouting and gunfire. He began to stumble over his own feet and had to fight to hang on to consciousness. But before he blacked out, he completed the most important – and secret – part of his mission.

He put a bullet through the young senator's head.

12

The voice on the phone told her that Samples had fallen from the window of his eighth-floor apartment. Although neither suicide nor foul play was officially suspected, Susan wasn't sure whether she heard or imagined a slight emphasis on the word 'officially'. Then he apologized and said he couldn't talk any longer because he had to go into a meeting. She asked him his name, and he said Tom Schiller. She thanked him for his time and hung up.

Next day, without telling anyone what she planned to do, she flew down to Baltimore and found the office where Tom Schiller worked. It was much as she'd imagined, except for being over Jack's Radio Shack instead of a Chinese take-out. There was a solid-looking street door with several locks and an unmarked entryphone. She pushed the button and waited. After a moment a light went on even though it was broad daylight, and she became aware of being scanned by a video eye. A woman's voice said, 'Can I help you?'

Susan explained who she was and apologized for not making an appointment. The woman asked her to wait, then after a moment said she could come up. The door clicked open. She climbed a narrow staircase at the top of which was another solid-looking door, also with several locks and a spyhole. She rang, and was admitted by a surprisingly attractive young woman in jeans and a roll-neck sweater. She looked as though she might normally have had a pleasant smile, though her manner that morning was tense and preoccupied. But there was no hint of the surly distrust of the world in general that Susan had half expected.

She found Tom Schiller also surprisingly open and easy to talk to. He couldn't have been much more than thirty. He had a casual, clean-cut look and was obviously bright. He ran the place, he told her, with a couple of assistants, one of whom Susan had already met. The other was a gangling young man with a beard who ran the computers. Writers and contributing editors, of which Dan Samples had been one, drifted in and out, said Schiller, as the mood took them. She got the impression that the latter were probably the ones who were dedicated to 'the cause', while Schiller himself had merely found a publishing niche from which he planned to build a wider empire. Nonetheless, he obviously cared about the things that were going on and which 'my team', as he called them, were investigating.

They went for lunch to an Italian place around the corner. She insisted he be her guest. He accepted graciously and ate with a healthy appetite. Schiller had no idea who she was or why Samples had been in touch with her. He knew only that Samples had been pursuing what he called 'his bionic man story', and that he had recently been to Russia for that purpose. He knew that Samples had come up with something there, but he didn't know what.

'Most of these guys play their cards pretty close to the chest. I guess they figure the less people know what they're up to, the less they're going to get hassled and pushed around – and maybe out of windows.'

He closed his mouth on a forkful of ravioli and watched her coolly to see what reaction his words had provoked in her.

She blinked a couple of times and felt her eyes narrowing as she met his gaze. 'Are you telling me Dan Samples was murdered?'

Schiller dropped his eyes while he casually forked up a few more squares of ravioli. 'Isn't that what you think, Dr Flemyng?' he asked. 'Otherwise what brings you here? You said you'd only met him the one time. He must've said something that got your interest pretty well revved up.'

He raised the fork to his mouth and his eyes to her, and awaited her response.

'I can't help saying, Mr Schiller, that you're taking all this very calmly. Almost as though it's an everyday occurrence to have one of your employees, or colleagues, or whatever he was, fall out of an eighth-floor window.'

Schiller gave a barely perceptible shake of the head. 'On the contrary,' he said, 'I'm very concerned indeed. I just like to be sure who I'm expressing my concern to before I speak.'

She held his gaze for a second or two, then reached into her purse and took out the polaroid that Samples had given her. 'Do you know who this is?' she asked, pointing to John.

Again he shook his head, more firmly this time. 'Where was this taken?' he asked.

'Siberia. Somewhere called Ostyakhon, about a hundred miles south of Noril'sk.'

Schiller listened impassively while she told him the whole story, omitting only the fact that she had suggested to Latimer West that he might like to take some legal action against Samples and his publisher. When she was done, Schiller took a deep breath, pursed his lips thoughtfully and suggested they take a walk.

She didn't ask where they were headed until they'd gone a couple of blocks. In reply he pointed to a run-down apartment building over the road. 'Dan Samples lived at the back. Come on. I'll show you.'

As they crossed the road her eyes went involuntarily to the eighth floor. It was a considerable drop to the sidewalk. The thought continued to preoccupy her until she realized that Schiller had fished a set of keys from his pocket and was heading for the scuffed and graffiti-covered main door. She followed him into the dark and gloomy lobby. There was no furniture other than a semicircular desk where a doorman must have sat in better days. Now the place didn't look as though it was even swept very often. There were no pictures on the walls and the air had an unpleasant staleness. They didn't speak until they were in the elevator, rattling uncertainly towards the eighth floor.

'I suppose you've been over the place already,' she said.

'I got the keys from the building super. Hadn't ever been in when Dan was alive, but I offered to clear his things out by the end of the month. The rent's paid till then.'

It was obvious when they entered the apartment that the clearing-out process had not yet started. Susan found herself in a drab but fairly light and spacious living room. Everything about it reflected a man who had been obsessively organized and wholly work oriented. Or, she corrected herself, research oriented. There were filing cabinets along the walls and folders on shelves, everything carefully labelled and arranged in a specific order. Other shelves bore dictionaries, directories and reference books of all kinds. There was a television and a laptop computer alongside a printer.

She exchanged a look with Schiller.

'If the evidence you're looking for is here,' he said, 'maybe you can find it. I couldn't. In fact there's no reference anywhere – and I've been over the place with a fine-tooth comb – to the Pilgrim Foundation or the bionic man story. Not on paper, not on his computer, which I had Greg – that's the guy you met in the office – check out. If you want to go through the place yourself, you're welcome.'

She thought a moment, and shook her head. Not only did she find the idea distasteful, but she was prepared to believe that Schiller had done a thorough job.

'Of course he may have hidden it somewhere else,' she said.

He tipped his head in a way that acknowledged she could be right. 'I talked to the people who live downstairs,' he said. 'An elderly couple, both a bit hard of hearing. All the same, about an hour before he went out the window they said they'd heard about five minutes of thumping and banging, as though he was jumping up and down. They were going to call up and complain, then it stopped as suddenly as it had started.'

'So you're implying,' she said, 'that somebody killed him, then spent an hour searching the place and removing whatever it was they were looking for – then threw him out.'

He shrugged. 'Company policy,' he said. 'We just report the facts as far as they can be established. We don't editorialize.'

She looked at him, then glanced once more around the room, then back to him. 'I want you to know,' she said, 'that I appreciate your having shared these "facts" with me. I think we should keep in touch.'

13

At the time of John's death, before his body had been brought home for burial, Susan had been asked if she wanted to fly out to view the scene of the accident. Several wives and relatives of the other victims had accepted the offer, but she had not. Her main reason was a reluctance to leave Christopher; she felt that he needed her just then more than she needed to make this particular pilgrimage. There were no raised eyebrows, however, when she told Frank Henty that she now felt ready to fly out to Russia and see for herself where John had spent the final days and hours of life. It was a wish that everyone understood without her having to explain.

It had occurred to her that if the agency made the arrangements for her, then she would be afforded at least some measure of protection against . . . she wasn't sure what. All she knew was that she didn't want to be out there on her own and unaccounted for.

She told no one of her ulterior motive for making the trip, not even her father. No point, she thought, in worrying him unduly. Besides, she didn't even know what she expected to find. She knew only that several people had died mysterious deaths, first her husband and his team, and now Dan Samples. And those deaths were somehow connected with a town called Ostyakhon in Siberia.

Christopher was delighted at the prospect of staying over at his friend Ben's house for a few days. Susan decided against explaining to him that she was going to see the place where his father had died, just saying that she was going away because of work. Her friend Carla, Ben's mother, supported her in this minor deception, which made her feel strangely better about it.

She had been once before to Moscow for a neurological conference, not long after the collapse of communism, but she had had no time to see anything outside the city itself. This time she didn't expect to get beyond Sheremet'yevo airport, to which she took a direct flight from JFK. Frank Henty had made a call to the airline and made a plea on compassionate grounds to have her economy seat upgraded to business class. In the event they found her a seat in first class, which allowed her to grab a few hours of reasonably comfortable sleep. In principle she had a three-hour stopover at Moscow-Sheremet'yevo before boarding an Aeroflot flight for the two-and-a-half-thousand-mile flight to Noril'sk. However, she had been warned to expect delays of up to six hours or more; this, after all, was Russia.

All she hoped was that the guide whom the agency had arranged to have meet her at Sheremet'yevo would actually show up. She had been told to go to the transfer desk and make herself known; in fact she was told by a stewardess just before the plane touched down that someone would be waiting for her when she disembarked and would take her through passport control. So far so good.

'Dr Flemyng? I'm Irina Lomova. Everybody calls me Ika, I hope you will.'

The woman, whose handshake was warm and welcoming, was around thirty and spoke excellent English with only a trace of an accent. She had thick blonde hair swept back from a face that was coarse-featured though attractive and open; it was the sort of face, Susan decided, that would grow on you.

'Susan,' she said. 'That's what everybody calls me. So tell me, Ika, how long a wait are we in for?'

Ika screwed her mouth up to one side and made a wavy gesture with her hand. 'The good news is the official time is still three hours. The bad news is that maintenance have lost a fuel truck, probably stolen, which could mean a delay of . . . who knows?' As she spoke she gave a shrug which seemed to come from deep down in the core of her being: a very Russian response, Susan thought, to a very Russian situation.

The best thing about the delay was that Ika had arranged for them to wait it out in the first-class lounge of the US airline that had flown them in. She advised Susan to eat as many sandwiches, fruit and biscuits as she could manage, because there wasn't going to be much on the five-and-a-half-hour flight to Noril'sk – whenever it got off the ground.

Ika, Susan discovered, had helped organize John's trip. There was genuine emotion in her voice when she spoke of her shock and sadness at the accident. The cause had not been properly ascertained and probably never would be; such things were difficult in Russia. It had been a charter plane, well maintained, and with a good pilot. The inquiry was officially continuing, but offered little hope of a solution. Susan nodded, grateful for the Russian woman's kindness, but said nothing about the darker suspicions that had brought her here to find out what she could for herself. Time alone would tell her whether Ika was someone she could confide in fully or not.

In the event the delay was only a little over four hours, though it was followed by a further forty minutes on the ground before take-off. Ika said they were in luck, as this was slightly better than average. The plane itself came as a shock to Susan. The seats appeared to be made for dwarfs and nearly half of them were broken. The cabin hadn't been cleaned for some time, and the floor was covered in greasy wrappers and discarded paper cups. Ika's last advice to Susan before boarding had been to make full use of the first-class lounge toilet facilities, because no human being should ever have to enter an Aeroflot toilet on a domestic flight. Unfortunately, Susan had drunk one cup of coffee too many, and after an hour or so the need was irresistible. She returned to her seat white and sickly, and had to close her eyes and breathe deeply for some minutes.

Noril'sk, Susan had read in the guidebook she'd had picked up in New York, was a town of roughly 170,000 inhabitants. It had been founded in 1935, and lay in the Rybnaya Valley amid the Putoran Mountains and was two hundred and fifty miles north of the Arctic Circle. It was one of the world's leading centres for the production of nickel and platinum. Copper was also mined. But perhaps the most distinctive thing about it was its gigantic airport, which provided the only link to Moscow and the rest of civilization within a 1,200-mile radius.

So much for the abstract information. As she felt the plane begin losing height she looked out of the window to see what the reality looked like. What she saw was a flat, featureless landscape stretching away to the horizon, mostly just bare ground or rock. There were no trees, just scatterings of scrub-like grey-brown vegetation, which Ika said was chiefly moss and lichen. It was a picture of the most uninhabitable bleakness that Susan had ever seen, and she found it almost impossible to believe that people actually lived down there. She glimpsed Noril'sk only as a cold, grey and unwelcoming sprawl before they touched down. There must have been almost a hundred planes on the tarmac, from huge intercontinental jets to old crates that would have looked more at home in a museum than the air.

Ika had already warned her that there would probably be another delay on the ground before disembarkation. The usual reason given, she said, was too many planes arriving at the same time and not enough buses to transport passengers to the terminal. Sure enough, they sat there for another fifty minutes after the engines had stopped.

Susan was beginning to feel a deep passivity, a withdrawal into the self that immured her against the kind of frustrations and obstacles that would normally have driven her to distraction. Perhaps, she thought, she was picking it up by osmosis from Ika and all the other Russians around her. Time for them was not what it was in the West – a commodity with measurable value. Here it was an abstraction, something that ceased to exist when it wasn't being used to some purpose.

They would be staying overnight in Noril'sk, Ika explained, because there was no flight to Ostyakhon till the following day. They took a taxi to the Arktika hotel where Ika had made reservations. The taxi stank so strongly of diesel oil that Susan tried to wind the window down to get some air, but it jammed after barely an inch. At least the battered vehicle got them to their destination, though shock absorbers would have been a welcome comfort.

Susan's room was, Ika assured her, the height of luxury, having its own bathroom. There was marble everywhere, and very little else. The taps spat scalding water and gave a trickle of cold. The bed was hard, though not broken. That evening they ate in a gloomy dining room enlivened only by a group of Russians at a neighbouring table consuming vodka by the gallon. Ika advised Susan to stick to the cabbage soup and sausage, and avoid the wine. They retired to bed early, and Susan was glad she'd brought some sleeping pills.

Ostyakhon was a mere ninety-five miles south of Noril'sk, which prompted Susan to ask why they didn't rent a car and drive down rather than fly; she'd already had more than enough experience of domestic air travel in Russia to last a lifetime. Ika explained that it was autumn, which meant that the roads, which were muddy and almost impassable in summer and swarming with giant mosquitoes, had not yet frozen into the hard tracks that were slightly more negotiable in winter. It would be a horribly uncomfortable two-day drive, at least. This way they could get down there in relative comfort (all comforts in Russia, she reminded Susan, were relative), check into the only establishment that could loosely be described as a hotel, which was where John and his group had stayed, then make trips out in an old jeep she had managed to rent from one of the local apparatchiks.

The plane they boarded in one corner of the giant airport did not fill Susan with confidence. It was a single-engined bi-plane, an Antonov 2, Ika explained, built in the 1940s and still in use as a reliable flying bus and freight carrier. There were four passengers in addition to Susan and Ika, all men, and all apparently suffering from gigantic hangovers. Whether or not they had got into this condition together or separately was unclear, since none of them was in the mood for conversation either among themselves or with Ika and Susan, a fact for which Susan considered herself fortunate.

Despite an alarmingly noisy and bone-jolting take-off, the plane took on a more dependable and solid feel in the air. There was actually something strangely reassuring in its age and much-used appearance, as though the act of flying over this bleak landscape was as casual and risk-free as hopping on municipal transport to travel a few blocks in the city. Indeed, the experience was not all that different, allowing for the difference in topography. The plane touched down four times to let passengers off and take on new ones; also to unload and replace various crates and packing cases. The landing strip was never more than a stretch of cleared, hard earth, sometimes incorporating cracked asphalt or large cement and steel slabs left behind, Ika explained, by the Americans after World War II. They were never on the ground more than fifteen minutes, and each time Susan peered from the window at a remoteness so extreme that she could hardly understand how human beings could inhabit it.

About a half hour before they were due to land at Ostyakhon, and by prior arrangement with the pilot, they made a detour over the site where John's plane had crashed. The other passengers either didn't notice the change of course, or had been forewarned, or were merely indifferent to such things, another example of that strange and rather touching Russian fatalism where matters not in their own hands were concerned.

There was little to see. All the wreckage had long since been retrieved. But for the fact that Ika said this was the place, there was nothing to indicate what had happened there. Susan tried to imagine the scene, as she had often, both awake and in her nightmares, but the reality of John's death still remained curiously remote – a lingering effect of shock, perhaps. She still had to come fully to terms with her loss.

'We can drive out tomorrow or the day after, if you would like,' Ika said softly beside her, as though knowing what was going through her mind.

'Yes, perhaps, I think I would,' Susan murmured. She saw the pilot give a discreet glance in Ika's direction, wondering if he should circle the spot again. 'Tell him to go on,' Susan said, 'and thank him, please. This was very kind.'

14

The landing at Ostyakhon was along the northern bank of Lake Khantayskoye, a stretch of water about a hundred and fifty miles long and varying between two and eight miles in width. From the air, Ika had pointed out the fish cannery on the lake shore, which had been the cause of John's coming to this place. The town itself, just a haphazard scattering of buildings from the air, was a mile or so away.

Ika explained that the long, derelict-looking shed which was the first thing they saw when they got off the plane was the local school. The jeep that Ika had arranged was waiting for them. The driver gave her the keys, then hopped on the back of a friend's waiting motorbike. The jeep was a two-seater, and they threw their bags in the back.

Architecturally, Ika explained as they drove into it, Ostyakhon was a good example of state model E3. Susan wasn't sure whether this was meant ironically or literally. Almost every building was a near-identical, three-storey concrete block. They were linked by a network of pipes which Ika said were 'utilidors' – conduits for water, electricity and gas which could not be buried underground because of the permafrost. Even at the warmest times of year, she said, when the surface became pure mud, the earth remained rock hard just beneath.

Here and there an old wooden 'isba', a traditional wood-built cabin with ornate doors and windows, broke the visual monotony. Most of them were oddly tilted or askew – a consequence, Ika explained, of movement in the permafrost beneath them. The only remotely distinguished piece of architecture was the People's Palace, a whitish Greek temple structure, in which a couple of broken windows had been boarded up with pieces from an old Coca Cola crate.

The hotel, Susan had already been warned, would make the one in which they'd spent the previous night look like a czar's palace. John, when he stayed there, had told her about it on the phone, so she was prepared for the worst. What she wasn't prepared for was the immediate and unsettling sense of déjà vu that she experienced the moment she stepped through the door. It took her a moment to realize that she was in the place where the polaroid of John with Dan Samples had been taken. She didn't even have to take it out to recognize specific details – a lamp with a faded blue shade, a hideous still life on the wall (which she could now see was an original), and beneath it a long sofa covered in some sort of coffee-brown artificial leather.

It was over dinner in the hotel that evening that Susan first showed Ika the picture of the two men together and asked her if she'd ever met Dan Samples. Neither the face nor name meant anything to her. She asked who he was. Susan side-stepped the question, saying she wasn't sure. She said her husband had sent her the photograph along with several others in a letter that he'd posted just before the fatal flight, and she would be curious to know, just for sentimental reasons, who the man was.

With Susan's permission, Ika showed the picture to

their waiter, the barman and the hotel manager, but drew a blank. Susan shrugged, said it was of no real importance, and put the picture back in her purse.

It was not long after nine when she went up to her room. She had just undressed and was about to take a sleeping pill when there was a knock at her door. It was Ika.

'I'm sorry, I hope you hadn't gone to bed.'

'No, I was just going to.'

'Only, I just talked to the night manager, and he says he might know the man you were asking about. He says that there is something here that the man left, and he wants to know what he should do with it.'

'Left? What did he leave?'

'A package of some kind. Papers.'

Five minutes later, fully dressed again, Susan was standing with Ika in the windowless, cupboard-sized office behind the reception desk. The night manager was a pale, overweight individual whose face and shortness of breath betrayed a wear and tear beyond his years – something Susan had observed in just about all the men in this place. When shown the polaroid, he confirmed that he had met Dan Samples. Not only that; it was he who, at Samples' request, had taken the picture of the two men.

He went on to recount how, on that same night that the photograph was taken, Samples had spent an hour using the ancient and very slow photocopier in the night manager's office – the one that Ika was leaning against at this moment. He had no idea what the document was or how many copies Samples had made. All he knew was that Samples had left one copy, or possibly the original, in an envelope in the night manager's safe, promising to phone or fax in a few days and give instructions about what should be done with it. By now several weeks had passed and nothing had been heard. Perhaps, as Dr Flemyng knew the gentleman, she might care to return his property to him, because the safe was very small and they didn't have room to store things indefinitely.

That night Susan did not take a sleeping pill. She didn't sleep at all, even though the forty or so pages Samples had left were quickly read, then re-read.

Sleep, after she had absorbed what was contained in them, was impossible.

15

Ika Lomova would tell her friends later that something had obviously happened to Susan Flemyng overnight. Clearly it must have been connected with the papers that had been left in the hotel safe, but Susan volunteered no explanation, and Ika sensed that questions would be unwelcome.

When Ika came down for breakfast at seven-thirty the next morning, she found Susan already in the lobby and barely able to contain her impatience while Ika swallowed a quick cup of coffee and a stale bread roll.

'Do you know how to find this?' she asked, producing a scrap of paper on which she'd scribbled down a name.

'The Igatrov Marshes? It's about an hour away.'

'I want to go there.'

Ika looked puzzled. 'It's the opposite direction from the crash site. There's nothing to see, just an old agricultural research station.'

'I'd like to go. Can we, please? Right away?'

'Of course, if you wish.'

They didn't talk much on the journey. Any effort Ika made to start up a conversation was met by a polite but monosyllabic response. Susan did not want to talk. She was preoccupied with her thoughts and preferred to keep them to herself. Only as they grew closer to their destination did she start asking questions.

'This agricultural research station? What d'you know about it?'

Ika shrugged. 'Not much. I think it was set up in the fifties. I've driven by it. The people who work there live on the premises. You don't see much of them outside.'

'And what exactly do they do?'

Again Ika shrugged. 'Whatever they do in all these places anywhere, I suppose. Try to develop a new strain of wheat or a higher milk-yielding cow.'

'And is it guarded?'

Ika's smile was vaguely sardonic. 'In Russia, everything official is guarded. It used to be the army, now it's some private organization, but I think it's the same men in a different uniform.'

The place itself when they arrived still had a military air about it. The buildings which were visible some distance beyond the wire fence had an ugly, functional appearance. Some were constructed of breeze-blocks, some of creosoted wood. Few were more than one storey high. Occasionally a lone figure would be seen walking from one building to another. Sometimes a vehicle moved between them. Ika said it was rumoured that there were sizeable underground installations, but nobody knew for sure.

Susan asked her to drive by a couple of times and then to stop while she got out and took some photographs. This activity aroused the interest of the guards at the gate; Ika saw one of them start to watch them through binoculars, then another began talking on a portable phone. Ika never knew whether there was any connection between this and what happened next, but a large unmarked helicopter clattered over the horizon and landed at some point inside the compound, where it was hidden from view by a cluster of buildings.

The incident had distracted Ika just long enough for her not to observe the unmarked though military-style jeep that had swung out of the compound's gates. She didn't see it until it swerved smartly across the nose of their own vehicle, blocking any attempt they might make to get away. Two men got out, both with revolvers in waist holsters. One held back, ready to cover his partner in case of any trouble; the other stepped forward and spoke to them in Russian.

Ika answered, trying to let neither Susan nor the man confronting her see how unnerved she was. There was much gesturing towards Susan as they talked. After several exchanges the man turned more fully to Susan and barked something at her.

'He wants to see your papers – passport and visa,' Ika translated.

Saying nothing, Susan produced them from her purse and handed them over. The man examined them sullenly, then reached abruptly for Susan's purse. Susan held on to it angrily.

'Stop it!' she said. 'Ika, tell him to stop this. He has no right.'

Ika didn't say anything, just watched anxiously as the man finally wrenched the purse from Susan's hands and then glared at her as though by resisting she had committed a serious offence against his authority.

'Tell him to go to hell, Ika! Who does he think he is?'

'Better stay calm, Dr Flemyng. Just let him show his masters that he's doing his job, then we go on our way.'

It was an attempt at reassurance, but her voice sounded less confident than she would have liked it to.

Susan continued to glare angrily at the man as he rifled through her belongings. Nothing seemed to interest him much until he found the polaroid of John with Dan Samples. He took it out and looked at it for a few moments, frowning. Then he turned and said something over his shoulder to his partner.

'What's he saying?' Susan asked.

'He's telling the other one to call the office,' Ika replied.

The man by the jeep had pulled up a dash mike and was speaking into it. As he did so, he glanced beyond the fence to the distant buildings.

'I think there is someone watching us,' Ika said, pointing, 'from behind a window over there.'

The man in front of her said something sharply. She replied with equal sharpness. His mouth tightened, and for a moment Susan thought he was going to hit Ika. But he was distracted by the crackle of a voice from the jeep radio. The man standing by it spoke briefly into the mike again, then hung up and turned to say something to his partner.

'They want you to go with them,' Ika said, her own fear vanishing in the face of her concern for Susan. She addressed several animated sentences to the two men in Russian, but her arguments were dismissed by a curt headshake and a few words.

'What did you say to them?' Susan asked.

'I say you are American citizen, they have no right to do this. Your ambassador and government will make big scandal, these men lose their jobs.'

The failure of this threat to make any impact on the men in question was underlined by the none-too-gentle pressure Susan felt on her arm, urging her to move to their jeep and get into the back seat. Once again Ika launched a torrent of protest in Russian, her voice rising half an octave in anger. This time the man who was pushing Susan into the jeep swung around and aimed a menacing forefinger at a point between Ika's eyes. Susan didn't need a translation to tell her that the few words he snapped out were a final warning to Ika to back off if she didn't want to suffer the same fate herself.

'Ika, it's all right,' she said, shouting to make herself heard over the general scuffle and crosstalk. 'I'll go with them, I'm not worried.'

'I call somebody for you – the embassy.'

'It's all right . . .'

Ika said something else in Russian, then added for Susan's benefit, 'I tell them take me with you – you need translator.'

Susan didn't have time to respond before the other guard, the one who'd spoken on the radio, pinned Ika's arms from behind and pushed her roughly towards her own vehicle, where he wrenched open the door and threw her in. Then he climbed behind the wheel of his own jeep, reversed into the road and drove them at speed back towards the gates.

That was the last, Ika would tell people later, that she ever saw of Susan Flemyng. She continued to watch through the fence as the jeep headed for what looked like the main block among the scattered buildings, then swung left and headed between two of them. Seconds later, it and its occupants had disappeared from view.

16

The room into which Susan was shown had no furniture except for a bench attached to one wall. It was clearly a security holding area because there was no handle on the inside of the door and the single window was barred and fitted with opaque glass. The plastered walls were painted in a faded green and were absolutely bare. She glanced at her watch and saw she had been sitting there for a little over ten minutes when she heard a key turn in the lock and the door opened. The guard who gestured for her to follow him was one she hadn't seen before.

She was shown into an office that was a little more welcoming than the room she had just left, though not by much. A coal fire burned dimly in a grate, there were a few prints and what looked like diplomas on the walls, and two windows (without bars) that looked out on to a kind of inner courtyard formed by the central cluster of buildings. Behind a desk sat a man in a threadbare suit with a few pitiful strands of hair carefully fixed in place across his bald head. He looked like the eternal and universal petty bureaucrat, and he did not get to his feet when she entered. In fact he didn't even look up from the document he was studying, occasionally tapping a line with his ballpoint pen as he mulled over its significance.

The guard who had brought Susan in had withdrawn

93

respectfully and shut the door after him. She stood waiting for several moments before breaking the silence.

'I hope you speak English,' she said, not disguising the resentment she felt at this high-handed treatment. 'Because you seem like an offensive little man, and I'd hate to waste my breath telling you so if you can't understand what I'm saying.'

He gave no sign of being aware that she had spoken, just went on tapping his pen down the page he was reading, then turned it over and continued on the other side.

'I would like some kind of explanation,' she continued. 'I don't know where you've spent your career until now, but you obviously have no idea of the kind of trouble that taking an American citizen prisoner in this way is going to cause.'

The man drew a long, slow breath, then sat back and looked at her. A faintly supercilious smile played over his bland features, as though he wanted her to see that her attempts at sarcasm had merely amused him.

'Please explain your interest in what we're doing here, Dr Flemyng,' he said, in perfect, near-accentless English.

'I trust you won't mind if I sit down,' she said, 'because I'm going to anyway – as you haven't the manners to ask me.'

He tipped his head slightly and made an open-handed gesture, inviting her to be his guest, but still didn't move. She pulled a chair over from the wall, and sat facing him across his desk. Even though their eyes were now level, he created an illusion of superior height by tipping his head further back and peering at her down his nose.

'I am still waiting for an answer to my question, Dr Flemyng.'

'The answer is that I know what you're doing here. And very soon the rest of the world will know. So I think that's all we have to say to each other, Mr . . . whoever you are. Perhaps I'll wait to find that out from the newspapers.'

The man sighed in a way designed to emphasize yet again how empty her threats were. 'There will be nothing in the newspapers, Dr Flemyng. Or on television. Or, for that matter, anywhere else.'

'I wonder what makes you so sure of that.'

In reply, he looked past her. She sensed that someone had entered the room without her hearing. She turned.

A man stood there, astrakhan coat hanging open over an expensive suit, a pair of soft black leather gloves clasped almost foppishly in one hand.

It was Latimer West.

The room they had adjourned to was again more comfortable than the previous one. With its armchairs and drinks cabinet, it struck Susan as a kind of visiting VIP lounge, although there was no doubt in her mind that the VIP was West and not herself.

'We're going to have a civilized conversation, Susan,' he said, after offering her a drink, which she had refused. 'I know what you think and how you feel. Nonetheless, I'm sure I can persuade you to see things differently.'

'You murdered my husband. Is that what you call civilized? D'you think you can persuade me to see that differently?'

There was a hangdog sadness in the way he looked at her. She wondered for a moment if it came from regret over his crime or simply from her bad taste in bringing it up.

95

'I am not the principal in these matters, Susan. I do not make final decisions. I am what I have always been – an administrator.'

'And you think that puts you above the law? Or any consideration of right and wrong?'

He sighed and nodded thoughtfully, as though he understood and sympathized with all she said. 'You know that your work has been, as you would claim, "misused". But you also know now that you are not alone in this. Indeed, you would be disingenuous to pretend that the possibility of such "misuse" had never occurred to you.'

'I thought there were safeguards. No, let me correct that. I *knew* there were safeguards. I *thought* they worked.'

West gazed down ruefully at his hands, which lay loosely clasped over his stomach.

'Of course they work.' His voice took on a note of weariness, as though restating the obvious was beginning to test his patience. 'Otherwise quite the wrong sort of people might have got their hands on this project by now.'

She wanted to laugh at the sheer arrogance of the remark, but somehow couldn't bring herself to do it.

'How strange,' she said, 'that the depth of your cynicism fails to surprise me, Dr West. I barely knew you at the foundation, but I always sensed it.'

He looked at her and raised an eyebrow. It was an ironic gesture, mocking almost.

'Your problem, Susan, is that you forgot the most fundamental law of science – which is that there is no such thing as a free lunch. That is something every scientist has known since Archimedes lowered himself into his bath and shouted "Eureka!" So we must begin to wonder why scientists such as yourself turn your backs on that eternal truth. Perhaps because, like all hypocrites, you know perfectly well what's going on, you just don't want to see it. You tacitly approve, but you don't want to say so openly.'

'That is absurd!'

'All science is a double-edged sword. It is pure only in the mind, at conception, as an idea, an equation, or just some new way of looking at things. But once it's out there in the world, it becomes whatever the world wants it to be. Germ warfare, nuclear holocaust or a cure for cancer.'

'There's no comparison—'

'You want the right to do your work on your own terms and the wherewithal to do it.' He was on his feet now, his impatience with her growing into open irritation. 'You want the luxury of thinking your own thoughts in your ivory tower. All right, you can have it – but read before you start telling us what we can and can't do.'

'You don't have the right to use any of my work without my agreement.'

He tossed his head with scorn and gave a murmur of bitter amusement.

'In a court of law no doubt your view would prevail. But the world is not a court of law. It is a court of common sense, of which the law is only one part.'

'A very small part in your world.'

He stopped the pacing he had begun and looked at her sharply out of the corners of his eyes.

'My world is your world, Susan. Ordered the way you

like it, for your comfort and pleasure and security, where you are able to get on with your work and avoid confronting the necessary unpleasantnesses of life . . .'

It was as far as he got, because Susan had sprung from her chair and attacked him with a ferocity she didn't know she possessed. She knew that the voice she could hear screaming obscenities was hers, but she felt strangely detached from it. As indeed she did from any sense of physical contact with him. Her rage was so deep and inexpressible that violence could not assuage it. She knew only that she was pounding and kicking and tearing at him, but it was doing no good. And yet she couldn't stop, until she became aware that she was being stopped by force. Two guards had entered the room and were dragging her away from him, pinning her arms behind her back. Only now did she see that his collar was torn, his hair disordered and his face streaming with blood from a long scratch under his eye.

'All right . . . all right . . . give her a moment to calm down.'

West was breathing hard as he spoke, dabbing his wound with a handkerchief. His words were translated into Russian by the little bureaucrat who had also entered the room. Slowly the guards released their grip on her, as though wanting to be sure that she wasn't about to launch herself at him again.

But the worst of her rage had gone. She allowed herself to be led back to the chair she had been occupying, and didn't resist the pressure on her shoulder to be seated. She wanted to sob helplessly, but knew this was something she would never permit herself to do. Instead she sat like a sullen child, staring at the floor, her hair a tumbled mass covering half her face.

The guards stepped back, but remained by the door. West remained standing, breathing slightly easier, still dabbing at his wound and brushing back his hair. He became crisp and businesslike.

'Now, Susan, I'm going to put some questions to you, and I want answers. How did you find out?'

She looked up at him through her hair, not bothering to brush it from her eyes. Somehow she felt such a gesture would have shown a kind of respect for him, and she didn't want to risk that.

'I got a copy of the file that Dan Samples had given to my husband. How else?'

'Where did you get it?'

'At the hotel in Ostyakhon.'

West froze and looked at her in disbelief.

'The hotel?'

'You mean you didn't think of searching there? You're not as efficient as you like to appear, are you?'

'We checked. Your husband had left nothing at the hotel.'

'But Samples did.'

West looked doubly surprised. She didn't try to hold back a faint smile she felt playing around her mouth.

'This is all most encouraging, Dr West. I was afraid you people might be infallible. I see you're not.'

He ignored the jibe and snapped, 'Where is that file now?'

'I won't tell you, and even if you torture it out of me, it won't do you any good.'

'You know we can make you tell us without torturing you.'

'True. But the file is already beyond your grasp. It's too late.'

She felt a kind of elation now. Suddenly she was winning this confrontation. She hadn't anticipated trouble when she came to photograph the camp. All the same, she had been ready for it. She had made sure that Samples' file was in safe hands. That was her only protection. She was terrified, but she could see from the look on West's face that it was a protection that might work.

West contemplated her a while. She could almost see the wheels turning behind his forehead as he weighed the implications of her words.

'Of course you realize, Susan, that the information in that file is effectively useless unless you are there to back it up and explain what it all means. It amounts only to accusations, which are always deniable.'

She tipped her head, acknowledging he had a point. 'All the same, the media will have quite a time with those "accusations".'

West continued to dab at his scratch, then contemplated his blood-stained handkerchief for a while as though he could find some guidance in the spreading red Rorschach.

'You have a point,' he said eventually. 'It is something we would prefer to avoid. Fortunately, it is a contingency, one of many, against which we are already prepared.'

Something in the way he spoke checked the feeling of relief that Susan had started to enjoy. There was an enduring confidence in him that she didn't like. Without thinking, she brushed back her hair to get a clearer view of him.

He noticed the gesture and knew that she was worried. The balance between them had swung back in his favour. She sensed his satisfaction as he turned to the little bureaucrat who had remained in the room.

'You might care to put through that call now,' he said.

Susan watched as the shabby little man dialled a long-distance number. It was answered promptly. 'One moment please, Mr Hyde,' said the little man, 'I have your daughter here. She would like to speak with you.'

Susan watched, too shocked to react, as West took the phone from the little bureaucrat and handed it to her. Automatically she said, 'Hello, Daddy?'

'Hello, darling,' he said.

She could tell at once that something was wrong. The vibrancy had gone out of his voice. He sounded older.

'It's Christopher,' he said, and went on quickly before she could react. 'He's not hurt or anything like that. But I'm afraid he's disappeared.'

'How d'you mean "disappeared"?' She could feel her heart beating, and felt strangely suspended between fear and relief that the news wasn't worse. 'You mean somebody's taken him?'

'I'm afraid that's the way it seems. There's someone here now, insisting I make this call.'

'Daddy, are you hurt?'

'No – don't worry about me. We must think of Christopher. I've been told to tell you that you must do as they say.'

'Daddy, d'you know who "they" are? It's the Pilgrim—'

At a signal from West the little bureaucrat had broken the connection. Susan looked up at him.

'I swear, West, if anything happens to my son . . .'

'Nothing will, Dr Flemyng – provided you take your father's advice, and do as you are told.'

17

They took the helicopter that she'd seen arrive earlier. It flew for about twenty minutes, then landed at a small military airbase. At least it seemed military from the way it was guarded, but most of the planes she could see were private jets. They boarded a 737. The interior was done up like a luxury hotel. At least they gave her a private cabin. She had a bathroom, a fridge – everything she needed. Nobody interrupted her during the flight. She was sure there was a fibre-optic lens watching her but she didn't try anything to test her theory.

She tried to rest, but she couldn't sleep. When dawn came up she looked out and saw they were still over the sea. A while later there was a knock at her door. She called 'Come in,' and a young man entered. He was one of the crew she had observed when she boarded the plane.

'Dr West would like to talk with you before we land, Dr Flemyng. If that's convenient, would you follow me, please?'

They went through to a conference room. West sat in a deep leather armchair with a swivel base. He didn't get up, but gestured to a similar chair opposite him. She sat. Between them was a low table, a pot of coffee, and a tray of croissants and conserves.

102

'We shall be landing in California in about an hour,' he said. 'Please, have some breakfast.'

She accepted a cup of coffee, but nothing to eat. Before they boarded the plane she had told him everything there was to know about the two copies of Samples' file that she had been planning to get back to America. Two because, like Samples himself, she had spent several hours labouring over the hotel's ancient photocopier. Then she had paid the night manager extravagantly to make sure that one copy was posted first thing in the morning – addressed not to her father, in case West's people should be watching the mail, but to an old college friend who lived in New York. Inside the envelope was a second envelope with a note asking her to deliver it by hand to Amery Hyde. The other copy she had hidden in the lining of her suitcase, but that had already been handed over to West.

'You're undoubtedly wondering, Dr Flemyng, where we all go from here,' West began. 'You're an intelligent woman, highly intelligent. You must have thought through all the possible scenarios.'

The look in her eyes was as flat as her voice. 'There's only one,' she said. 'You have to kill me. If you harm my son you'll have to kill me, because nothing else will stop me. And if you don't harm him, even if I make promises, you'll never trust me. You know I'd figure out a way to get you. So you can't take that risk. Which means I have no more life. I know that. So it's my son's life we're talking about, not mine. All I want is to know he gets out of this unharmed.'

West looked at her for a moment, as though weighing and measuring the suppressed anger in her voice. 'Dr Flemyng, I didn't ask you or your husband to involve yourselves in any of this. Your own choices have brought you here, not mine. Neither I nor anyone connected with this project would have attempted to involve you against your will. All we required was that you mind your own business. But apparently that was too much to ask. You have forced your way into things, and that's where we find ourselves now. We must try to live with that fact. We shall all live with it far more comfortably if from now on you give us your full cooperation.'

Susan frowned, not quite sure that she had heard him correctly, and quite sure that he couldn't have meant seriously what he seemed to have just said.

'Are you suggesting that I take part in this programme?'

'Exactly that.'

She almost laughed, but instead a gust of scorn blew from her lips when she opened them to speak.

'It's monstrous! I'll have nothing to do with it!'

He nodded slowly several times, as though this was the answer he had expected.

'Dr Flemyng, your father has already called the person in New York to whom you sent the file. When it arrives it will be collected, ostensibly on his behalf, by one of our people. It may be several days before the package arrives. If you wish to delay your decision until it does, so you will finally know you've lost the game, be my guest.'

A silence hung in the air between them. She wondered if all evil was the same – this casual disposal of other people's lives: deal-making to let them live, but no qualms about killing, or at least ordering the kill when necessary.

'You must see that your participation in the programme is the only way we'll ever be able to trust you at all from now on.'

'You think I wouldn't still blow the whistle the first chance I got? Forcing me under duress to take part isn't going to keep me quiet.'

He smiled faintly, as though everything she said merely confirmed his expectation of the way their conversation would go. 'Of course I don't imagine anything so naive. But I think you'd like your life, and your son's life, to return to normal, or something as close to normal as can be arranged. Isn't that right?'

She didn't reply at once. As her silence continued, she realized she had confirmed his supposition. Again he nodded, just once this time, acknowledging the deal she had unwittingly shown herself willing to make. She did not contradict him.

'To all intents and purposes,' he went on, 'you would be free. Of course there would be nothing to stop you telling what you know to the press or anyone you chose, but you would be under a considerable disincentive to do so, knowing that your son's life would be immediately forfeit. You wouldn't be able to hide or protect him from us. His whereabouts and yours would be monitored at all times. Even in the event of your death, his safety would depend on whether you had left anything unfortunate behind, in the form of a document or memo in some lawyer's office or bank vault.'

'Dear God,' she whispered softly, almost in awe of the ruthlessness she found herself facing and the terrible power that seemed to be behind it.

'Come along, Dr Flemyng, even if you can't entirely trust me, you know that going along with what I'm saying is your best bet. Yours and your son's.'

She remained silent for a moment, absolutely and unnaturally still, hardly breathing, her eyes fixed on his.

But there was no contact in the gaze. She was looking at him not as at a living thing, but rather as she might regard some compound in her lab, wondering how best to break it up into its parts and find out how it was assembled, how it worked.

'What do you want me to do?' she asked after a while, her voice cold and sterilized of all emotion.

West pushed himself up from his seat and went to look out of one of the cabin windows. She could feel that the aircraft was beginning its descent.

'We've taken certain aspects of your work further than you ever envisaged – you already know that.' He turned back from the window but didn't resume his seat. Instead he stood there, hands thrust casually in trouser pockets, looking down at her. 'The whole psychological architecture we've created is working almost better than we could have hoped. But there is a problem, just one, that so far we haven't been able to get over.'

He looked at her, as though waiting for her to ask what it was. But she wasn't going to do that. He folded his arms and continued.

'Visual memory,' he said. 'We've had some problems with his visual memory.'

Part Two

Part Two

18

Control sat back in the hospital chair by Charlie's bed. 'It went well,' he said. 'We're lucky you weren't more seriously hurt.'

Charlie noted the 'we'. Control seemed genuinely pleased that Charlie had come out of that embassy affair alive.

'Another inch and that bullet would have severed your brain from the top of your spine. You got another in your shoulder – nicked the bone, you'll have to go easy for a while. But your rib will feel better in a few days. Have you any idea how you broke it?'

'I hit a tree when I came down. It could have been then.'

They chatted a while more, going over some of the details of the job, but without a formal debriefing. Maybe that would come later, if at all. Control seemed happy with the outcome. Everything, aside from Charlie's injuries, had gone to plan.

When Control left, Charlie reached for the remote and switched on the TV. He surfed a few channels, then found CNN doing a piece on the end of the embassy siege. It led with the tributes still pouring in after the tragic loss of the young senator's life. There was more about international cooperation against terrorism, about coordination and training, about the resolve of governments to stand firm and so on. The military action was re-hashed in detail, minus any reference, naturally, to Charlie. He was used to that. If he'd been mentioned, it would have meant something had gone badly wrong.

Bored with the news coverage on TV, and feeling suddenly tired, he flipped off the set and settled back to rest. He closed his eyes. An image filled his mind. A woman's face. At first he couldn't put a name to her. Then he realized, with a shock, who she was. He was looking at the face of Kathy Ryan.

The image was so startling in its clarity that he opened his eyes and tried to sit up, forgetting the restrictions imposed by his injuries. But even the brutal stab of pain that shot through him didn't dislodge the picture from his mind's eye. He stared at the blank wall opposite; but he saw, as clearly as if she had been standing there, the face of Kathy Ryan. The memory that had been lost for so many years was suddenly – magically – restored to him.

He wondered how this could have happened. How could he have forgotten that familiar young face that he had loved so deeply? Why did he suddenly remember it now? Was it somehow connected with the injuries he had suffered? That blow to his head from the bullet that so nearly killed him? There was no way of telling.

Maybe a shrink could make sense of it. But he didn't know any shrinks. He couldn't offhand think of anyone who might help him with this. But almost as quickly he decided he didn't want any help. This was his affair, his memory, his life, and it would stay that way.

There was no living soul he would choose to discuss it with.

19

Susan had done what they had asked of her, but it wasn't over yet. She paced her comfortable and spacious quarters, unable to leave, unable to relax. The procedure to improve the subject's visual memory had been successful, yet she was expected to remain on standby in case anything else important or urgent came up. The carrot of a return to 'normal life' for herself and Christopher, not to mention her father, still dangled out there, but whoever controlled it was not yet ready to bring it within her grasp.

Not that she had any guarantee they ever would. She knew she had accepted a gamble, the only alternative to which was probably too dangerous to risk. For the moment, however, there was nothing she could do except wait and let the game play out.

Her phone rang. It was West. 'Would you like to talk to your son?' he asked.

'Of course I'd like to talk to him,' she snapped. 'Where is he?'

'He's in good hands,' West said. 'I assure you he's quite safe and perfectly happy. Hold on, I'll patch him in.'

She heard various connections being made. Then suddenly, down the line, came Christopher's voice.

'Mom?'

'Christopher?'

'Mommy? Where are you? When can I come home?'

'Soon, darling, I promise. How are you? Are you all right?'

'Okay, I guess.' His tone was grudging. 'They said you sent me here. Did I do something wrong?'

'No, of course you didn't, darling. Nothing at all.'

'So why'd you send me here?'

She thought fast. There was sure to be someone listening on the line, maybe even West himself.

'It's just that I have to be away for a while. I'll make it as short a time as I can.'

'Why d'you have to be away? What are you doing?'

'Later, darling. I'll tell you all about it when I'm back.'

'Why can't I stay at Ben's house?'

'Well, a couple of nights is okay, but . . . you know, you can't stay too long with people, not even your friends. You'd start to get in each other's way.'

'Why can't Grandpa come to the house and look after me again?'

'He's . . . I'm afraid he's busy. He'd like to, but he can't. Don't worry, darling, it won't be for long.'

There was a silence, but she knew it wasn't the kind of silence that meant he'd finished. There was still something he wanted to say, but didn't know how.

'What is it, Chris? What's on your mind?'

There was a tremor in his voice as he spoke. 'Mom, I thought maybe you were dead.'

She felt her throat tighten and tears come to her eyes.

'I'm perfectly all right, darling. You mustn't worry. Everything's going to be all right. We'll soon be together again.'

'Will you call me again?'

'Of course I will.'

'There are horses here. They say I can learn to ride.'

The remark took her by surprise. Or perhaps it was the change of tone and the sudden enthusiasm behind it, like a child phoning home from summer camp, unhappy and homesick at first, then wanting to stay longer than planned.

'That's good, darling. Where are you? On a ranch somewhere?'

'Yeah. They said you arranged it.'

Again she had to think quickly. It was a lie she realized she couldn't afford to deny.

'Of course I did, darling. I just didn't know . . . what kind of ranch. I haven't been there.'

'It's kind of neat. And there's a helicopter.'

'That sounds wonderful, Chris!'

She heard a door bang and a dog barking in the background. The sound was oddly familiar.

'Is that Buzz?'

'Sure. They said I should bring him with me. He's having a great time.'

'I'm glad.'

Oddly, it was the news that Christopher had his dog with him that reassured her more than anything else. There was a click on the line and West's voice cut in.

'Time to wind up, Susan. Christopher can't hear me – just do it naturally.'

Another click.

'Darling, I've got to go now. I'll call again soon. I love you.'

'Love you, Mom.'

20

They sent Charlie home after a week. He was driven in a private car, not an ambulance. Control had visited him once more and said he was to have as much time off as he needed to get well. They could arrange a vacation if he wanted, but he chose to stay home. Why spoil what he knew would be a good time by adding elements of the unpredictable? He got enough unpredictability in his work.

He painted, swam and worked out at the gym as he got better. Every night he'd have a date with one or another of the girls – sometimes two, if it was Savannah and Jane, who always worked as a team. The girls would come over around six-thirty and they'd go to bed for an hour or so. Then they'd go out, eat something, maybe dance a little sometimes, then they'd come back and screw themselves to sleep. In the morning the girls left after breakfast and maybe a little fun in the shower, leaving him on his own again and looking forward to a bright new day.

Virgil Fry came by to pick up the latest batch of Charlie's paintings. He showed no interest in how Charlie had received the injuries from which he was recovering. It was as though the little man had somehow known what to expect; as though, Charlie reflected later, he had been fully briefed before arriving. He wondered whether that could be the case, and made a mental note to question him the next time he saw him.

He glanced at his watch. It was time to go down to the gym, work out, take a swim, then back home to prepare himself for the evening's amusement. The girl he was seeing tonight was Lila, pronounced 'Lie-la'. At least, she said that was her name. Charlie had a feeling it was a made-up name. He'd once known a girl called Eileen, although she spelled it 'I-lean', as in on a gate or against a wall. She had ambitions to be an actress and thought a novelty name might be a useful gimmick. Charlie had seen her in a TV movie on television and decided that talent would have been more useful.

He and Lila had met soon after he'd come out of the hospital. He'd been passing this little perfume store in the lobby of his apartment building at the marina when he'd seen this statuesque and lavishly proportioned woman with a shock of red-gold hair. He'd gone right in there, pretending he had to buy a gift for his sister. He'd asked for her advice, but she'd seen through the ploy at once and laughed – a friendly laugh that told him she was flattered by his attentions. He'd suggested they go somewhere for a drink. The place they went was his apartment, and it was a while before they got around to the drink.

Since then they'd been going out a couple of times a week. She was older than most of the girls in his life. At a guess, he'd have put her a year or two older than himself, but she was great looking and loved sex. Plus she was easy to have around.

They went to a new restaurant. It was her idea; she'd read about the place and wanted to try it. The cooking was part Chinese, part French. Charlie said that sounded great.

At some point in his special training, in between an advanced course on how to kill with his bare hands and another on survival in sub-zero terrain, he'd done a course called 'Social Etiquette'. They'd done classes in everything from polite conversation to which knife to use with the cheese. Wine tastings had been arranged, and Charlie learned how to steer his way between a Californian Cabernet and a decent Bordeaux. He would never be an expert, but he knew enough not to make a fool of himself. Wine waiters accorded him a proper respect and did not take on airs when he asked their advice about some out-of-the-way label or lesser-known vintage. In fact the role of man-about-town was one he enjoyed and had taken to with surprising ease. It amused him that even very limited knowledge, if presented with authority and just the right degree of understatement, could be passed off as sophistication.

He and Lila ate and drank well that evening, talked, told stories, laughed. Then they went back to his place, where the evening only got better. About three in the morning he awoke drowsily with the sense that something was happening. He found Lila getting dressed. She said she'd been trying not to disturb him.

'Why are you leaving?' he asked, propping himself up on an elbow.

She gave a little shrug, as though it was something she couldn't or didn't wish to talk about. 'I'd rather,' she said.

'Is something wrong?'

She shook her head.

'Well, come on . . . come back to bed.'

'I'd rather go, really.'

He looked at her. She continued dressing, businesslike and brisk, avoiding eye contact with him.

'For God's sake, Lila, it's three in the morning!'

'I've got my car.'

He swung his feet to the floor but remained sitting on the edge of the bed. He felt annoyed but didn't want to let her see it. That wasn't the best way to handle this situation, he decided.

'Talk to me. What's on your mind?'

No reply.

'Lila?'

She seemed to think a moment, then looked at him very directly as though she was about to deliver some kind of ultimatum. Only it wasn't an ultimatum, just a blunt statement of fact.

'Charlie, I'm here for the same reason you are – for an evening out and a good time in bed. I don't ask any more, and I don't want you to ask any more from me. I don't want you to ask if I've ever been married or if I have any kids, or whether my parents are alive and where they live. You don't ask anyway, but I never expected you would. So everything's fine, let's keep things the way they are, and if you don't mind I'd like to go home.'

'But I do mind.'

He was standing now, hands by his sides, suddenly aware of how easy it would be to settle this small difference between them. At the same time he knew how meaningless that would be. It wasn't that he was against the use of force on moral grounds; it was just that force, in some circumstances, simply couldn't deliver. Rape wasn't his idea of good sex. A partner had to be as willing and enthusiastic as he was himself.

So let her go, if that was what she wanted.

He raised his hands and held them palms out, pressing on some invisible space between them. 'Okay, you do what you want. What am I going to do – keep you prisoner?'

He gave a little laugh to underline the fact that everything was cool and she had nothing to fear. She looked back at him and something softened around her eyes. 'No,' she said, 'I know you wouldn't do that, or I wouldn't be here.'

As she spoke, she pulled on her high-heels and undulated across the floor to him.

'I had a great time. Call me soon.'

She kissed him lightly on the mouth, then turned and headed for the door. When she reached it she paused and flashed him a big smile over her shoulder.

'See you.'

Then she was gone.

Charlie pulled on a robe and wandered through to his bar in the main room. He thought about putting on some music, but couldn't decide what. So he took out a cold beer, sank into a chair and swung his legs over the arm.

There was only one thought in his mind, one image overshadowing all else. Lila was forgotten and so were all the others. It was the face of Kathy Ryan. Did she ever think of him, he wondered for the millionth time? What had become of her? She didn't have an easy start in life, no more than he did. But he'd been lucky. He hoped Kathy had been lucky.

And he wondered if, one day, he'd ever figure out a way of finding out.

21

Charlie had never spoken directly with Control about sex before. One of the things that gave him confidence in the man, however, was that he never dodged a question or failed to give a clear answer.

'For Christ's sakes, Charlie! What d'you think your right hand's for?'

'Sir?'

Control lowered his head and pushed it forward, his eyes burning into Charlie's head.

'Your dick won't drop off if you don't have sex for a few days.'

'This could be weeks, sir. You said so yourself.'

Control sighed irritably and sat back. They were sitting outside a coffee and doughnut pull-in off the 101 going north. They had met there in separate cars.

'I'll tell you what,' Control said, after drumming his fingers on the table for a while, 'we'll give you a phone number. You can have them send some girls over now and then, and we'll pick up the tab – within reason.'

'Thank you, sir, that sounds good. But I'd prefer to make personal contacts in the community.'

'You know the rules, Charlie.' Control's gaze hardened. 'Anything that could threaten the security or success of the operation . . . you don't want to know what would happen to you if you did that. Do you understand?'

'Yes, sir.'

'Rule one, Charlie. What is it?'

'Don't fuck up, sir.'

'And rule two?'

'Don't fuck up, sir.'

'And three?'

'Don't fuck up, sir.'

'And all the other rules?'

'Don't fuck up, sir.'

'Right.'

Control let the last few words hang in the air – no doubt, Charlie thought, for his improvement. But he'd got the point. Everything came second to getting the job done.

The cars swished by with a metronomic regularity.

'I won't fuck up, sir.'

He figured that surveillance was a convalescence job. Control had said as much. 'It'll get you back into the swing of things, Charlie. A warm-up, nothing too demanding.'

They'd rented him an old fisherman's cottage, decorated and done up comfortably, with a studio attached. Whatever he needed was delivered from Old Harbour, which was the name the residents had given to the most recently developed and prosperous side of their community.

Charlie liked New England. He had never spent time on the East Coast before, but he'd been told that life there wouldn't differ in any important way from California, except that both the climate and the people would be cooler. His cover was an artist on vacation painting a series of landscapes. It was an obvious choice and had the advantage of making him master of his own time, so he could stick around as long as he had to without arousing suspicion.

It was early spring and nature was coming back to life. In the mornings he painted outdoors, early, while the light was best. In the afternoons he might run, swim, and do some more work in his studio. Sometimes he took his four-wheel drive into Old Harbour to get dinner, or just to see a few faces. The drive took him past the house he was supposed to be watching. He could also see it through powerful binoculars from his cottage. So far it had remained closed up and uninhabited. It was built of white clapboard and overlooked the ocean. It had green shutters and a carefully tended garden ringed by a picket fence. Several times in the first week he saw a gardener at work, but by keeping him under discreet observation he discovered that he lived a couple of miles away and never entered the house. So far as Charlie could see, no one ever entered the house. It looked like the kind of place that some wealthy family might keep for use at weekends or a month in the summer. Other times they might rent it out. But certainly, nobody was using it now.

Charlie had been told that somebody would be coming to live in the house. He wasn't told who, or what they would be doing there, not even how many of them there would be. Only that any new presence was to be reported immediately to the number Charlie had been given.

On the matter of sex, a compromise had been worked out with Control. Charlie was to invite any of his girl-friends from California to come and stay with him when-ever he wanted. Alternatively, if he preferred not to have them in the house, there was another little cottage about half a mile from his own which they could use. Savannah and Jane came out for a few days. He installed them in the separate cottage because, frankly, he enjoyed his privacy. The arrangement worked well. When they left, he had Carol (he had ascertained there was no 'e') come out to replace them.

It was a Wednesday morning about eleven. Charlie had set up his easel as usual on a stretch of coastline from where he could see the house in the distance, checking occasionally with his binoculars for signs of movement, though making it look as though he was just scanning the horizon generally for anything of interest. He found he enjoyed the sound of the sea and the gulls wheeling and diving overhead. The whole atmosphere was restful and somehow cleansing. But he didn't lose his sixth sense for danger, and he knew at once when someone was approaching him from behind, moving silently through the sand, hoping he wouldn't notice they were there.

He turned casually, but ready for action. The woman he saw was about his own age. She had dark hair, thick and fairly short but falling naturally around her face.

It was a strong face, not quite classically beautiful – too individual, too special for that, but beautiful all the same. Her eyes were dark, almost as dark as her hair, with a look that suggested understanding and intelligence as well as an ability to surprise. Her nose was fine and her mouth full, with lips slightly parted, as though taken unawares at the same time as about to speak.

He knew that look. He knew that face – better, perhaps, than any face he'd ever known. But it took him a long moment to speak the name of the woman who stood before him.

'Kathy?' he said at last, his voice suddenly dry and faintly hoarse.

22

Her face took on a strange fixed look – surprise, he supposed. Her eyes searched his, looking for some clue as to why this stranger knew her name. But recognition would dawn soon. She would – she must – remember him.

'Kathy,' he repeated, 'it's me, Charlie. Charlie Monk.'

She continued to stare at him in the same odd way.

'Charlie Monk?' she echoed.

'My God, Kathy . . . I can't believe this . . . I've thought about you so much for so long, wondered where you were, what became of you . . .'

He got to his feet, clumsily for him, knocking over the little canvas stool he'd been sitting on. She stepped back instinctively, though there was nothing threatening in his movement. He still had his brush in one hand, but then realized that the other was reaching out to touch her. He withdrew it.

'Kathy, it's all right. It's me, Charlie. Don't you re-member me?'

He realized he had taken another step towards her, and she had backed away again. He felt a sudden alarm. He couldn't be mistaken, could he? No, this *was* Kathy; there could be no question of it. But why was she so afraid of him?

123

'Look,' he said, 'it's been a long time. I understand, you're surprised, you're a little bit in shock. So am I. My God, if I'd had to list the ten things I least expected to happen this morning, this would have been top of the list!'

This brought a faint, nervous smile to her face. Her eyelids flickered briefly. Charlie felt reassured. He'd been afraid for a moment she was going to turn and run. He put his brush down carefully on his palette.

'You do recognize me, don't you? Kathy? You remember me?'

'Yes, Charlie, of course I do. I recognized you right away.' She paused slightly. Then added, almost guiltily, 'It's good to see you.'

It was all the encouragement he needed. He moved forward to take her in his arms, to wipe all the lost years away with one great, joyous hug of reunion. But he saw her stifle a gasp of alarm as she instinctively took another step back.

'Kathy, it's all right. I'm not going to hurt you.'

She must have seen the pain that her fear caused him, because she visibly relaxed a little. She didn't come any closer, but at least she stopped looking as though she was about to take flight.

'I know you're not,' she said. 'It's just, as you say, quite a shock. I'm sorry.'

Charlie stayed where he was, respecting the distance she seemed to need to keep between them.

'That's okay,' he said, 'let's take our time. After all our time's our own.' He corrected himself. 'Well, I'm saying that, but I don't know about you. I don't know anything about you . . .'

He glanced at her hand. She wore a wedding ring. The

sight of it caused him a sudden, unanticipated stab of pain. Aware of his glance, she covered her left hand almost guiltily with her right, then just as quickly uncovered it, as though conscious of the absurdity of the gesture.

'You're married,' he said, and hoped the disappointment in his voice wasn't too obvious.

'I was,' she said. 'My husband died.'

Something about the way she said it shocked him more than he could have anticipated. 'I'm sorry. What happened?'

She gave a little shrug. 'I'd rather not talk about it.'

'Of course.'

He'd been about to ask her if she had any children, but decided to leave it. Give her time, he told himself. They both needed time.

'So what are you doing here?' he said. 'Do you live around here?'

'No. Just visiting. And you?'

'The same.' He gestured towards his easel. 'I've taken up painting.'

'Looks like you're pretty good,' she said, looking at his canvas. 'I'd like to see some more of your work.'

'I'll be glad to show you. Are you going to be around for a while?'

She hesitated. 'It's hard to say.'

He wondered what that hesitation meant. The sense began to grow on him that she was struggling with more than just the fact of meeting him again so unexpectedly. There was something else, some other problem troubling her.

'Can you tell me where you're staying? Can I call you?'

Again she gave a slight shrug, as though not wanting

to answer directly. 'I usually walk along the beach in the morning. If you're here, we'll find each other.'

'I'll be here.'

She looked at him. He sensed that she wanted to turn the conversation away from herself. 'So, you're an artist,' she said. 'D'you make a living at it? Do you exhibit? D'you have a dealer?'

'Yes. I mean, I have a dealer. I don't exactly make a living, I have another . . .'

He stopped himself, realizing he was about to say more than he should. He had a cover story, and as long as he was here on this job he had to stick to it.

'Well, I guess I do, in a way – make a living.'

She tipped her head to one side and looked at him quizzically.

'In a way? Are you just being modest? Or were you about to say you have another job?'

'I was in the army for a while. After they took me away that last time, they put me in a kind of military training place.' He paused, watching her, waiting for some reaction. 'You remember that last time, after they caught us in the rail yard?'

She nodded almost imperceptibly. 'Yes, I remember.'

'Kathy, it's so good to see you again.'

She looked at her watch. 'I have to get back,' she said. 'I have things to do.'

'Can I walk back with you?'

She looked unsure.

'Just up to the road,' he said. 'The place I'm renting's over that way.' He pointed vaguely.

'Of course,' she said, 'to the road. Then I go that way.' She pointed in the opposite direction.

It took only a few moments to fold his easel and pack

away his paints, then they started walking. They talked, but it was strangely difficult. In a few moments they had reached the road, where they turned to face each other.

'Well,' he said, 'I'll be here tomorrow.'

She smiled. There was a touch of sadness in the smile, he thought, but also relief, as though in some way the worst was over, the shock of meeting now behind them, the future brightening.

'Take care, Charlie.'

He wondered for a moment if they were going to shake hands. But it was too formal. And a kiss, even on the cheek, would be too intimate. Neither of them was ready yet. In the end they simply held eye contact a moment more, then went their separate ways.

Was it some instinct that made him look back after fifty yards or so? Or just the wish to see her again, the need to be sure that he hadn't hallucinated the whole unlikely episode?

But no, she was there, as clearly as she had been when she stood before him moments earlier, walking away now, her figure growing smaller and more distant with each step.

He watched as she changed direction slightly, not looking back, unaware of his gaze.

And walked briskly into the white clapboard house that he'd been sent to watch.

23

Charlie faced a dilemma. He had to call in, but what should he say? Simply failing to report her arrival was impossible; there were too many other ways they could find out. Of course, he could just say that 'a woman' had arrived without admitting he knew her.

The fact that Control wanted the house watching meant that something was going on, with the implication that anyone involved could be in trouble. In the worst of all possible scenarios, Charlie could imagine being ordered to kidnap or even kill whoever was in that house. Of course he wouldn't do anything to Kathy, but there were limits to the extent he could protect her.

In the end he said merely that a woman had arrived and gave a vague description, but nothing more. He certainly didn't say he'd spoken to her. There were no awkward questions from the anonymous voice on the phone to whom he made his reports, no suggestion that Control might want to talk to him about this. He hung up with a sense of relief and looked forward to the following morning.

That night he dreamed of Kathy. It was a fractured, disconcerting dream. They were on the run again, two kids who knew nothing except that they wanted to escape from their lives, and they wanted to escape together. He knew he was dreaming. The emotions were powerful and genuine, but set against a surreal landscape that told him he was inside his own head, not out in the real world. At the same time Kathy's presence was more than that of someone in a dream. He felt the softness of her skin as he brushed her arm; the sweetness of her breath as they clung together in the shadow of the vast unspoken horror they were running from; the contoured warmth of her body against his.

And yet there remained a monstrous gulf between them. In part it was the gulf of dreams, the strange intangibility of things: the book from which you have to read that opens to show pages with no print on them; the long cold drink that doesn't slake the burning thirst; the furious dash for safety followed by the realization that you are running without movement. Worst of all, the object of desire who remains untouchably remote despite the casual, naked intimacy in which you find yourselves together.

It was partly that, but something more. He began to fear he would go mad if he couldn't solve the mystery. What was missing? Something he was hiding from? Something he wouldn't, couldn't, even dare not let himself remember?

He woke turning and perspiring in his bed. Sleep had flown and could not be coaxed back, so he got up and walked down to the beach. He passed her house. There were no lights. But then – he glanced at his watch – it was three in the morning.

For a while he stood there, watching in the darkness. Should he go knock at the door, tell her he knew something was wrong, persuade her to confide in him? But suppose she wasn't alone. He hadn't seen anybody else, but there could be other people in the house, and he might be putting more than just himself and the operation at risk by blundering in there in the middle of the night. He might be putting Kathy at risk. Better, he decided, to wait until the morning when they would meet on the beach. He would talk to her then, persuade her to confide in him.

He turned and started back towards his cottage, but he knew that sleep would not return. Instead of waiting out the long hours until he saw her again, he ran down to the water's edge, threw off his clothes, and dived into the languid surf.

It was dawn when he eventually got home. He shaved, prepared himself some breakfast, then collected his painting things and started out once more for the beach.

He glanced at his watch for the twentieth time that hour. Anybody watching would have recognized an anxious man. It was almost midday and there was still no sign of her.

From where he sat at his easel he could see the house clearly even without binoculars. There had been no movement all morning. As the minutes ticked by, he abandoned even the pretence of painting; his concentration was shot to hell, and he knew in his bones that something was wrong. He made up his mind to get into that house and find out for himself what was going on. His only regret was that he hadn't followed his original instinct and done so in the night.

The rear of the house was shielded from any neighbour's view by trees. He vaulted over the fence then slid along the back wall and peered cautiously in at a window. To his amazement, he found himself looking into a completely bare room – a kitchen, in fact, but without a stick of furniture except for a sink and some fixtures on the walls. He moved along to another window. This looked into a good-sized living room with windows on the far side overlooking the sea. But again there wasn't a stick of furniture in the place, just bare floorboards and wires hanging where light fittings had once been.

Charlie began to have a very strange feeling. There was something unreal here. This was the house he'd seen Kathy enter. She had produced a key and opened the front door. So why was the place abandoned? Obviously he had to get in and check out the whole house. Maybe the upper floor was in use. He tried the back door, but it was locked, not surprisingly. What was surprising was the feebleness of the lock used. Charlie reckoned that an average teenager with a pin could have opened it in under five minutes; his own expert touch coaxed the levers into submission in seconds. He checked the door frame for metal contacts whose broken circuits might have triggered an alarm in some local police station or security office. There were none. And no electric eyes or floor pads, which would anyway have been impossible to conceal without carpets.

He slipped off his shoes and left them at the foot of the stairs. Even though they were soft moccasins, a trained ear would have heard their approach. Only bare feet guaranteed silence and the advantage of surprise. Before starting up, he listened carefully to the sounds of the house. There seemed to be nothing out of the ordinary. He started up the wooden staircase, arriving at a landing which was as bare as downstairs. He started cautiously along a corridor, checking doors as he went. The whole floor was the same: unfurnished and without any sign of life. It was not with any great final hope that he climbed the narrow back stairs to the attic. That, too, was empty. He went back downstairs, reclaimed his shoes and left as he had entered, carefully re-locking the door.

Back at his cottage he pondered what he should do. Obviously he had to report that the 'mysterious woman' was gone. He made the call and did so. No questions were asked, though there were plenty he was asking himself. Had she run away because of him? But why? Or had she been taken? In which case, by whom? Maybe she needed his help, but where was she?

For a moment he even toyed with the idea that he had dreamed or imagined the whole episode. But no, that wasn't possible. Such things didn't happen.

And yet how strange to have met her again as he had, so soon after his memory of her had suddenly returned with a clarity that had eluded him for years. One moment he'd remembered what she looked like, and the next she was there.

Were such coincidences ever what they seemed? Was something he didn't understand going on?

His phone rang. This time Control himself was on the line.

'Charlie. Are you absolutely sure there's nothing more you can tell us about this woman?'

He hesitated fractionally, though not long enough, he thought, to make Control suspicious.

'Nothing I can think of, sir.'

'You spoke to her?'

Was that a trick question? He had definitely reported that he hadn't spoken to her, but then he hadn't reported directly to Control, so maybe there was nothing to worry about.

'No, sir. I just observed her.'

'Entering the house.'

'That's correct.'

'And today you didn't see her, so you broke in and took a look around.'

'That's right, sir.'

'What made you suspicious?'

'Hard to say, sir. There was something wrong about that place.'

'You should have called in first.'

'I understand, sir. But then the opportunity arose, and there was no guarantee I'd get another chance.'

That was bullshit, he knew. He could have got in and out of there any time he wanted. But Control seemed to buy the story. He sensed a change of tone down the line and imagined Control nodding his head and pursing his lips the way he did as he mulled over some information and made a decision.

'All right, Charlie,' he said after a while, 'it doesn't seem like there's much more to be done for the time being. We'll arrange for you to fly back west. I'll be in touch.'

24

As good as his word, Control summoned Charlie to a face-to-face meeting on the following day. The location this time was an anonymous office building in Santa Monica just off Wilshire. Charlie looked at the names listed in the lobby. There were management companies, business consultants, and a handful of film and TV production companies with tortuously inventive titles. Alongside suite 304, however, which was where Charlie had been told to report, there was no name.

He rang the bell and the door was opened by a slim young man who stood politely aside to let him enter. The office suite was almost as bare as the house on the east coast had been. Only one room of the four Charlie could see had any furniture, and then just a couple of chairs and a table with a computer on it. A fat balding man sat working at the keyboard. Control was standing a little to one side. He nodded a greeting to Charlie and told him to pull up a chair next to the fat man.

'We need to know what she looked like, Charlie,' he said. 'Anything you can remember, anything at all. It's important.'

Charlie sat down. The on-screen program was one of those used for building up pictures of suspects and most wanteds. Charlie played the game solemnly, creating an image that was close and yet not her. Control then asked him some questions, mostly the same ones he'd asked on the phone. It was a routine debriefing, but it was obvious from Control's interest in Kathy that she was involved in something that Charlie didn't like the feel of.

'Very well, Charlie,' Control said eventually, exhaling his words on a sigh, 'you can stand down. Take a few days off. We'll be in touch.'

The past, Charlie heard once, was a foreign country. In his case it was a country he'd had no intention of revisiting, until now. But meeting Kathy had changed everything, and her mysterious disappearance left him no choice. There was nothing he'd been told not to do, so a casual stroll down memory lane seemed, in Charlie's view, perfectly normal and unlikely to arouse suspicion.

He'd never been quite sure how much Control actually knew about him. Sometimes he wondered if he was checked on when he was off duty. Not that he was ever off duty really; he was always on call should he be needed. He carried a pager and a mobile phone every-where. These, he knew, could be used to trace him if that was what they wanted to do. The thought had never troubled him until now, because until now he'd had nothing to hide.

He wasn't sure, now he came to think about it, that he'd ever known the name or even the general location of Kathy's orphanage. It was just 'the girls' place' across town. They'd bussed over every morning for school then bussed back at night. The school itself was attached to the boys' orphanage that he'd been in. That was the logical place to start. He remembered that it had been way down town. He could recall the general area, but no street names, so he decided just to drive around until he found it.

As he recalled, it had been a big dark building with a strangely permanent gloom about it, as though this were magically the one part of the city where the sun never shone. It was a building designed to break the spirit of those who lived in it. How else to explain those airless dormitories with their high barred windows, those winding corridors and endless staircases, and above all those narrow stone steps leading down to the black steel door behind which was the 'hole'?

He thought of Kathy as he drove. In particular, he thought about the first time they met. There'd been a fight – which was nothing new, except this time it wasn't just one or two kids but a gang of them who'd started in on him. He didn't remember much about it, except that he must have gone berserk. They'd all fled, except for two who couldn't. One was trying to crawl away on his hands and knees, the other lay whimpering with blood streaming from his mouth. Then suddenly, out of nowhere, the gorillas arrived. Huge hands grabbed Charlie by the hair and throat. Others took him by the arms and legs. He found himself lifted up and held level with the ground, like a battering ram. That was when Kathy stepped in front of them.

'It wasn't his fault,' she said. 'There was a gang of them. They started it.'

One of the gorillas had muttered something obscene and pushed her aside. Charlie saw her stumble and fall over. It was in that moment that their eyes met. His last memory of the outside world, before they threw him in the 'hole', was that look of hers. Something had passed between them in that moment. He hadn't known what, but he'd been unable to think of anything else until he saw her again. It had been only a couple of weeks after that day that they'd run away together. Then that whole relationship, which still meant more to him than any in his life, had ended – until that strange meeting by the sea the other day.

What surprised him, as he wound his way through the same streets for the third or fourth time that morning, was the way that nothing whatever struck him as familiar. Of course it was possible that the orphanage had been torn down – best end to it, no doubt of that. But could literally everything else have been razed to the ground and rebuilt? He was sure he was in the right part of town, so why was there absolutely nothing that he recognized?

He parked his car on a meter and got out to look around on foot. If he couldn't find any clue to what had happened, he was going to have to go to the city authorities. He'd been hoping to avoid that; it could set off all kind of warning bells. But he was determined to do whatever it took to find Kathy.

It was then that he realized he was being followed. He hadn't spotted them in the traffic. There were two men, casually dressed, driving a dusty blue sedan. It had a couple of dents and some bad rust around the fender, the kind of car you wouldn't glance at twice. In fact it wasn't the car that Charlie glanced at first. As he walked past it, the two men in it sat talking. Charlie happened to notice that the one behind the wheel was wearing a shirt very like one he had himself, perhaps identical. The design was marijuana leaves on a red background. It was something he'd picked up on a trip to Maui a few months ago.

He thought no more about the coincidence until another one happened. Charlie had crossed the road and was standing on the sidewalk, trying to get a feel of which of the buildings around him might have been there for more than fifteen or twenty years and so would date back to his time. He thought he might find somebody he could talk to and ask a few casual questions about the vanished orphanage and school.

It was then that he saw the man in the marijuana shirt on the far sidewalk, gazing into the window of a TV and radio store, but positioning himself so that he could still see Charlie out of the corner of his vision. It was a stance that Charlie knew well from training and field operations, and it triggered an immediate question in his mind: where was the other man?

Then he saw him, seated in the window of a deli, reading a paper and taking a sip from his cup of coffee. It was all the confirmation that he needed.

Charlie was under surveillance.

25

They were, Charlie decided after about twenty minutes, competent though fairly low-level operatives. Affecting no suspicion that he was being watched, he sauntered in and out of several shops, buying a couple of ties, some socks, a magazine. Always he kept a wary eye on the movements of the two men, and soon established what pattern they were following. Then he strolled up to an amusement arcade and slipped inside.

He knew that one of them would come in after him in about five minutes. The other would by then have gone around to cover any possible rear exit. That was standard practice. He went straight to the men's room, locked himself in, then forced open a rusty window of frosted glass and crawled out. He found himself in a narrow chimney-like space. The only way up would be through sheer muscle power, arms and legs braced against the walls. He decided it was worth a try.

Every fibre in his body strained almost to breaking point, but after the first few feet he knew he was going to make it. He hauled himself on to the flat roof and moved crab-like to the edge. Looking down, he could see the guy watching for him by the arcade's rear exit. Marijuana shirt was probably still waiting out front, or might by now have started looking around inside. This gave

Charlie just enough time to pick them off individually, which would be less messy. He waited till there was nobody passing the end of the alley, then jumped.

The guy didn't know what had happened until he felt himself grabbed from behind. He tried to reach for the gun under his jacket, but Charlie twisted his arm up behind his back and made him gasp in pain.

'Who are you?'

'You're breaking my arm.'

'Oops – there it goes.'

'Aaaaarrrggh . . .!'

'Relax, it's only dislocated. Now, who are you?'

'My name's Jack Cooper. I'm a private detective.'

'Who hired you?'

'I don't know. Ow! Christ! I don't know the client's name.'

Charlie didn't have time to get the truth out of him. He had to be ready for marijuana shirt, who would be out any moment. He gave a jab to the neck and the guy dropped stone cold. He'd be fine, but he'd have a headache as well as a painful shoulder for a while. Charlie dragged him out of sight, then slipped into the shadows and waited.

After ten minutes he began to wonder if he'd misread the situation. Then he guessed what had happened. Suppose they'd feared that Charlie was on to them, what would they have done? Marijuana shirt wouldn't have bothered to make a thorough search of the arcade. He would have assumed that Charlie had given them the slip and he would go – where? To watch Charlie's car, of course. There was only a slim chance that Charlie would return to it, but it was the next logical step in the game plan these guys were following.

So Charlie moved up the alley intending to find a cab. When he reached the street, he turned left, away from where he'd left his car. He found two cabs on the rank a little way along, and let an elderly man with a stick take the first: haste and discourtesy were a sure way of making yourself stand out in a crowd. It was just as his own cab pulled away that he heard a distant shout of 'Hey!' behind him. Looking back, he saw marijuana shirt running after him. The cabbie hadn't noticed and drove on regardless. The last thing Charlie saw was marijuana shirt standing in the middle of the street and reaching inside his red and green shirt for something. Charlie couldn't believe he was going to start shooting right there in the open. But he didn't pull a gun. There was something in his hand, a small black object, but it wasn't a gun. All the same, he held it like a gun, as though he was about to fire after the departing cab. But at that moment a container truck made an unexpected right turn and blocked him from view.

At the same time something strange happened to Charlie. He found himself opening his eyes, but with no memory of having closed them. It wasn't just a blink. This was like opening his eyes after falling into a light doze. He saw right away that the cab wasn't in the same place it had been a moment ago – if it *was* only a moment. It seemed incredible, but he must have fallen asleep.

'Hey, mister, are you all right?'

It was the cab driver looking at him in his mirror.

'Yeah, sure . . . I'm fine.'

'You flaked out back there. I thought you'd had a heart attack.'

'No, I'm . . . I'm okay . . . How long was I out?'

'I don't know. I just looked up and saw you with your head back and your mouth hanging open.'

'But . . . how long have I been in the cab?'

He saw the driver's face in the mirror crease into a frown.

'Are you *sure* you're all right, mister?'

'Just tell me how long I've been in the damn cab!'

'Two, three minutes, tops.'

So what the hell had happened? Had he passed out? Or had marijuana shirt used something on him? But what?

His thoughts were interrupted by the phone in his pocket. He answered it.

'Yes?'

'What d'you think you're doing, Charlie?'

It was Control's voice. Charlie felt an odd sense of panic, something he was unaccustomed to.

'Charlie, talk to me.'

He didn't know what to say. He was too busy coming to terms with the fact that Control must have been behind what just happened. Control was having him followed because he knew, or at least suspected, that he'd lied about Kathy. That was the only explanation.

'Charlie!'

On an impulse, he cut the call off. It rang again almost at once. This time he didn't answer, he just flipped open the back and disconnected the battery. Of course that didn't mean it couldn't still be used to trace his movements. There could be something in it sending out a signal. He took out his pager, then felt for a space under his seat and wedged it and his phone firmly in there.

'Pull over on this next corner,' he told the driver, 'I'm getting out.'

'You said the marina. That's a thirty dollar fare!' The driver's voice was pained and indignant.

Charlie saw there was only six bucks something on the clock this far. 'Here's twenty,' he said, pulling out his wallet and handing over a couple of bills. 'Now pull over.'

The driver did so. Charlie got out and watched the cab disappear in the traffic. Then he looked carefully around. He was pretty sure he hadn't been followed. He started walking.

Was he crazy, he asked himself, defying Control like this, going out on a limb? For what? For somebody he hadn't seen for fifteen years or more? Who, for all he knew, might have been a lot less excited to see him than he had been to see her?

Okay, maybe he *was* crazy – crazy enough to decide now that he was going to go through with what he'd started. If Kathy was in trouble, it was beginning to look as though the trouble was coming from his own side, not from the amorphous 'enemy' out there that he'd always taken for granted. The thought disturbed him. He intended to find out what the game was, and who was playing it.

As he walked he ran through his options. He'd noticed when he paid the cab that he didn't have much cash on him. Obviously he couldn't use his credit cards and leave a paper trail. Various solutions presented themselves, theft being one. Then he noticed he was passing an art gallery, and he thought of Virgil Fry. Fry owed him for his last batch of paintings. If he could get to Fry he could demand cash instead of having the money transferred to his bank. He knew he'd have no difficulty persuading the weasel-faced little man to do this one small favour for him.

Luckily he remembered Fry's address from the few pieces of correspondence he'd had with him. It was in Pasadena. He checked his wallet again; he had just about enough money to get down there. He found another cab rank. Twenty minutes later he paid it off a few blocks from where Fry's place should be located.

If he hadn't been looking out for the street numbers he would have walked past it without a second glance. It didn't look much like a gallery at all; more of a junk shop, Charlie would have said. True, there were a few paintings on sale, but none of them Charlie's. And they were stacked alongside a couple of ancient armchairs, a brass bedstead and a marble fireplace.

He paused in the mouth of an alley across the street and watched for signs of life. After a moment he saw Fry moving about in the dark interior. He was about to step out and cross over when he caught sight of something that made him pull back sharply into the shadows and press himself against the wall.

It was the dusty blue sedan with marijuana shirt at the wheel. He pulled up outside Fry's door and went briskly inside.

26

Charlie could see the two men through the window. They obviously knew each other, though it was impossible to say how well. They talked urgently for several minutes. Marijuana shirt seemed to be impressing something of great importance on Fry, and Fry was nodding vigorous agreement. Then marijuana shirt left and drove off as abruptly as he had arrived.

Fry then went methodically into action, closing up the shop, pulling down blinds and locking the door. He seemed to be alone and without the assistants who sometimes came with him to collect pictures from Charlie's apartment.

Slipping from his hiding place, Charlie moved cautiously some way along the street and then crossed quickly to the other side. He found another narrow passage, similar to the one that he'd been standing in, that looked as though it might lead around to the back of Fry's shop. He ventured down a little way and saw that it did. A white van was parked outside a garage door that had been rolled about three quarters of the way up into the roof. Fry was ducking back and forth under it, loading things into the back of the van. They were Charlie's pictures – including some of the most recent that he'd painted on the East Coast and left there, not expecting to see them again. Who had brought them back, and why? And where was Virgil Fry taking them now?

As he watched, Fry rolled down and locked the garage door, slammed shut the rear of his van, and got behind the wheel. Charlie realized he needed to find a car fast if he was going to follow him. He'd done a course on stealing them, and learned enough to know that modern alarms and clever circuitry made that a very skilled and essentially full-time profession. The surest way was to commandeer one. The course on how this was accomplished had been far simpler to understand.

Taking out his platinum American Express card, he ran the fifty yards to a stop sign. It wasn't a busy intersection, but visibility was limited, which meant that everybody obeyed the law and stopped. A black Toyota was pulling up as Charlie got there. Flashing his credit card, but holding his fingers so it wasn't readable, he shouted: 'Police!' The driver, mild-looking in a hat and rimless glasses, looked up in alarm. His first instinct was to dive for the lock, which he found, to his relief, was already on. Charlie confirmed this by tugging the door handle to no avail.

'Police!' he repeated. 'I need this car.'

'Let me see that ID again,' the man behind the wheel said with a tremble in his voice, shouting so he could be heard through the closed window.

Charlie's hand moved like a jackhammer. He used the side that had been specially hardened, not just by training but injections too. Held the right way, it was like a ridge of steel. In a single movement he shattered the window behind the driver and reached over to unlock his door. His other hand snatched it open. The driver didn't even

146

have time to cry out before a jab to the neck sent him slumping sideways, unconscious. Charlie bundled him over to the passenger side and slid behind the wheel.

A few minutes later when Fry pulled out on to the road, all he would have noticed, if he'd noticed anything at all, was a black Toyota with two men in it, one of whom seemed to be enjoying a refreshing snooze while his companion drove.

Fry headed out on the 405 southbound towards San Diego. Charlie stayed three, sometimes four cars back, occasionally switching lanes so that he wasn't an eternally hovering presence in Fry's rear-view mirror.

Nothing in Fry's behaviour suggested he knew he was being followed: no double turns or other tricks to test out the car behind. Instead he just stayed on the main highway. Charlie checked the gas, anxious about how far Fry might be intending to go, but he saw he had nearly a full tank and needn't worry for a while yet.

The man in the passenger seat stirred and moaned faintly. Charlie glanced over but paid no particular attention. He had already checked that he wasn't carrying a weapon, nor was there one hidden within easy reach. He waited for the man to wake up and fully take in what was happening. When he did he jerked upright and instinctively cowered away from Charlie, pushing himself against the passenger door and groping for the handle.

Charlie's hand shot out and took the man's arm in an iron grip, pulling him away from the door and exerting a painful warning pressure.

'Don't panic. Nothing's going to happen to you. You got a headache?'

The man nodded and tried to speak, but he was trembling too hard to get the words out.

'Try anything stupid and you'll get a worse one. Just do as I say and you'll be fine. Understand?'

The man nodded more vigorously this time. 'You're not really a cop, are you?' he managed to say.

'What's the difference?'

'Are you on the run?'

'Empty your pockets.'

'You're not a serial killer, are you?'

'Did you hear what I said?'

'Okay . . . sure . . . look, I've got about two hundred dollars . . . take it . . . please take it . . .'

'Maybe I will.' Charlie took the money held out to him and slipped it into his jacket. He didn't want to rob the man, but he was still short of cash and had no idea how much he might yet need. 'Now empty your pockets, like I said.'

'But I don't have anything else—'

'Do it.'

The man fumbled through his pockets, pulling out bills, papers, envelopes. 'I've got some credit cards. If you want my credit cards . . .'

'I don't want your credit cards. Gimme that in your hand.'

'It's just personal things, letters . . .'

Charlie made an impatient gesture. The man handed over a couple of envelopes. One was handwritten, the other a printed bill. Both bore the same address.

The man caught the look in Charlie's eyes, and realized what had just happened.

'Please . . . my wife, my children . . . I won't say anything about this . . . please don't do anything to my wife or my children . . .'

Charlie pocketed the envelopes ominously. 'You better be damn sure you don't say anything.'

The man swore on his life that he wouldn't. They then drove on in silence for a while. Charlie was pretty certain that the guy still hadn't figured out that they were following the white van several vehicles ahead. He thought Charlie was on the run, which was fine with Charlie. The fewer people who knew what he was up to, the better.

They drove past signs for Long Beach, Seal Beach, Huntingdon Beach; past shopping centres, offices and auto dealers all incongruously interspersed with fields of cauliflower and potatoes. They drove past the huge South Coast Shopping Plaza, after which the signs for John Wayne Airport began to appear. For a moment Charlie worried that Fry was going to take to the air, which would make him more difficult to follow, especially if he took a flight out of the country.

The freeway had widened to six lanes in both directions. Charlie tightened the distance between himself and Fry as far as he dared, ready to follow if he made a right into the MacArthur Boulevard exit. Planes were coming in to land, hanging low in the air above their heads.

But Fry didn't make a turn. Instead he drove on for another ten minutes, then pulled across two lanes of traffic and signalled he was about to pull off the freeway. He took the Bristol Road offramp towards something signposted as the Irvine Spectrum. This turned out to be a massive area of high-tech corporate buildings, acres of glass sparkling in the late afternoon sun. Some of them had their own areas of green and cultivated garden. In between were vegetable fields, well farmed by the look of them.

Charlie saw a sign offering industrial spaces between 2,700 and 100,000 square feet. Looking around him, he thought some of them must be even larger than that. Most were open on all sides, but several were fenced and looked secure.

They drove on quieter streets now, Charlie still hanging back as far as he dared without losing sight of the white van ahead. After several blocks, Fry signalled a right and pulled over to the middle of the road. Luckily a pick-up truck was making the same turn, so Charlie didn't wind up sitting right on Fry's tail.

The street they turned into was quieter still and narrower. Charlie sensed the guy in the passenger seat was beginning to eye him suspiciously. He wasn't driving like a man in a hurry to get away from something, and any minute now the guy was going to make the connection with the white van up ahead and realize they were following it.

Just then Fry made a sharp left. Charlie didn't respond, just drove calmly on. Out of the corner of his eye he glimpsed big iron gates set back amongst a long row of mature Eucalyptus trees. Fry's van was already through them and heading up a winding drive, waved on by security guards.

Charlie drove on, intending to put a mile or so between this place and himself before dumping the car and doubling back. When he saw an empty picnic and rest area, he pulled into it. Without a word, he killed the motor, removed the ignition key, and got out. Then he leaned in through the open window and addressed the vehicle's still-terrified owner.

'Unless you want to see me again, forget this happened.'

'I will.'

'Remember, I know where you live.'

The man gulped and swallowed and went a shade paler than he was already. Charlie tossed him the keys; the man flinched as though he'd been thrown a grenade. Charlie turned and walked into the nearby trees. He heard a screech of tyres and an over-revved engine and glanced over his shoulder. The car was already back on the road, travelling faster than was wise. He hoped the guy wouldn't get picked up by the cops too soon and spill everything in his panic. That was why he had started walking in the opposite direction from the one he intended taking once the car and its driver were out of sight.

Now he turned and started back towards where he had last seen Fry's van.

27

It took him less than fifteen minutes to find a tree-covered spot that gave him a view of the place Fry was visiting. It looked similar in design and layout to most others around there: labs, workshops, offices, arranged in a grid-like pattern, with newly created strips of lawn and bits of garden here and there to break up the symmetry.

Yet Charlie could see there was more to this one. It had a ring-fence made of chain link with steel posts every few yards. The fence didn't make it unique; he'd already seen several like it. There was nothing particularly intimidating about it, no spikes on the top or deathly warnings about dogs or electric current. But it was just high enough to make a big deal out of climbing over it. If you made the attempt, you would certainly be spotted. He could see cameras over the main entrances to most of the buildings. There were also two patrol cars: one was always making a slow tour of the estate while the other was stationed near the gate. These people, Charlie decided, didn't want strangers in there.

Virgil Fry's white van was nowhere to be seen. Charlie wondered if he'd parked somewhere out of sight or if he'd left already. If the purpose of his visit had been simply to deliver a load of Charlie's paintings to some mysterious collector, then he could well be on his way home by now, leaving Charlie with the difficult job of finding out who took such an interest in his artwork, and more importantly why. Just at that moment a door to what appeared to be a subterranean garage beneath one of the main buildings swung open and Fry's van emerged. Charlie couldn't see clearly enough to be sure it was Fry at the wheel, but he assumed it was. He watched the van drive to the gate, then turn on to the road and start back the way it had come.

At least, Charlie told himself, he now knew in which building to start looking. All that remained was the question of how to get in. He glanced at his watch, then at the security patrol car touring the tidy, antiseptic avenues set at perfect right angles to one another. For the next hour he timed them. They had a set routine with minor in-built, and equally routine, variations. It wouldn't be hard to get past them, but first he had to get over the fence.

He looked around from where he sat in the boughs of the huge Eucalyptus. A set of power lines ran from behind and down towards one part of the fence, but not over it. He looked further, and saw that a little way on they crossed another set. This set, Charlie saw as he traced them with his eyes, came back and passed close by one corner of the estate. A little way inside the fence were more trees like the one Charlie was sitting in. They had probably been kept to break the monotony of concrete and glass rectangularity.

Charlie calculated the distance between the two sets of power lines, and decided he could do it. The lines, he knew, were strong enough to take his weight. He knew they carried enough raw electricity to fry him like a piece of bacon at a single touch – but only if he was grounded at the same time. That meant he had to find a way of breaking contact with anything else and just land on the power line like a trapeze artist. He needed to find somewhere to jump from. He looked around again.

There was a pylon – tall, narrow, almost sheer concrete. It was his only chance, but it would be like climbing a pole.

He decided to wait until it got a little darker.

Bracing himself, with the force coming entirely from the grip his feet had on the pylon, he launched himself into space. His outstretched hands began to close even before they felt the touch of the cable. He swung hard and felt his skin burn from the friction, then he used his whole body to steady himself. He hung there a few moments. There had been no noise; that was good. Nothing had broken or given way. Now all he had to do was pass himself along hand over hand, sometimes hooking his feet to get a little speed, until he was as close as he could get to the second set of power lines.

It was a big leap to make from a hanging position. He looked down. The ground was rocky and hard and a long way off, and there was nothing to break his fall. He started to swing, gently at first, then building speed.

He didn't know where he found that extra final kick: in the air, or so it seemed. Wherever it came from, it took him those vital last few centimetres. Even so, his left hand failed to get a grip, though his right held on. When he was steady, he started to calculate his next jump, and wondered whether this whole thing was going to work at all. The distance to the trees was definitely more than it had looked from where he'd been observing earlier. This simply couldn't be done. He moved a few yards to his left and peered again into the shadows. The chances were better there, but he went on looking.

Pretty soon he found something that was still difficult but worth a try. It was a downward jump, clearing the fence and landing right in the heart of one of the trees. The big danger was that the branch he would have to catch might not be strong enough to take his weight and would break with a dangerously loud snap. He couldn't know until he tried.

The branch started to give way as he'd feared. But the moment before it broke he let go and fell to the ground. The tree had slowed his fall, and he landed on all fours with no more than a rustle in the leaves above him, as though a gust of wind had passed through or a bird taken flight.

He stayed in a crouch and looked around. Then he checked his watch. He was waiting for two things. One was to find out if he'd been spotted or not. Any device set to detect a man, or any other object, flying through the air and clear over the fence would have got him, that was for sure. Which meant that any moment now there would be guards and probably dogs out looking for him, and he'd rather be near the fence if that happened.

The second thing he was waiting for was to see the patrol car pass next time, because after that he'd have a minimum of seventeen minutes, and just over thirty at the most, before they came around this way again.

As the seconds went by and became minutes, Charlie knew that his guess had been right. This place was as secure as anyone could make it without drawing unwelcome attention to themselves, which meant there were holes in their system. He'd just got through one; now he had to find another.

He heard the patrol car approaching, then saw its headlights, which were dipped. Other lights about the place were coming on as dusk gathered. He imagined that most people must have gone home, though some could be working late. Perhaps some of them lived on the premises.

When the patrol car's tail lights had disappeared around the next corner, Charlie made his move. He headed for the garage door from which Fry's van had emerged. When he got to it he could hear the whine of an electric motor. It was coming closer. A hydraulic thump was followed by a lighter, faster whine, and the doors that had opened for Fry swung up again into the ceiling.

Charlie flattened himself against the wall on one side. A front-loader trundled out pulling a small cart. It had a cargo of something he didn't recognize at first. Then a shaft of light as the doors closed caught something. Charlie recognized one of his own paintings. Then he saw that they were all his recent paintings: Fry's vanload.

Keeping low, he ran along the edge of the ramp, following the loader, finally hopping on the back. The man driving felt only a slight bump behind him, as though a wheel of the trailer he was pulling had passed over a stone.

28

He made himself so small that nobody would have noticed, at a casual glance, that he was there. The cart bumped and swung along like a children's ride at the funfair. They were heading, Charlie calculated, for the residential part of the estate.

When the movement suddenly stopped and he heard the motor die, he moved fast, and was in the cover of nearby bushes before the driver came around to start unloading. He watched as the pictures were carried inside, three or four at a time, about a dozen of them.

Somewhere above a light went on. He looked up. It was an apartment block that looked, he thought, as though a lot of expensive television sets had been stacked together at slightly odd angles. The windows had curved edges and looked out on to the world like screens, yet the whole effect was softened by carefully cultivated ivy and other climbing plants. What could easily have been forbidding and strange became merely suburban.

The thing he noticed in this particular window where the light had just gone on, the thing that kept him watching, was the sight of one of his paintings being held up to be examined. He could see only one hand, and no sign of the person it belonged to.

He could either go in and ring the bell or break the

door down, or he could do the sensible thing. Some days, he found, and this was one of them, his climbing skills came in more useful than others.

There wasn't much in the way of finger- or toe-holds, and any attempt to use the climbing plants would be rash, but he managed, going carefully, to get there. Each apartment had its own small terrace; in this case it was just around the corner from the window Charlie had observed. He pulled himself up and flipped over the rail. Now he could see into the room fully.

It was a comfortable, conventional living room. It obviously belonged to someone interested in books and art generally, and particularly the art of Charlie Monk.

Kathy Ryan was going through his pictures, pausing to look at each of them for a few moments. When she'd gone through them once, she started again, spending longer over some this time, less over others. Charlie had the feeling she'd already done this repeatedly.

The glass door from the balcony into the apartment was open slightly, but Charlie checked his impulse to walk in unannounced. Instead he took a step closer so that she would see him if she turned. Then he spoke her name quietly.

'Kathy . . .?'

She didn't jump. She just stopped what she was doing and looked at him. There was no fear in her face.

'Come in, Charlie,' she said. 'I was told you'd probably get here sooner or later.'

He reached out and pushed open the door, then took a step inside the room, and waited for her to speak. She looked at him with a strange kind of sadness that touched and troubled him. Something, he knew now for sure, was badly wrong with her life.

'Kathy,' he said softly, 'just tell me what's going on, please.'

She looked down, as though she found it difficult to answer his question. She was playing with something in her hand, something small and black, though he didn't pay it much attention for the moment.

He waited a while for her answer, then said, 'Kathy, tell me.'

She looked at him.

'I'm not Kathy,' she said. Her voice was flat, drained of emotion. 'There is no Kathy Ryan. My name is Susan – Doctor Susan Flemyng.'

He could feel the puzzlement gather on his face like a hot flush. He opened his mouth to protest at this nonsense. But she – Kathy, or Susan as she now chose to call herself – lifted the small black object in her hand slightly, and suddenly he remembered the thing he had seen marijuana shirt pointing in his direction before that truck had come between them, and after which Charlie had lost consciousness for several seconds.

This time nothing came between him and the small black object that she aimed straight at him. Charlie's world came to an end.

A strip of light opened horizontally across the centre of his vision. He tried to focus, but everything was strangely blurred, as though he had suddenly become short-sighted. He could see movements and what looked like reflecting surfaces, but he could make out no detail.

'That was quite a game you played there, Charlie,' someone said. It was a man's voice, a voice he didn't know. And somehow it didn't seem to be addressing him quite as directly as the words implied.

'He must be feeling wiped out,' another voice said, also male, also unknown.

'He'll be okay in a couple of minutes,' said the first voice.

They were talking *about* him, Charlie realized, not *to* him. He tried to ask where he was and what was happening, but found he couldn't speak. All he heard was a strange sound coming from his mouth, as though he was half-drugged.

Then an extraordinary thing happened. The strip of light he'd been staring at shot upwards suddenly and disappeared from view. There was a brief passage of blackness, then the whole of his field of vision opened up. He realized that something had been lifted off his head. It was a kind of helmet. He could see it now in the hands of one of the men who had spoken. It had a dull metallic colour and several strange-looking leads coming out of it. The man holding it wore a white lab coat. So did the other man with him. Charlie had never seen either of them before.

'He's awake,' one of them said. 'Look, he's watching us – be careful.'

'It's okay, he can't move.'

The one who'd just spoken reached out a hand towards Charlie's neck. Charlie made a superhuman effort to pull himself together and say something. But the sound that escaped his lips was no more coherent than before, just louder and with an edge of frustration to it.

'Jesus Christ, he tried to bite me!'

The man who'd reached out to Charlie snatched his hand back in alarm.

'I told you to be careful. He can take your fingers off with those teeth.'

Charlie heard all this with a strange sense of detachment. He was beyond shock or even surprise now. This was simply absurd. Someone had to tell him what was going on, and soon. Or maybe he just needed to wake up.

'Listen, we'll pull the seal and let him get the damn thing off himself. If he's pissed off, we'll be out of here.'

This was said by the man whom Charlie had – allegedly – tried to bite.

'Okay, fine,' the other man said, sounding nervous and relieved in equal parts.

Both men then reached cautiously around the back of Charlie's neck, jumping slightly as he twisted in whatever kind of harness it was that held him. Once again he tried to speak; once again without success. This time he managed only a curious, rough-edged rasping noise.

What had happened to his voice?

There was a hissing sound, like a vacuum being punctured. It didn't come from him but from something he was wearing. He felt a curious kind of pressure change all over his body. Not uncomfortable, just strange. He looked down.

His whole body was encased in some kind of silvery suit, like a spaceman. Cables of differing thickness were attached to various parts of it, snaking away across the floor.

He heard a muffled clang and looked in its direction, and saw the two white-coated men pulling a door to after them. It was a cage door made of vertical bars. They were on the outside, and Charlie was inside.

In a cage!

He struggled to get to his feet, but something still encumbered him. It was the spacesuit. But as he moved and tried to free himself, it fell away, just sliding down

161

his torso first of all, then falling with a surprisingly heavy thud to the bare concrete floor. He continued to look down.

But it wasn't the spacesuit that held his attention now. It was his own body. He was naked, and yet not naked. Every inch of him – broad chest, long powerful-looking arms, muscular legs and feet – was covered in thick, black, coarse-textured hair.

His head spun. He thought for a moment that he might pass out. But of course he didn't. Because this wasn't possible. This was some kind of aberration, some brief hallucination.

A hand rose towards his face. His own hand. Without consciously willing it to move, he brought it up and held it before him, examining it, turning it over in wonderment.

It wasn't his hand at all. Not Charlie's hand. Not Charlie Monk's. It was an ape's hand.

He stared in silence, as though hypnotized. The hand grew larger, filling his field of vision. Unknowingly, instinctively, he brought it to his face to feel what was there.

The hardness of the hand itself, the texture and thickness of the skin, made feeling anything at all difficult. Like wearing gloves. Except that these weren't gloves. This was a living hand.

And the face that it was feeling – his face – was similarly rough and covered in hair, and strangely rounded. He felt his lips. They were wide and thin, but with a leathery edge. And where he should have felt his nose, there was none; just a small mound in the middle of his face.

Something moved on the floor by his feet. He looked

down and saw the discarded silvery suit being towed by its various attachments towards a recess in the wall. When it had been pulled all the way in, the recess swivelled and disappeared, leaving only a smooth wall.

He looked around him now, taking in a wider aspect of his surroundings. It was true: he actually was in a cage. Two sides were bars, two sides concrete wall. Beyond the bars he couldn't see much. A passage went past one side; there was nobody in it for the moment. On the other side was a more open space with a brightly lit area visible in the distance. It looked like a high-tech lab. There were benches with microscopes and computer screens, and people working at them. Nobody was paying him any attention at all.

There was a movement in the corner of his vision. He swung to his right – and found himself looking into something he hadn't noticed before. On the far wall of the corridor, opposite his cage, was a full-length mirror. He could see a reflection in it – a reflection of whoever was in the cage.

He raised one arm, and then another. Then, just to be sure, he took a step forward and another step back.

There could be no doubt about it. The reflection was himself.

He was a full-grown chimpanzee.

Part Three

Part Three

29

They were in Montana: that much she knew. As the executive jet lost height, the relief-map topography below them gradually transformed itself into pine- and aspen-covered slopes against a background of soaring mountains. They were aiming for a plateau where she could see a landing strip on what looked like a big private ranch. A helicopter sat on a circular pad nearby. Some way off she could see a sprawl of buildings. There was a luxurious ranch-style house surrounded by lawns, a swimming pool and tennis courts. Behind it were a couple of barns with corrals and horses.

Susan and her father were the only passengers. There were two pilots, both of them professional and courteous; they wore uniforms and even put on their caps as they came back from the cockpit to open the door. The senior of the two said he hoped they had enjoyed their flight and wished them a pleasant stay.

A station wagon waited, driven by a pleasant young man in jeans and a lumberjack shirt. As they covered the half mile or so to the house he told them the ranch was twelve hundred acres and stood at an altitude of fifteen hundred feet. The whole state, he said, was around a thousand feet above sea level – no finer air in the world, he added with proprietorial pride.

It had been Amery's idea to come with her on the trip. West hadn't objected when she'd told him she would like Amery to accompany her. It would help her get through the whole difficult experience as much as it would reassure Christopher.

'Okay,' he'd said after a moment's reflection, 'I've no doubt you'd tell your father all about it anyway, so he might as well be there in person. You see, we're trying to make this whole experience as painless for you as possible.'

She hadn't replied to that, but she hoped the expression on her face had conveyed her feeling that the remark, like West himself, was beneath contempt. Did he really expect her to feel gratitude for being allowed to visit her kidnapped son?

Christopher was waiting for them on the porch of one of the buildings she'd seen from the air. He leaned out, waving, as their car approached. Buzz ran barking at his heels. There was nobody else in sight. Christopher flew into his mother's arms while the dog danced around them, delirious with joy. They clung to each other, the child ecstatic to see her, she fighting to hold back tears of happiness.

'Let me look at you,' she said after a few moments, and held him at arm's length. 'You look so well. Are you having fun?'

'Sure, sometimes. But I miss you, Mom.'

'Me too.'

They hugged again.

'I'm sorry,' she said. 'I'll try not to make it much longer.'

'Why can't I come with you? Have I done something wrong?'

'No, darling, it's not you. It's some work I have to do. It's creating problems just now, but they won't go on for long.'

She paused, looked him in the eyes, and knew he'd understood – at least the important things. He knew it wasn't his fault, and their separation wasn't her choice. It was something else, and neither of them could do anything about it. He also saw that she hadn't changed, and that was good. The same with his grandfather.

'What d'you do most of the time?' she asked him.

He brightened.

'Like I told you, I'm learning to ride. I'm getting real good. You want to see me ride?'

'Of course I do . . .!'

'And there's my tree house . . . and some great videos . . .'

'Sounds like you're doing fine . . .!'

The sound of a door on the porch made her look up. A tallish woman in jeans and a white blouse had emerged. She was around fifty, with grey hair pulled back and fixed in a bun. She had a long, bony face which might have been stern except for kindly blue eyes with laugh lines around them.

'We do an hour or two of schoolwork every day, just so he doesn't get too rusty.'

The woman came down the steps towards Susan.

'I'm Mrs Hathaway. Christopher calls me Auntie May.'

She did not offer to shake hands; nor did Susan, but their eye contact was direct and steady.

'You seem to be looking after him well, Mrs Hathaway. At least I'm grateful for that.'

'He's a nice boy. We're all very fond of him here.'

She looked past Susan to where Christopher was now hugging his grandfather. Susan looked back at them. She was overwhelmed suddenly by a sense of unreality. This wasn't happening. It was a dream from which she would wake up and breathe a sigh of relief as everything returned to normal: John at her side, Christopher running through the house getting ready for school.

'Come on, Grandpa, you gotta see Polly – that's my horse. Well, she's a pony, really, but she's like a horse.'

He began tugging his grandfather along by the hand.

'Come on, Mom – I want to show you my horse!'

'Go with them, Dr Flemyng. It's best if you let Christopher show you around, then we can have a cup of coffee back at the house.'

Susan looked at this woman who called herself Mrs Hathaway, wondering if that was her real name. What sort of a woman did it take to do what this woman before her was doing? Could she appeal to her? To her maternal, female instincts? Or was she as cold as the people she worked for obviously were? Anyway, what kind of appeal could she make? Christopher was clearly being well cared for, not abused or ill-treated in any way. What more could she ask in the circumstances? Only that the circumstances change, and this woman couldn't do that for her.

'Go on, Dr Flemyng – they're waiting for you.'

She realized that the woman had just read in her eyes every thought that had passed behind them. She felt herself blush faintly. She felt suddenly foolish, naked almost.

'Christopher's been so excited about this visit, he's been planning everything he wants to show you. Go on, now.'

Susan felt a soft pressure on her arm. Not coercion of

any kind. Not a warning or a threat. Just reassurance, a promise that everything would be all right in time and that for now she should just enjoy the moment. She gave a nod. It felt like an odd, jerky movement, but it shook her free of the paralysis that had gripped her. She opened her mouth to say something, but the words refused to form. She half-mumbled something under her breath, then turned quickly and walked to where her son and father waited for her, hand in hand.

Christopher was indeed showing signs of decent horsemanship. Susan met the man who was teaching him. He was called Michael, was around thirty, good-looking and open, with impeccable, rather old-fashioned good manners. She could see at once that Christopher and Michael were fond of each other.

But who were these people? What were they doing with her son? She wanted to shake them, make them explain how they could do this. By what right? But she couldn't do that without making things much worse for Christopher, and that was the last thing she had come here to do.

'Well, if you ask me, you're a very lucky young man,' she said, as Christopher finished showing them his room. It was filled with every toy and gadget a boy his age could want.

'I wouldn't mind a vacation some place like this myself,' Amery said.

'Why don't you stay here, Grandpa?' Christopher shot back, aglow with the certainty that an idea this good could not possibly be turned down.

Amery looked taken by surprise. 'Well, I . . . I'd love to, Christopher . . . but I don't know if I could get away . . . or even whether there's room for me here . . .'

'Oh, we've got lots of rooms.'

'I'll try. I can't promise, but I'll try.'

'You're welcome to stay with us as long as you wish, Mr Hyde.'

Susan and her father turned to see Mrs Hathaway standing in the door.

'I'm serious. We have no problem with that. We'd be delighted.'

Amery looked at his daughter, then back at the older woman, more shrewdly this time.

'Are you telling me that this would be agreeable to your . . . associates?'

'Perfectly.'

Amery looked at his daughter. She said, 'Do it, if you can.'

Christopher watched these exchanges closely, though their meaning went over his head. He was aware only that it was some kind of game that grown-ups got into when they had to make a decision; all he cared about was the outcome.

'Very well, then,' said Amery, 'I shall stay.'

Christopher gave a whoop of joy and started to cheer, doing a dance of triumph around his grandfather.

An hour later, when it came time to go, Susan kissed Christopher goodbye, hugged him, and promised to come back as soon as she could. Then she kissed her father, and stepped down from the porch. Mrs Hathaway walked with her to the car. As the driver held open the door, she turned back to see her father and Christopher standing hand in hand. They waved. She waved back. She felt better than she'd expected to feel at this moment; better than she'd felt in some time.

As she turned to get into the car, she paused again,

facing Mrs Hathaway, searching that kind and pleasant face for some clue as to what lay behind it.

'Who are you?' was all she could think of asking.

'I told you,' the older woman said with a gentle smile, 'Christopher calls me Auntie May.'

30

The door in the back of his cage slid silently into the wall, leaving a dark opening. He waited a while before approaching it, in case something came out. When nothing did, he looked cautiously over his shoulder. Nobody was watching him. There was activity in the part of the laboratory that he could see, but none of it directed his way.

He took a step or two towards the opening. Now he could see a faint wash of light coming from somewhere. He moved closer, and saw a tunnel, curving slightly down and to the left. The source of the light was somewhere around the curve and not visible from where he stood.

Once again he looked behind him. Still nobody was paying him any attention. Of course that didn't mean there weren't cameras on him. He suspected there were; they were just so small these days you never saw them. And that hole in the wall hadn't opened up all by itself. Something was going on here. He knew he was being provoked or challenged in some way.

At least that was the assumption he made. It was the only way he could make sense of the craziness going on around him. He had decided he was in some artificially created nightmare. That was the only explanation. Maybe it was a training course, introduced without warning, meant to take him, if he passed it, to a higher level. Maybe he was learning how to survive mental disorientation induced by drugs and perhaps other methods, and still remain sane at the end of it all. He could see that might be a skill worth learning. He knew brainwashing was a possibility you had to be trained for.

The thought also struck him that maybe this wasn't training. Maybe this was the real thing, and he had fallen into enemy hands. The last thing he remembered was blacking out in Kathy's apartment. What was it she had called herself? Doctor something. Dr Susan Flemyng, that was it.

Who was doing this to him? And why? And what was Kathy's part in it all? Or, rather, this woman who'd said she wasn't Kathy, who'd said there was no Kathy?

That wasn't possible, was it?

He realized that, almost without thinking, he had taken the first few steps into the tunnel. He checked himself: he must keep his concentration. That was always rule one: be in the moment. He walked on.

The tunnel walls were smooth, made of prefabricated sections. There was no sound except the soft pad of his own feet on the concrete floor. As he walked, he became aware of certain odours which he couldn't quite identify although he knew them. It was a kind of open-air smell, which made him suspect that the source of the light he could see might be daylight.

He stopped again, waiting for something to happen, some trap to be sprung. But there was nothing; only a sense, even stronger now, of the sounds and smells of nature, as though someone had left a window or a door open just around the corner. He took a few more cautious steps, and suddenly everything opened up in front of him.

He found himself standing on the edge of a vast open space. Tall trees, mostly oak and beech, rustled gently in a light breeze. He could hear voices somewhere. He couldn't make out what they were saying, but when he listened more closely he realized they were just hoots and grunts. Then he saw them, scattered around singly or in groups, some climbing trees, some grooming one another, here and there babies playing together or huddling by their mothers. It was a colony of chimpanzees, at a quick guess somewhere between twenty and thirty of them.

None of them seemed to have noticed him yet, but he had a distinct feeling that this would change very soon. He was an outsider and he would be seen as a threat by the dominant males. How he knew this with such certainty he couldn't say, but he knew it as surely as he had known anything in his life. There would be one dominant male, or possibly a coalition of them, and he would have to face them – unless, of course, he went back the way he had come.

But that wasn't his way. Besides, he was pretty sure that the door back into his cage would have closed by now. There had been a purpose behind its opening, and that purpose had been to get him out here with the other chimpanzees.

'Other' chimpanzees? Was that really the thought that had gone through his head? He looked down at himself once again, at the thick black hair, the bent legs with their prehensile toes, the long arms on which, he realized with a shock, he was instinctively leaning, taking the weight of his upper body on the knuckles of his massive hands.

Shocked, he pulled himself upright. It was that movement that attracted the attention of some member of the group. He heard a different kind of hooting noise, more urgent and with a harder edge. It was picked up and transmitted from one group member to another. He saw an arm outstretched, pointing his way, then more arms and many pairs of eyes. The air was alive now with chattering and calls, and with hurried movements as mothers herded their children to safety and the various members of the group took up their different places.

The two most powerful of the males who stepped forward were working, Charlie thought, as a team. That was obviously how they ran things in the group. But right now the group was behind them – 'to a man', Charlie thought, not without a sense of irony.

Because he knew he *was* a man. He knew that this thing, whatever it was, was being done to him, though he didn't know how. It was too clear for a dream; it was a remarkably sustained hallucination. It could have been induced by drugs or virtual reality, or a combination of both. He knew little about either, other than that they existed.

Something glinted in an upper corner of his vision. He looked up and saw a camera. When he looked around he saw another, perched up on poles and protected by wire that must have been electrified, otherwise they'd have been torn down and vandalized long ago.

The two chimpanzee leaders were still making great physical displays, hauling themselves fully upright, inflating their chests and making their hair stand on end so they looked even larger than they were. For one extraordinary moment he felt himself start to do the same thing, out of instinct. But he checked the impulse at once: any fool could see where it would lead.

Maybe that's what this was, he suddenly thought.

Some kind of response test – rational response versus irrational, that kind of thing. He stood his ground, but made no attempt to show belligerence. Instead, having faced them, he turned in his own time and ambled off in another direction, making it clear, he hoped, that he had no interests or ambitions in anything that might concern them, and that if they left him alone everything would be just fine.

That was when he saw the other figures moving somewhere beyond the trees – human figures this time, but far off, at least a hundred yards away. They seemed to be watching what was going on between him and the other apes. Now that he looked more closely he could see families walking by, couples hand-in-hand, women pushing kids in strollers, a group of senior citizens on what looked like an organized day out. They were on a winding path, and the path, he saw as he got closer to it, was on the far side of a stretch of water, and this, he could see as he looked along it, was a kind of moat. There was no way of telling how deep it was, but he could swim across in a few strokes.

What was obvious was that he was in a zoo. This whole 'open space' he'd wandered into was in reality an enclosure. He couldn't see how big: an acre at least, maybe much more. In another direction he could see a high wall. There was another camera on the top of it. Further to one side something jutted out over the top of the wall. It was a curved glass window about thirty feet above the ground. Beyond it he could see half a dozen or so people watching him and everything that was going on. He couldn't make out any details, just their silhouettes.

How strange, he thought. This really was incredible –

in the sense, he corrected himself, that it was incredibly well done. The feel of it all was amazingly real. But not *quite* real, although maybe that was mainly because he knew it couldn't be. Would he have known all this wasn't real if he hadn't already known that it couldn't possibly be? That was an interesting question.

A grunt of surprise and anger burst from him as something hit him on the shoulder. He looked down; a rock lay on the ground. There had been nothing 'virtual' about the pain it had caused him; it was as real as pain got. He spun around.

There was no mistaking which of the two leaders had thrown the missile. He was displaying and roaring and stamping the ground. His number two backed him up and the others looked on expectantly. Very well, Charlie thought, if that was how they wanted it, then so be it.

As he moved into position to fight, he realized that his body, despite its changed appearance, felt like the body he'd always had. His reflexes were the same, his sense of balance, his sureness of the strength and speed he had at his command. He was still himself, Charlie Monk, inside this ape suit, and he was going to have no problem making it work. That seemed to be how this whole thing was set up. Those were the rules of the game. He had all the physical strength of the apes around him, but he also had the intelligence of a man. He could give direction and control to his strength, which meant he could do things they couldn't.

To begin with he tried out a few evasive moves. The leader tried to provoke him with slaps and shoving – punches that were hard enough to knock down a man and even injure him badly. But to a chimpanzee they were little more than taps, designed to arouse anger, to provoke a confrontation; and to Charlie they weren't even that, shifting his weight as he was doing from foot to foot, so that the force of the blow was absorbed into his own movement. He waited till the moment was perfect, when the other's frustration was beginning to mount, then delivered a colossal blow to the side of his head.

His opponent gave a cry more of surprise than pain and stumbled backward. Charlie waited for him to get over the shock, confident that he could handle whatever was coming and maybe even enjoy it. When his opponent charged him with teeth bared, Charlie knew he'd got him mad. That made it easier to swing his weight to one side and bring it down in a terrible punch to the lower back of his opponent's skull. It didn't quite connect as Charlie had intended, but the other ape still went down. He was shocked and winded, and it took him a moment to scramble to his feet. Charlie waited, and put him down again. This time he stayed down, unconscious.

Charlie looked at the shocked and fearful faces around him. The cry that came from his throat was harsh and defiant. He wanted to say, 'All right now? Is that enough? Can we get along now without any more of this?'

It was still a strange feeling to hear the words in his head while being unable to say them.

When he fell silent, nothing happened. There were hoots and murmurings, but nothing that sounded to Charlie like a concerted response. The chimpanzee he'd knocked unconscious stirred; two or three others went over to him solicitously.

Charlie sensed the movement but couldn't turn before the teeth sank into his side. He hadn't been ready for that much speed, but he made up for it with his own. He spun his new opponent's arm, then stamped him underfoot.

The other shrieked with pain and struggled to get away, but Charlie didn't let him until some of the other males attacked him from behind with bites and punches. They didn't know how to fight, but he was forced to turn around to chase them off. That was when his opponent got away. Charlie saw him shin up a tall oak. This particular oak was absolutely stripped of all greenery and transformed by constant use into a natural climbing frame. Nearby were a couple more like it. The rest of the trees, Charlie saw now, were protected by electric fences.

He quickly shinned up one of the other two defoliated trees. The rest of the group all remained on the ground looking up while the two antagonists displayed and threatened each other from neighbouring branches. It was Charlie who made the first leap; he was getting bored and thought this farce should end. He was fighting, he knew, with a strange detachment, almost as though he wasn't really there. The thought suddenly crossed his mind that perhaps he was a figure in a computer game. Then he wondered who was playing him, and who was playing the other guy. Or was he himself playing both sides? Was this a feedback game?

The pain that followed a split second later made him realize he'd been kicked in the stomach. He hadn't seen the blow coming – hadn't even seen the chimpanzee climb the tree. Careless again. That was obviously the thing he had to watch in this game. He mustn't let his mind go wandering off into irrelevant reflections and philosophy. What mattered was what was happening now. And to get through what was happening now, he had to forget about what it all meant, if anything.

He made a leap to the third oak, as stripped and polished by daily use as the other two. The move gave him a moment to gather his wits and get his breath back. Then the first of his opponents played right into his hands. Charlie could see him calculating a leap across into the same tree as Charlie, but a branch or two higher, from where he could use his feet in an attack. Charlie leapt at the same time as the other did. He saw the look of shock on his opponent's face as he thought they were going to collide in mid-air, then horror when he realized that Charlie had completely outmanoeuvred him. Executing a perfectly timed flip, he kicked the other ape so hard on the behind that he spun out of control, crashing through several branches, even breaking a couple, before he got a hold on one. Then he scampered back down to the ground as fast as he could go and ran for his life, screaming.

None of the others followed him. They just stood watching Charlie uncertainly, but not yet in submission. There was still hostility in the air. He was going to have to hurt one or maybe two more before they got the message.

He glanced up towards the glassed-in observation post he'd noticed earlier. The silhouetted figures stood there still, watching. Some of them now had binoculars to their eyes.

Turning back to the apes, Charlie saw that this brief distraction had been taken as a sign of weakness by at least two of them. One held his hand out to another, and the other moved closer. They were forming an alliance. Two or three more shuffled into positions behind them.

Charlie looked at the ground. He needed a weapon to get this over fast. He saw a stone, shaped almost like a small club. He picked it up, curling his fingers around it, ready for action.

Then suddenly he felt a hand take his. He looked and saw one of the older female apes standing next to him. She had approached unobtrusively, without any menace or bad intent. She met his gaze directly, and there was a deep intelligence in her eyes. It seemed to be seeking out the intelligence in his. She was offering reason in place of madness.

Very gently she began uncurling his fingers from around the stone. He put up no resistance. He knew somehow that there would be no more fighting if he made this gesture, allowing her to disarm him while still standing his ground and challenging any of the males to try their strength against his.

None did. The old female walked a little way with the stone, then tossed it aside. She knew it wouldn't be needed any more. A moment later the group leader who had thrown the first stone at Charlie came loping back through the trees. He made straight for Charlie, but there was no threat in the way he moved. Instead, once he got up to him, he crouched down low so that he had to look up to make eye contact with Charlie. Then he emitted a series of soft grunting sounds which, Charlie realized, was the ape's open acknowledgement of Charlie's superiority. It was Charlie's cue to draw himself up to his full height, at the same time making his hair stand on end to exaggerate his size and underline the dominance–submission, giant–dwarf roles that they had now adopted. Then he realized, as though recalling some half-forgotten ritual not performed for so long that the memory of its details had begun to fade, that something more was required of him. The ape before him continued to cower low on the ground and now raised his hands as though to protect his head. But it wasn't any kind of blow or further attack that he feared. Rather, Charlie suddenly knew, it was an invitation to him to perform the final symbolic affirmation of his victory. Without further thought or hesitation, he swung his leg high and stepped boldly over the crouched figure of his former attacker.

Immediately afterwards, the others he had fought presented themselves in similar fashion, and Charlie went through the same ritual with them. It seemed natural now. This was how things were done, the way life was lived among these creatures. He knew that.

There was only one nagging question on his mind: how did he know?

31

Latimer West's office was on the top floor of the main building. She imagined, when she thought about it, that the view must be impressive, but she never seemed able to take note of it when she was there. It was like an office in a private apartment, not some corporate place. She suspected there were living quarters attached, though she didn't know if this was his permanent home, at least while he held the job, or whether he had some other place of his own. Somehow she imagined him in New York, on the Upper East Side, leading an elegant bachelor existence and going to cocktail parties and the opera with women older than himself. She wondered if he was gay, and decided he was simply sexless. Intimacy, she suspected, would be as disturbing and repulsive to Latimer West as it would to any other unfortunate individual involved – although, she reminded herself as the elevator slowed, this was perhaps a biased view.

The elevator doors opened directly into West's office, and closed behind her as she stepped out on to the thick, soft carpet. He was expecting her, so he made no pretence of being too engrossed in work to acknowledge her arrival. He didn't get to his feet but looked up from his desk with a smile – the kind she thought of as a diplomatic smile, suggesting that as both right and might were on his side, this interview was going to be pretty much a formality.

'Well, Susan,' he began, leaning back and steepling his fingers in a way that she had always thought should carry a capital penalty, 'what's so urgent that you have to talk to me this afternoon? I'm really rather busy.'

'Why don't you take a wild guess?' she said, abandoning every resolution she had made on the way up to avoid losing her temper. 'It's just possible you may hit something not too far from the bull's-eye, something you said we'd get around to discussing when I'd done what you wanted me to do. Now I've done it, so if it's all the same with you I'd like my life back, and with it my son and my father.'

He continued to lean back looking up at her, his smile not slipping an inch, his fingers apparently glued at their tips. 'Nothing was ever said,' he intoned piously, 'about a specific time frame. Your work has been first class, I'm genuinely grateful for all you've done. I know at times it hasn't been easy.'

As though to forestall any remark she may have been about to make, he swung his chair around and slid his elbows on to the edge of his desk. It was a manoeuvre of such fluid, practised grace that, to her annoyance, she found herself almost admiring it.

'But let's be sensible about this, Susan. The project's not complete yet, and your work isn't over. You've seen your son, he's being well looked after and he's quite happy – especially now that he has his grandfather with him. Maybe you're not able to see him as often as you'd like, but you see him often. So I'm afraid that, for the time being, our present arrangements will have to remain in place.'

She looked down at him coldly. It was odd: she actually had the sensation of a physical chill behind her eyes, like a splinter of ice where his image struck her retina.

'One day,' she said, and realized that her lips were dry. She darted her tongue over them, annoyed by what she knew would be seen as a display of weakness. 'One day,' she began again, more deliberately this time, 'you'll pay for what you're doing now. Believe me, you'll pay for this abuse of my work, and other people's work.'

'We've had this discussion before, Susan. I've tried to make you see that knowledge is nobody's private property. To pretend that some piece of knowledge is yours and yours alone is a far worse theft than anything you're accusing us of here. Scientists don't create knowledge; we uncover it, but it was always there, waiting for somebody to lift up that corner of the map.'

'I never claimed to own anything. All my work has been done out in the open, published and talked about. Anyone could use my work the way you have, but most people wouldn't want to, and society wouldn't let them.'

The smile on his face grew a little thinner and the impatience growing behind it began to show.

'There's no point in you and I debating the morality of this, Susan. We see things differently. That's all there is to say.'

'Maybe we can agree on one thing.'

He looked up at her. Was this a trap? The set-up for some parting insult? He didn't much care.

'Tell me.'

'From now on stick to "Dr Flemyng". I don't like your using my first name.'

'As you wish, of course.'

He tipped his head in a slight bow. It was a gracious gesture, yielding her the point, though he remained seated.

'Just tell me one thing, Dr Flemyng? Despite all your abstract moral objections, aren't you just a little bit excited by all this, as a scientist? Just the tiniest bit?'

She felt the anger mount inside her like a surge of electricity. This was the moment at which she risked losing all control, lashing out or throwing something, inflicting whatever damage she could and damn the cost. She recognized the moment, and as soon as she did she knew it was over. She held in her anger and maintained an icy equanimity.

'When what you are doing here becomes known, Dr West, even though my part in it was under duress, I shall be deeply ashamed.'

'Rest assured, Dr Flemyng, it never will become known. At least not until society takes such things for granted, which it will very soon, just as it now accepts spaceships and television. It's progress, Dr Flemyng. Evolution. There's no stopping it.'

She realized that as he spoke he had pushed himself up from his desk and walked over to the window. Her eyes had followed him every inch of the way. They were still fixed on him when he turned to face her, standing in partial silhouette against the light.

'Stopping it,' he said with the finality of an emperor delivering judgement, 'is the only thing that can't be done.'

On her way down in the elevator, Susan reflected that she had yet again failed to ascertain whether the view from his office was as she supposed it must be.

32

Charlie pondered the question. How had he known? How had he known that stepping over his beaten adversary was the way to seal his victory? Why was this whole strange experience starting to feel like coming home and resuming old habits, slipping into comfortable and well-worn clothes?

The thought of clothes made him look down at himself again, at the thick black hair and alien body which, strangely, didn't feel quite so alien any more.

Meanwhile the rituals continued. One of the males he had fought brought him a branch with some leaves which, mysteriously again, Charlie knew were edible. He tasted one: it had a rich and satisfying flavour. Someone else gave him a handful of twigs; he didn't know the significance of that, apart from it being a gift, but then he saw there was a certain delicacy in the arrangement of the tiny branches. It was a work of art, a creation, a treasured object.

Another gave him a piece of dried fruit. Others, males and females, approached him nervously at first, then embraced him, planting kisses on his face and stroking him with unexpected tenderness. It seemed that once the issue of dominance had been settled, all-round affection and companionship were the natural order of things, often expressed in the most tactile of ways.

Suddenly he realized that one of the younger females was presenting herself to him in a manner that left nothing to doubt and little to the imagination. She was backing towards him while looking over her shoulder to make sure that she had his attention. Her genitalia were red and hugely swollen, like some inflated rubber doughnut growing out of her nether regions.

But it was the shock of his response that shook Charlie more profoundly than anything that had happened so far. He felt an abrupt stirring in his groin, and looking down saw that his penis was erect. But it was a thin, long, spiky thing, not the robust human penis he was accustomed to. And yet it had a life of its own, and he was attached to it, and he knew what it was about to make him do.

Something shifted in his head, an abrupt change of mental perspective from immediate detail to a more comprehensive awareness. With it came a terrible sense of panic, the worst he had experienced since this whole episode began. He felt for the first time that he was trapped in something from which he might never escape. All his psychological defences fell like a house of cards. He could no longer pretend this was a game, or a dream, or a test. All those mechanisms which had allowed him to step back from the experience and view it with an outsider's detachment had vanished with that visceral sexual impulse that had just so irresistibly and unstoppably run through him. He was, he realized, what he seemed to be, and nothing more.

Except, and always – no. It wasn't possible. As though physically tearing himself from the fabric of this new reality, he turned about, then turned again, his gaze clawing the air for some sign of something else. He saw the cameras, and the silhouettes of those people still watching from behind their glass partition. He picked up another stone, smaller than the one the older female had taken from him, and flung it with all his strength at those impassive observers. It bounced harmlessly off the glass, which was obviously unbreakable. No one on the far side flinched.

There was a chattering of excitement around him. Some of the other chimpanzees also picked up stones and flung them up at the glass. It was, he got the impression, an occasional pastime they were accustomed to, and which they were indulging in now as a courtesy to the new number one in their group, who seemed to find it amusing. He turned away in tired despair, and saw again the strolling figures of the public on the distant far side of the moat.

It was then that, amongst them, he suddenly saw Kathy. She stood watching him, not moving, her gaze fixed on his with a stillness that was almost hypnotic.

Charlie gave a cry of recognition. It burst from his lips as a howl of something close to pain. Kathy didn't budge as he began loping towards her at a rolling all-fours gallop. He felt his lips curl back as he trumpeted his anguish, his need for someone to explain how long all this was going on and why.

She did no more than watch as he approached the moat, but at the last moment, as it became obvious he wasn't going to stop but plunge headlong into the water, she thrust out her arms in a gesture of alarm, as though trying to hold him back.

He took no notice, pressing on as the smooth floor of the moat slipped steeply away beneath his feet. As the water closed around his chest, he pushed off and began to swim – and sank, struggling and choking, beneath the surface.

For a moment he didn't know what had happened. Some stupid miscalculation, a lack of familiarity with this new physical form that he was saddled with, had made him slip and stumble, miss his stride and bungle his normally powerful swimming stroke. But that could happen to anyone. Charlie was a champion swimmer. All he had to do was move his arms and legs in the usual way and his head would break the surface, then he would cover the last few yards to Kathy in seconds.

Except that whatever he tried, he couldn't find the surface. No matter how he writhed and turned, he remained just a flailing mass of limbs, no more able to direct his movement than to float. He felt himself sinking helplessly to the wide V-shaped bottom of the moat. He tried to scramble up one side, then the other – which was which no longer mattered to him. All he needed was to reach the air and fill his bursting lungs. But the surface was too smooth to give him purchase. All that happened every time he struggled up a painful inch or two was that he slid down and landed, rolling over, on the bottom.

He knew with a sudden and terrible clarity that he was going to drown. If there was any way out of this, he told himself, he would have found it by now. All that remained was to await the point at which his self-control would break and give way to the final scream of dying rage that would fill his lungs with water. The swirling blues and whites and slashes of shadow that he saw now would fade to darkness. His heart would stop, his brain would die, and the body that would eventually be fished out would be no more than a lifeless hulk: man or beast, what matter?

Suddenly he felt the hard surface on which he was lying give way beneath him. As he fell he gave an involuntary gasp of shock, gulping water, but found that with it there was air. He landed in a huge curved pan of stainless steel or something similar. It sat at an angle so that the water still pouring from the moat on to his head drained off into a narrow trench beyond his feet. He shifted to one side and looked up. The section of the moat that had opened to let him out was already swinging shut like a powerful jaw closing on the cascading water. In a moment it was back in place, and everything was silent.

All he could think of at first was what an extraordinary piece of engineering this was. He could see now that the whole underside of the moat was constructed in sections, each one of which presumably could open as the one above him just had to free a drowning . . . what?

He looked down at his matted wet black hairy body. So, he thought, it continues. He tried to stand up, but the polished steel surface was too slippery. He slid down, ending up with one foot in the narrow drainage trench and the other on the concrete floor beyond. He stepped over and looked around. There appeared to be only one way out of the area, an opening about the size of an average door, and a lighted corridor beyond. He started up it, no longer hesitant or cautious; fear was something that belonged in another, more rational life. So far as this life he found himself in now was concerned, Charlie was all 'feared out'.

The walls and ceiling of the corridor were again made

of some prefabricated substance in a dull beige colour, with lighting from a strip embedded in the ceiling. After a few yards it turned abruptly to the right, and came to an end. He looked for some crack in the blank wall facing him that might indicate a hidden door, but there was nothing.

A sound behind him made him turn. He saw a panel sliding swiftly across and closing off the corridor behind him. He was boxed into a space about six feet square. Instinctively he ran back and threw his weight against this new fourth wall, but it didn't budge.

Still he didn't panic. All he felt now was a kind of stoic acceptance of his fate. Something, he told himself, of which he had no knowledge was taking its course, and it was a course over which he had no control.

He sensed movement, a brief pressure beneath his feet. The box he was trapped in was moving upwards, like an elevator. After about fifteen seconds it stopped, and the wall which had just slid shut now opened again. Before him was a round tunnel, about six feet in diameter. He was obviously expected to step into it, but he didn't move, just to find out what would happen.

After a few moments he felt a pressure on his back. The wall behind him was moving slowly forward with a power that he couldn't resist or even slow down. Silently and ineluctably he was forced out of his elevator and into the tunnel. It was silvery and had small holes punched in it in strip-like patterns. He heard an electric motor start up. The air grew warm and began to whip around him in criss-crossing currents. He was, he realized, in a giant hairdryer. The process lasted for a couple of minutes and was curiously pleasant. At the end of it his thick black hair was once again shiny and without the matted dampness that had made it look like some old sackcloth left out in the rain.

Another panel opened at the far end of the silvery corridor. This time he could see where it led – back into his cage in the corner of the laboratory. Once again he probably wouldn't have moved unless obliged to, which in a sense he was.

Because he could see Kathy standing on the far side of the bars, waiting for him.

33

'Hello, Charlie,' she said, as he walked towards her. 'I hope you're feeling better after your wash and brush up. We didn't want you to catch cold.'

Charlie reared up on his legs and seized the bars of his cage, trying to shake them, but they were fixed firmly in place. An agitated chattering noise came from his throat. He could feel that his lips were curled back and his teeth exposed. He wanted to close his mouth, but he couldn't make it happen; it seemed to be a reflex, beyond his control.

'I've brought you something,' she said, and looked over to one side of his cage. He followed her gaze. By the wall stood an easel with a fresh canvas, a palette of paints and brushes. He went over and reached out a hand to pick up one of the brushes. The movement felt surprisingly natural, just as it always had. He looked back at her. She was still watching him. Encouraged by the expectant look on her face, he dipped the brush cautiously in a whorl of green paint, then touched it to the canvas. He knew what he was going to do. If he couldn't speak, he could at least write.

'Go ahead, Charlie,' she said, encouraging him. 'Go on.'

The question he wanted to write was, 'What is happening?' He could hear the words in his head, and he knew how to write them. But somewhere between the order that came from his brain and its execution by his hand there opened up a yawning and mysterious gap.

He stood briefly paralysed, like someone who has forgotten a word but who knows that a moment's concentration will bring it back. He tried to visualize the words he wanted to use, to see them in his mind's eye as they would appear on the canvas when written. He saw them. They were absolutely clear. And yet, when he tried to look closer, to distinguish each letter, take it out of context and focus on its form enough to reproduce it, he found he couldn't.

It was almost too absurd to be frustrating, one of those moments when some chance collusion of synaptic firings creates a sense of déjà vu, or persuades you that a passing shadow on the edge of your vision is something it is not.

He waited for the lacuna to pass, but instead it drew out and still nothing happened. He made a renewed effort to visualize the first letter of the first word he was trying to write. It was a . . . what was the name for it? A 'W'.

Now he had it. Three – no, four lines – connected at angles. Tentatively, he reached out his brush and made a mark on the canvas. It wasn't, he realized at once, quite what he wanted. As the first angle of the first letter, it seemed somehow wrong. Could he incorporate it as one of the other angles? Had he left enough room for something in front, not to mention everything that had to come after, all those other lines and curves that made up the phrase he could still see in his mind's eye?

He *could* see it, couldn't he? He was sure that he could. So why couldn't he break it down into its parts, then execute them one by one? Surely he must be able to do that.

His brush struck out this way and that, but never in the way he wanted. Whatever was in his mind refused to project itself on to the canvas before him. He didn't know whether it was a failure of skill or of imagination. He had never imagined that such a sense of inner dislocation could exist.

The slashes of line and colour became wilder, until they became rents and tears in the canvas. Then, with a cry of outrage and frustration, and an indefinable but terrible fear, he broke the easel into splinters and scattered the paint and brushes. He only turned when he heard voices behind him raised in alarm. Two or three people in white lab coats had run in. After them came two men in suits and ties.

'Is there a problem, Dr Flemyng?'

It was the shorter of the men in suits who had spoken. His hair was brushed back sleekly from a pink and well-fed face.

'Just a tantrum,' Kathy replied, 'no problem.'

Charlie watched as the other man took a few steps towards his cage. He was probably around fifty, a year or two older than the one Kathy had just spoken to, but taller and wearing rimless glasses. He had the diffident though sharply observant air of a college professor, which is what Charlie would have guessed him to be.

'Is this the one?' he asked, peering more closely at Charlie. He spoke in a light and very clear but rather brittle voice.

'Don't lean too far over that barrier, General,' the sleek-haired man said, hurrying to the taller man's side and laying a hand respectfully on his elbow.

Charlie registered with some surprise the use of the

rank 'general'. He would never have guessed that in a thousand years.

'They're strong and they're vicious,' sleek hair continued. 'Not even their keepers ever get within striking distance of a full-grown chimpanzee. He's about eight times stronger than any human being.'

The general looked at Charlie critically. 'I always thought chimpanzees were friendly little fellows.'

'That's just the babies. The ones you see on cute TV shows. A full-grown male weighs over two hundred pounds.' He threw a glance over his shoulder. 'All right, everybody, there's no problem. You can go back to what you were doing.'

The three men in white coats departed, but Kathy remained with them. Charlie still thought of her as Kathy despite the name this man had called her by, and the name she now used herself. He thought back to the other night when he'd climbed into her apartment and found her looking through his pictures. Just how long ago was that? It seemed like a lifetime ago – which in a sense it was, he thought, not without irony.

'But they're not as tall as we need, are they?' the general asked, still eyeing Charlie with distrust, as though somebody was trying to sell him a suspect idea. 'Five feet . . . what? Five something at the most.'

'The height will come naturally as part of the genetic adjustment,' sleek hair said, smiling unctuously and rubbing his clasped hands slightly. 'It's actually a minor thing, largely a function of the upright stance. The physical similarities are extraordinary, both skeletal and muscular. D'you know, the sole of the human foot has exactly the same muscles as the chimpanzee foot. The only reason we can't grip things with our feet is because we've lost the habit.'

'Why aren't we using gorillas?' the general asked, twisting around to look at sleek hair almost accusingly. 'They're bigger and I imagine stronger than chimpanzees.'

'The process wouldn't work so well with gorillas,' sleek hair replied, holding up a soft pink hand in a cautioning gesture that made Charlie think of a priest about to pronounce the blessing. 'They're less intelligent and less aggressive than chimpanzees. More importantly, they're not as closely related to us. Human beings and chimps are as closely related as the African and Indian elephants. The difference between our DNA and his,' he pointed a plump finger in Charlie's direction, 'is 1.6 per cent. Between chimps and gorillas it's 2.3 – which means that chimps are genetically closer to humans than they are to gorillas. In fact they're practically human already.'

'Except for that 1.6 per cent.'

'But we know now where it makes the difference. Interestingly, it's not the brain. They have much the same brain as humans – slightly smaller, but not significantly. The human brain is more dominated by the left hemisphere, but that's a result of our having evolved speech and sequential thought – which is where the human branch of the chimp family really scored. Chimps communicate between each other quite effectively, though on a fairly basic level. A few chimps have been taught to use sign language amazingly well, and of course they have quite a visual sense. They love to paint, some of them, especially in captivity where they need something to do. But without spoken language they could never build the Parthenon or a rocket to the moon.'

'But given language, they could do all that?'

'Not overnight, of course. But that's not what we want, after all.'

The general looked at Charlie thoughtfully, pursing his lips and blowing a little burst of air out through his nose. 'No, you're right,' he said, 'that's not what we want.' He paused, still thinking something over, then added: 'I must say, though, I was surprised to learn chimps can't swim. How d'you explain that in evolutionary terms?'

'I'm not sure I can. Maybe they didn't evolve around enough water.'

'But it won't be a problem with our fellow – swimming, I mean?'

'Oh, no. He'll swim far better than any normal human being – not to mention all his other accomplishments.'

The general continued to look, Charlie thought, somehow unconvinced. Then he turned to the attractive young woman he'd not had a chance to speak with yet. 'Do you really believe that this can work?' he asked her. 'Can we really create this prototype just by giving some chimp DNA a tweak here and a push there?'

'Genetics isn't my side of things,' she replied awkwardly. Charlie had the impression that she didn't want to get into this conversation.

'Dr Flemyng has been working on some special neurological aspects,' sleek hair said quickly. 'We had problems with visual memory – all solved now, thanks to her.'

The general looked her up and down, then gave an appreciative smile and inclined his head in a courtly, old-fashioned bow. 'I'm bound to say, Dr Flemyng, that you would have a beneficial effect upon anybody's visual memory.'

Before she had time to make some anodyne, polite reply, they were interrupted by a fusillade of angry screeching from Charlie. Turning to the cage, they saw that he had hauled himself halfway up the bars and was wrenching wildly at them as though trying to pull them loose.

'We mustn't keep you, Dr Flemyng,' sleek hair said. 'I know you have things to do, thank you for your time.'

Charlie saw her murmur something to the two men and leave. He continued his screeching and tugging at the bars, though he didn't know quite what he was hoping to achieve. Gradually, overwhelmed by the sense of his own powerlessness and the futility of his rage, he slid down until he sat murmuring helplessly on the floor.

Sleek hair and the general had watched his performance with interest.

'Can he actually understand what we're saying?' the general said as Charlie quietened down.

'No more than the average dog or cat can. Tone of voice means more than anything else.'

The general looked at sleek hair with suspicion as well as puzzlement in his face now. 'But you said that these VR tests you've been doing have proved that he can handle language.'

'Ah, yes – but only while he's wired into the suit. The prototype that we'll grow from the genetically engineered egg will have the modified larynx as well as a fully human appearance. He will live the life that Charlie has experienced only through virtual reality.'

The general glanced from sleek hair over to Charlie, who stood motionless, staring back through the bars of his cage with a kind of dumb stupefaction. 'Hmm,' the general said, blowing out air through his nose again, 'fascinating.'

'We got a lot of data from this last VR trial,' sleek hair said, with an air of deep satisfaction. 'Charlie's helped us a great deal.'

34

Susan and her father sat on the porch in comfortable rockers, drinking the coffee that Mrs Hathaway, Christopher's new 'Auntie May', had brought them. They were watching Christopher go through his paces on his horse under the careful supervision of Michael, the young man who seemed to have become something between a father, brother and best friend to him. Christopher's dog, Buzz, sat obediently and rather primly watching nearby.

'He misses home, his friends, school,' Amery was saying, 'but otherwise he's fine here – it's a beautiful place, after all.'

Susan shifted uneasily in her chair, frowning as she brought the mug of coffee to her lips.

'I know you don't like to hear that,' Amery added quickly. 'Neither do I. But as long as we're in this situation, it could be a lot worse.'

'As long as,' she echoed flatly. 'How long is that going to be, I wonder?'

Her father sighed. 'I went back to Washington last week for a couple of days. I had some business to attend to, so I spoke to Mrs Hathaway – if that's her real name. I somehow can't believe it is. Anyway, she put a call through to somebody, and within five minutes I had

Latimer West on the line. They had someone fly me to the airport in the chopper, fixed my ticket up and everything – the full VIP treatment. In fact West said that not only could I make this trip, I could come and go as I pleased. He said he knew he could rely on my discretion as long as Christopher remained here.'

He looked over at his daughter, watching her reaction. She sat hunched and tense, her head sunk into her shoulders, her gaze still fixed on Christopher though without really seeing him. Amery set his coffee mug down on the table, then sat back, rocking slightly, picking his words carefully.

'Something else he said to me. He said he and others – I don't know who he meant by others, but there obviously are others, quite a lot of them, and in high places – anyway, he said that he and others would very much like to see this situation normalized. I asked him what he meant by normalized, and he said exactly what the word implied. I said, you mean Christopher and his mother could return home, resume their lives? He said that's exactly what he meant.'

Susan was looking at him now, unblinking. It was impossible to tell whether she was outraged or encouraged by what she was hearing.

'The thing is,' Amery continued, 'they feel they've made their point now. They have the power to do what they want, and they've shown that they'll use it if they have to. Now, if we're prepared to cooperate, we can all go home.'

'And live under house arrest?'

'Live like normal people, with something we've agreed not to talk about.'

'And if we do talk, they'll kill us.'

It wasn't a question but a flat statement of how she saw the facts.

Amery dropped his gaze. 'I didn't go into that.'

They sat in silence for a while. Christopher had completed a circuit of jumps and waved to them in triumph. They waved back mechanically. Michael started raising the bars a notch for another round.

'You know,' Susan said, 'the more I think about this, the more I can't believe it's happening. What kind of a country are we living in?'

Her father looked at her sadly. 'A country like any other,' he said. 'When those responsible for its security decide that something needs to be done, they're going to do it – without any discussion and in spite of any moral opposition. D'you really think there's any major country that doesn't have chemical weapons or nerve gas hidden away somewhere, just in case? We know they have nuclear weapons, but do we want that to be the only choice they have? Elected politicians pay lip service to fine principles, because that's their job. But behind them are the people who do the dirty work, who are guided only by necessity and pragmatism. Because when the chips are down, all the people who vote for politicians want to know is are we ready for this crisis? Can we handle it? Can we keep their houses warm in winter, cool in summer, their cars full of cheap gas and their refrigerators packed with frozen steak and ice-cream? So if the people whose job it is to guarantee all that decide that they need a new kind of weapon or a new kind of fighting man, they're going to get it.'

Susan had turned her gaze on to him again. 'You almost sound like you approve of this.'

He shrugged. 'My approval – anybody's – is irrelevant.

You may as well disapprove of the earth going around the sun. It's just how things work.'

They sat in silence a while, watching Christopher as he started his next round of jumps.

'So,' she said eventually, 'you're saying that if I continue to work on this project voluntarily and convince them I'm no longer a security risk, they'll let you and me and Christopher live our lives as though nothing had happened.'

'That's about it, as far as I can see.'

'Jesus, Dad, these people are all heart.'

The bitterness in her voice was so raw that he didn't say anything for a while. They both watched Christopher, who was going around the course without a fault.

'Look,' Amery Hyde said eventually, 'it's just something to think about, that's all. But it's your decision.'

She nodded a couple of times. 'You know,' she said, 'these people seem to think they're pretty powerful. But there's one thing they can't do.'

'What's that?'

'They can't bring John back.'

35

Charlie ate alone in his cage – a platter of fruit and vegetables that was pushed in through a slot. His sleep was surprisingly undisturbed and dreamless, and he awoke gently enough to re-absorb the ongoing strangeness of his situation almost calmly. Had they put something in his food or water, he wondered? A tranquillizer?

But he certainly didn't feel tranquillized when they let him out. His status as the dominant male didn't seem to have altered from the day before, as a result of which he was left alone as much as he wished. He stayed well back from the moat and paid little attention to the people who wandered by on the far side. He used his solitude to digest and reflect on what he had learned the previous day.

It seemed that he, Charlie Monk, was a chimpanzee who had been used in some kind of experiment to find out if he could think, speak and behave like a human being. That strange silvery suit they'd taken him out of had created the illusion that he was not only a man but a special kind of man, a secret agent who had enjoyed some very colourful adventures.

He thought back over that life – *his* life – trying to remember every detail. It was, of course, impossible. The past was irretrievable, beyond recall in a way that was more absolute than he had ever realized. How could he be sure that his memories derived from events and not from something else? What was it that sleek hair had said about Kathy, or Dr Flemyng, or whatever she was called? That she'd solved some problems with his 'visual memory'? What did that mean? That all his memories of being human had been somehow planted in his brain?

But if that was the case and he'd been an ape all along, where were his memories of life as an ape? Why were human memories the only ones he had?

And yet, as he looked around at his fellow chimpanzees, he realized he was coming to feel increasingly at home in this place. The smells, the calls, the playfulness, the whole rhythm of this life, were becoming familiar to a quite extraordinary degree, as though a veil had been drawn aside and what had originally seemed alien was now recognized as home ground, even fondly remembered. Had he truly been here before? Was this who he was, and all the rest some kind of electronic dream?

How could that be? Did he imagine for one second that these creatures all around him, intent as they were on the trivia of their daily routine and relationships, could possibly share any of what was going on inside his head? Sleek hair had told the general that he, Charlie, couldn't understand what was being said about him. But that was a lie. He'd understood every word. What was he to make of that? Was it some other kind of test?

He became aware, almost subliminally at first, of someone moving on the periphery of his vision, subtly creeping up on him. He tensed, but didn't move. If there was going to be a fight, his challenger must start it; he, Charlie, would then finish it, as he had the day before. He was surprised, after yesterday, that any of them still had the nerve to face up to him, but that was their problem.

After several minutes during which nothing happened he became bored and not a little annoyed. It seemed to him absurd that he should have to follow this protocol of sitting still and pretending he was unaware of what was going on. He stood up, stretched, and turned in a way that he knew would bring him into eye contact with his adversary. But what he saw was not an adversary at all. Seated about ten yards away, apparently paying him no attention and playing with a tuft of grass she'd pulled from somewhere, was the young female he'd noticed yesterday, her genitals still swollen and red, proclaiming she was ready for intercourse.

Charlie's visceral response to the sight of her shook him somewhat, as it had on the previous day. He knew she was aware of him though she didn't look his way; he suspected that she'd placed herself where she was so that he would have to notice her.

Well, notice her he had, and he felt the same familiar stirring in his groin that he'd felt before. He became aware that she was avoiding his gaze, playing coy.

Charlie's arousal now was total. He found himself sitting upright and leaning back on his hands, his legs spread apart and his erection displayed. It was then, for the first time, that she looked at him. And something happened in Charlie's mind. It was as though something had burst, flooding every cell in his brain with one sole purpose, wiping out all thought and leaving only physical desire and straightforward lust.

At that moment she turned and looked fully at him – at his face, his body, his pulsating, bursting penis. Charlie held out his arm in an instinctive gesture of invitation.

She got up from where she sat and came towards him. Her movements were confident but oddly shy, as though she were thrilled by what was happening though a little nervous. When she got close enough for him to touch her, she turned, backing the last few inches towards him, crouching low to facilitate his entry.

He felt her warmth and wetness, and thrust deep with all his power, gasping as he built to his near-unbearable release. She gave a sudden shrill scream of climactic pleasure, and Charlie felt a fireball of ecstasy explode somewhere deep within him and engulf his entire being.

It was over as abruptly as it had begun. Almost before he'd registered her departure, she had disappeared into the trees.

Charlie closed his eyes and tried again to recall himself as Charlie Monk, the man. He tried to recall that life: the smell, the touch, the taste, the whole sense and feel of that existence. But he couldn't. He had come too far. It was a memory now, another life, a dream.

He found he was holding his eyes tight shut, squeezing them, afraid to open them again.

36

Tom Schiller entered the narrow lobby, walked back past the stairs, and pressed the bell outside the peeling brown door. A light went on over the cheap tele-scanner in the wall. Tom held up his card, somebody buzzed open the door, and he entered.

The pretence at security, he knew, was bullshit. He could have held up his video-store card for all the old guy dozing on his stool in his grey uniform could care. It was just an excuse to charge more than necessary from people who, for one reason or another, didn't want some or even any of their mail sent to where they lived or worked.

Over the past five years Tom had always kept at least two of these drops active at any one time, always under different names. He didn't take the Great Conspiracy theory of government quite as seriously as some of the people whose writing he published; nonetheless, he knew that government worldwide had grown into a many-headed monster that needed to be feared, faced down and fought on practically all fronts. Because of this, he found it useful to have ways of receiving correspondence that he wouldn't want read by anyone else, certainly not anyone working for the political-military-industrial complex of which he was so critical – which pretty much included half the adult population.

He'd only had this drop for six weeks, and there was only one person he was expecting to hear from in it. He'd given the address and his code number to Susan Flemyng before she went to Russia. Just in case. If ever. Since then he'd heard nothing from her. He had also discovered after making a few phone calls that she and her son were away on some kind of trip, though nobody knew quite where or for how long. He'd tried to contact her father in Washington. He too was strangely hard to locate at the moment.

So Tom Schiller dropped by this address every two or three days – just in case. As always, he produced his key and went to his letter box in a wall of identical ones. To his right a business type in a good suit was poring over the contents of a thick plain envelope that he didn't want anybody else to see. To his left a middle-aged woman, ordinary looking in every way, slipped a handwritten letter into her purse then locked her box and hurried out. In the corner an unhealthy-looking teenage girl had torn open an envelope, tossed it and the note it enclosed into a bin, and was stuffing two or three ten dollar bills into the waist of her tights.

Tom didn't know whether he hoped to find something in his box or not. Something from Susan could mean a story; it could also mean she was in trouble. On the whole he'd have preferred a phone call to say she was all right and was maybe even letting the whole thing drop.

The postcard was a bland picture of orange groves. On the back were just two lines, handwritten. The first gave the date, time and number of a flight from Washington DC's National Airport to Great Falls in Montana. The second line said, 'Wear a red tie.'

37

There was nothing to stop Charlie going with the rest of them to the chimpanzees' sleeping quarters. There was also nothing to stop him returning to his own cage at the end of the day if he preferred. The choice appeared to be his.

By the same token, there seemed to be nothing to prevent any of the other chimps entering his personal cage and bedding down for the night if they chose to, but none did. Perhaps, he told himself, it was a mark of respect. Or perhaps they too felt there was something different and alien about him, something that meant he didn't belong. Perhaps they preferred that he slept in quarters of his own.

Charlie turned over all these possibilities in his mind, but by the end of the day felt such a weariness that coherent thought was becoming increasingly difficult. It was a mental weariness, not physical. His mind was spinning; there was no longer any centre he could cling to.

He ate, as on the previous day, from a tray that was pushed in through a slot. It was afterwards that Kathy arrived. He looked up and saw her standing some way off, watching him. Behind her, the section of the lab that he could see was almost empty; a couple of people were tidying things up before leaving. It was the end of their day as well as Charlie's.

When their eyes met she didn't react or respond in any way, just went on looking at him, her gaze locked on to his as though in search of something at the source of it.

'You understand what I'm saying, don't you?'

It was a statement of fact, not a question, as though she had no doubt. He was surprised, after that, when she asked for proof.

'If you can understand me, clasp your hands in front of you.'

Her own hands remained by her side. She was trying to ensure, Charlie decided, that she didn't give him any visual clues. Very deliberately he brought his hands together and interlaced his fingers, keeping his eyes on hers for her reaction. She murmured something under her breath. He thought he lip-read, 'Oh, my God.'

She looked down for a moment as though to gather her thoughts, then lifted her eyes to his. 'You can't speak and you can't write, but you can still understand. That's what I was afraid of. They said you wouldn't retain anything except a few visual impressions when you came out of the VR suit. You'd recognize me, but you wouldn't be sure why, and even that would fade quickly, like a dream. But you remember it all, don't you?'

He looked at her helplessly, not knowing how to answer. Realizing his predicament, she said, 'Knock on the floor, once for yes, twice for no.'

Charlie realized he'd fallen into his now customary pose, leaning forward and resting the weight of his upper body on his knuckles. He lifted his right hand and rapped the floor once.

She became utterly still, then closed her eyes as though

trying to contain an emotion that was too powerful to let go.

'This wasn't supposed to happen,' she said in a whisper. He wasn't sure whether the words were for him or whether they were spoken to herself.

He waited. After a moment she opened her eyes again and fixed them on him.

'That suit you were in. They call it the Demon Machine – it's a reference to Descartes. The name probably doesn't mean much to you. René Descartes was a seventeenth-century philosopher who imagined a demon manipulating all his senses, so that he could never be sure what was true and what was false.'

She paused, looking at him perhaps in search of some reaction. He offered none.

'They've been using your brain, Charlie. And your brain was where it's always been, and still is – in there.'

She turned and pointed to the mirror on the wall behind her. He looked at it, and his eyes met their own intense, enquiring reflection.

'They were testing your reactions, Charlie. They needed to find out if the chimpanzee brain was capable of doing what they wanted it to do.' She paused and looked away for a moment, her voice faltering. 'I'm saying "they", but I was one of them. What's happened to you is partly a result of things I did. But "they",' she drew in a deep, slightly unsteady breath, 'they're attempting to create a human lookalike – stronger and faster than any man on earth, and totally obedient to his masters. And they're going to make him out of a genetically mutated chimpanzee.'

Charlie listened impassively. He didn't know what felt more unreal: the fact that he was the creature he could still see reflected in that mirror behind her, or the fact that her story no longer surprised him. What he was hearing only confirmed what he'd heard and thought already. He wondered whether the strange numbness he felt was a defence mechanism, a kind of mental anaesthetic to keep at bay the madness that he feared had already overtaken him.

'What they're going to do,' he heard her saying, 'is take a fertilized egg, genetically modify it, then implant it in the womb of a female chimpanzee. The baby, a male, will be taken from her at birth. He'll be reared in a lab in isolation. When he's about eight years old he'll look like a fully-grown human being. That's when they'll send him to a place where they train killers. He won't know he's any different from the rest of them – just that he's the best. The shrinks say that knowing his true nature would make him impossible to handle. So he'll have been brainwashed in the lab – they've developed a total VR environment to give him the kind of background that will motivate him to become what they want.'

She looked at Charlie again and made a little gesture with her hands that he interpreted as a kind of apology.

'The key to brainwashing isn't just wiping memories, it's planting new ones. And the hardest kind of memory to plant is visual memory. That's where I came in. I'd discovered a way to plant visual images of things the brain had never seen before, and yet would recognize when they were encountered in reality. As a test, I even planted a picture of myself in your past – a past that never existed.'

She paused again, still looking at him with a strange expression on her face – almost, he thought, a mixture of guilt and denial.

'And you recognized me, didn't you, Charlie?'

He must have done something – a gesture, a movement, perhaps just the look in his eyes – that confirmed what she had supposed. She dropped her eyes.

'I'm sorry, Charlie.'

Without thinking, he took a step forward and held his hand out through the bars of the cage. He didn't know what he expected or even what he wanted from her, but his gesture wasn't an aggressive one; he meant her no harm. When she gave a little gasp and jumped back, he was surprised and strangely hurt. And angry. A sound came from the back of his throat, a grunt, almost a growl.

She seemed to understand and shook her head, not in denial but as though she was affirming what he thought, accepting his anger as her due and his right.

'I'm sorry, Charlie,' she repeated, 'so sorry.'

Then, turning away and refusing to look at him again, she hurried from his sight.

38

Tom Schiller spent the whole flight from National Airport to Great Falls scanning, as discreetly as possible, the faces of his fellow passengers. Susan Flemyng herself wasn't among them, but he hadn't expected her to be. The injunction to wear a red tie meant, he supposed, that someone who didn't know him was supposed to find him. But despite the slash of crimson at his neck, which he fingered significantly from time to time, no one approached him or even paid him any attention.

So he assumed somebody would be waiting for him at his destination. But there was no familiar face, and nobody holding a card with his name on it.

He went over to a lunch counter and bought himself a cup of coffee and a sandwich, still keeping his eyes peeled and his ears alert for an announcement, but there was none. He checked out the information desk. No message had been left. The woman asked if he wanted to have an announcement made himself; he thought about this for a moment, but decided against it.

The next flight back east was in three hours. He took it.

Susan's apartment in the Irvine Spectrum complex, in which she was effectively a prisoner, was spacious and had its own kitchen where she prepared herself a sparse breakfast of fruit and yoghurt. She had slept badly and had got up feeling tired and edgy.

The last time she talked to her father had been at the ranch. As they watched Christopher's latest display of horsemanship, she had told him about Tom Schiller and the secret post box by which she could contact him. That post drop was the last card she had left to play; surely she had been right to play it. Surely, she told herself, it was wrong, morally and in every other way, not to use everything she could lay her hands on to fight these people. Her only regret was that she was putting her father in the front line instead of herself, but what danger could there be in two strangers meeting on a plane and getting into casual conversation?

Amery had been nervous at first, reluctant for her sake and Christopher's to take any unwise risks. But in the end she had persuaded him. She told him she wasn't proposing they give the whole story to Schiller, or even any part of it. For one thing, nobody but the converted ever took seriously the kind of thing that Schiller and his kind published. Two months ago she herself would have dismissed talk of secret government and wheels within wheels as paranoid nonsense. Now she knew better. What she didn't know for sure was how far it went, this strange cancer of shadowy groups and secret powers. Obviously it went high, but maybe not everywhere. She couldn't believe that a major newspaper or TV network would not run with this story if they could be made to believe it. Then it would be up to the public to decide what they thought, and she had no doubt that most of them would share her revulsion for this project and any like it.

What she needed to know was where, who and what

were the Pilgrim Foundation's connections. What was the pattern of influence of which it was a part? Schiller and his cohorts would be better than anyone at digging up that kind of information. He would realize the significance of what he was being asked because it was she who was doing the asking, even if only indirectly through her father; but that alone wouldn't be enough to give Schiller a story to print because he wouldn't know enough of what was behind her questions. Besides, her father would pass on a message urging discretion, and she had sensed from the beginning that she could trust Schiller.

The phone rang and made her jump. It was an internal phone; she had no outside line, but it was unusual for anyone to call this early. She answered on the second ring. It was West.

'Just to let you know, Dr Flemyng, that a package is being delivered to your door as we speak. You'll find it on the small table outside. When you open it, you'll see just how foolish you have been in abusing the freedom granted to your father. I hope in the future you'll think twice before—'

She didn't hear any more. She was already wrenching open her door and reaching for the small, two-inch square box she saw there. It looked like a jeweller's box, and when she opened it she saw it did indeed contain a ring.

There was no mistaking it. It was her father's signet ring.

39

It was sunny. Charlie lay curled on a rock, enjoying its warmth. Through half-shut eyes he watched the cameras and the people behind the observation window. Was their attention focused exclusively on him? Chiefly? Partly? Or hardly at all?

He came to the conclusion that he was of no special interest, certainly no more than any other member of the group. Of course, it was always possible that they were putting on a performance to deceive him, to lull him into a false sense of security. But to what end? It was a hypothesis that he could only test in some practical way, and he intended to.

Stirring slowly, he stretched, yawned and glanced with studied casualness around him. Nothing special was going on: no fights, disputes, displays of jealousy or overt sexual courtship. Small groups were gathered here and there, some playing with children, some grooming one another. He spotted a couple returning separately but plainly from the same spot among the trees. It was one of the males he'd fought with and the female he had copulated with the day before. He turned away, ignoring the anxious glance in his direction from the male, and pretended he'd seen nothing.

He ambled off in no particular direction, moving not

in a straight line but zigzagging vaguely here and there until he found a patch of shade and slumped down in it. He looked back at the various cameras high in the trees; as far as he could see, none had moved to follow his progress. He looked up at the indistinct figures in the observation window; none of them seemed to be concentrating on him either. That was good. He would stay where he was for a while so as not to arouse their suspicions by appearing restless, and he would reflect yet again on the thoughts that had gone through his mind since his strange encounter with Kathy.

The thing that had struck him, not at the time but later when he had thought about it, was a curious inconsistency in what she had said. First of all she'd told him that he wasn't supposed to have remembered anything of his experience in the virtual reality suit, and later she'd said that she had planted a memory of herself in his past – a past that had never existed. But what was the point of planting a memory in his brain if he wasn't supposed to remember it later? It made no sense. But then very little made sense at the moment, and he wasn't about to puzzle over it endlessly. What he was going to do was get out of here.

He let some time pass, around twenty minutes he guessed, before he moved again. When he did, it was with the same careful casualness as before. He sat up and looked around, making sure he wasn't the object of anyone's undivided attention, then loped off further into the trees. He had the whole layout of the place clear in his mind now and knew where he was headed.

If he was right, there was a spot where the moat disappeared past a boundary wall in the north-east corner of the compound. He'd worked out it was the north-east corner by following the movement of the sun. It was a place generally ignored by members of the group. The ground was rocky and, owing to the height of the wall and the shade of nearby trees, never touched by sunlight. There was no camera directed towards that spot and it was invisible from the observation window. Obviously the people who designed and ran the place thought there was no danger of escape here because the wall was unscaleable and chimpanzees, as Charlie now knew to his cost, couldn't swim.

But Charlie wasn't just any chimpanzee, and even if he couldn't swim he could do other things. For example, he now knew the depth of the moat, and he could calculate how many rocks he'd need to roll in to stand in the middle and be no more than waist-deep. He had already selected, while casually wandering around, the rocks he was going to use. Also he'd found the log – in fact a heavy branch broken off one of the great bare oaks – that was going to form the second part of his plan. All he needed was about ten minutes undisturbed.

The first rock went in without a problem. It was big and took all his strength to move it, but it had an irregular shape and would wedge perfectly into the V-shaped bottom of the moat. Next he pushed in two smaller squareish ones alongside. They came to about the same level, creating a solid underwater platform; all he had to do now was reach it, and that was where the log came in.

He had already tested it and knew that it was strong enough to bear his weight, though he doubted whether it would be big enough to support him if he tried to float across on it. His first thought had been to find something of the same strength but longer that would go right across the moat, but a piece of such length would be difficult to handle without someone on the far side to help him place it. As this was impossible, he'd come up with his current plan, which involved dragging the branch over the hardened earth and then manoeuvring it carefully into the water so that the far end lodged in the niche where the three underwater stones came together.

This was accomplished quickly and with an ease he had hardly dared hope for. Satisfied that the log was secure, he climbed down it, and moments later was standing only waist deep in the middle of the moat. The next stage of his plan was to haul the log in and lever the end that he had originally fixed in the rocks up and on to the far bank. He had already identified the spot he should aim for where there would be least chance of the branch rolling and tipping him off. He looked at it again from this closer perspective, then turned to continue his work – and stopped, astonished and angered by what he saw.

One of the other male chimpanzees, who had probably been watching him from some hiding place throughout the whole operation, had climbed on to the log and was crawling precariously down to join him in the middle of the moat. Charlie gave a cry of anger and waved his arms threateningly, urging the other chimp to go back. His warning was ignored. The other kept on coming, showing his teeth and chattering nervously. He was one of the males that Charlie had beaten and then accepted a gift from the other day, and he seemed determined now to regard the incident as having created a bond between them. Wherever Charlie was going, he planned to follow.

The last thing Charlie wanted was a sidekick on this excursion. He didn't know what lay in store or where he might wind up, but he was going to get a lot further and travel much faster without a passenger. Beside himself with fury, Charlie stamped on the log, making it vibrate alarmingly. The other chimp hesitated, unsure now what he should do.

To make absolutely sure that he got his point across, Charlie reached down into the water and seized the end of the log, which he jerked sharply up and down several times. He wasn't trying to shake the intruder off and into the water, just make him go back.

At last the chimp seemed to get the message and started to turn. At the same moment the wet log slipped from Charlie's hands, and the jolt as it hit its underwater foundation was enough to make the chimp lose his balance and fall, screeching, into the water.

The noise, Charlie thought, would be sure to bring people running. That meant he had only a few seconds at most to make his getaway. Someone, he supposed, would see the damnfool drowning chimp and rescue him as Charlie had been rescued the other day.

He heaved the log up out of the water and pulled it towards him so that the far end slipped from the bank and the whole thing floated. He hauled it towards him, then, with considerable effort, picked it up and tossed it towards the other side. The tip landed, as he'd hoped, on the far bank, and he lowered the end nearest him back down to the stone beneath the water's surface, wedging it as securely in place as he could. Then he started to climb along it.

It alarmed him, looking down, to see the distorted image of his would-be companion still scrabbling and choking in the water. Any second now, surely, one of those sections, the one directly underneath the drowning chimp, would open and drop him to safety the way Charlie had been.

Yet, as Charlie watched, the seconds passed and nothing happened. He saw the chimp's eyes bulging, as though about to burst from his head, and he could sense the agonizing pressure of the air trapped in his lungs and that he daren't let go of.

Instead of moving on and making good his escape, Charlie found himself paralysed by the macabre spectacle. There was guilt, of course: he was partly responsible, though the other's stupidity in trying to follow him had been a far greater element in his fate. However, the fact that Charlie himself had almost drowned so recently created a powerful empathy – an emotion that he was unaccustomed to and which affected him surprisingly. In fact it came as a shock to realize that he was incapable of leaving the wretched creature to die, even if the price of saving him was the loss of his own chance to escape.

Another glance around confirmed his fears. There was no other help in sight, which left Charlie no choice. He started back down the log, planted his feet firmly on one of the two smaller stones, and, while clinging to the log with one hand, reached out the other to the drowning chimp.

The chimp understood the gesture and began scrambling desperately at the stones in an effort to grasp the proffered hand. But he still couldn't make it.

Charlie leaned out further – dangerously far. This time their fingers touched, and then, with an effort, they clasped hands. Charlie heaved with all his strength. The other weighed as much as he did himself, and the muscles of Charlie's arm burned as he hauled him up, as much by sheer determination as physical power. For a while he thought he wasn't going to make it, but suddenly the other's head broke the surface of the water and he opened his mouth for an almighty life-giving gasp of air. Charlie gave one last heave and pulled him up to safety on the rock – and as he did he heard something that made his heart miss a beat.

He heard the ominous splintering of wood as the log he was clinging to began to break.

It was, Charlie realized, too late to regain his balance. As the log gave way he pitched head first into the water. He felt himself executing a long, elegant and quite involuntary underwater somersault, at the end of which he lay spreadeagled on his back in the very bottom of the moat. Looking up, he could see the chimpanzee whose life he had just saved now gazing down on him in a bleakly ironic reversal of their previous positions. The other chimp was obviously distraught at his inability to help, hopping from foot to foot and calling for help which, mysteriously as before, was not forthcoming.

Charlie realized he would have to fend for himself, and the first thing he needed was a clear head. Shimmering before him in the water he could see the stones that he had rolled into place. If he got to them he would find a way up, as his companion had with his help; and as long as his companion remained there, he, Charlie, should also be able to regain his island of safety without too much trouble. Then they would make a pretty pair – two chimpanzees stranded in the middle of a moat with no way of reaching either side.

But the comic aspect of his situation did not preoccupy him greatly for the moment. All his effort was going into levering himself upright, or at least on to all fours. For some strange reason, however, he found he couldn't move. Perhaps he had injured himself in the fall, though he couldn't think how, and he felt no pain. Yet his body would not respond to the commands of his brain; it was as though all connection between the two had been severed. Could he conceivably have broken his neck?

A sense of panic the like of which he had never known before began to take possession of him. He could feel his body, but he could not move it. He could also feel the bursting pressure in his lungs, and felt sure that his eyes must be bulging from their sockets as his companion's had only moments ago. He knew he didn't have long. If rescue didn't arrive now, he was finished. But all he could see was the rippling, misshapen image of his fellow chimpanzee, jumping up and down and screaming on the rock, beside himself with helpless alarm.

Something happened to Charlie's vision: dark patches began appearing like burns on a film that has become stuck in the projector. It was something to do, he supposed, with a lack of oxygen in the blood reaching his brain. At the same time the pain in his chest became insupportable, and he knew that at any second his resolve to hold his breath would be undermined by the physical impossibility of doing so any longer. He would swallow death into his lungs as surely as if he had taken poison.

So this is how it ends, he thought. It made no sense. But maybe it wasn't supposed to make sense. That struck him as the scariest thought of all, and quite possibly his last, because he knew now that his endurance had reached its limit.

The end was surprisingly painless, just a distant roaring sound and a blackness that came from all around and devoured him.

He felt only gratitude that it was over.

40

'Mom, where's Grandpa gone?'

'He had to go away on business, darling. He's as sorry about it as you are.'

'When's he coming back?'

'I don't know, Christopher. I think what he has to do may take a while.'

'When are you coming again?'

'On Saturday.'

'Can you stay longer this time?'

'I can stay the whole day, like I always do.'

'Why can't I come home now? I don't want to stay here on my own any longer.'

'Darling, it won't be for long. I promise you.'

'I want to go home now.'

'I'm afraid we can't do that.'

'Why not?'

'Because I'm not there. I have to finish what I'm doing. Then we'll go back.'

'How soon?'

'Soon.'

'If Grandpa's in Washington, why can't I go stay with him?'

'He's travelling around. I have to go, darling. I love

you. I'll call you tomorrow, and I'll see you Saturday . . .
Christopher? . . . Darling? . . . Are you there . . .?'

'Yeah.'

'I'll call you tomorrow. Okay?'

'Okay.'

'I love you, darling.'

'I love you too, Mom.'

A pause, then: 'Mom . . .?'

'Yes, darling?'

'Can I go up in the helicopter?'

The question came as a surprise. 'The helicopter?'

'Michael's friend Joe says he'll take me up if you say
it's okay. Grandpa went in it last week to the airport, but
they wouldn't take me. Auntie May says I have to ask
you. Can I, Mom? Please? It's a really neat helicopter.'

Susan hated the idea. Flying and death had been
uncomfortably associated in her mind since John's murder, but she didn't see how she could refuse this request.
Christopher would only be more unhappy than necessary
if she said no.

'Of course you can, darling. But be careful.'

The warning was lost in his shouts of thanks and
happiness. She smiled at the sound despite her misgivings.
But when she hung up she buried her face in her hands
and fought back the tears of rage and frustration that she
was determined not to give in to.

West agreed to see her at once when she called. His outer
office was on the ground floor, where two assistants were
always on duty and in contact with him by video intercom.
West himself controlled the operation of the elevator from
his desk. There were cameras at the door and on the inside,
plus something that she suspected was a metal detector.

231

The ride up was fast, but she used the time to compose herself. She emptied her mind of all thought, even repeating in her mind a mantra she had learned years ago for meditation, though with one thing and another (marriage, motherhood, career) she'd never persevered with it. But now she wanted to arrive in West's office in a calm frame of mind, or at least as calm as possible. Going in with overt hostility wasn't going to achieve what she needed to achieve.

When she stepped out on to the thick carpet, he was sitting behind his desk as usual, looking up expectantly at her.

'Dr West,' she began, without greeting or rigmarole, 'I'm not going to fight you any more. I'll do whatever you ask of me.'

41

'Nobody can write a scenario for death, Charlie.'

It was a man's voice. He didn't recognize it.

'Come on, wake up, Charlie, it's all over. Open your eyes.'

His eyelids fluttered open. He found he was lying horizontally and a man was standing over him. The man was vaguely familiar, but only vaguely. He could have been the brother, almost the twin but not quite, of the sleek-haired man who had stood with the general in front of Charlie's cage a few days ago.

Seeing the look in Charlie's eyes, the man looked faintly amused, pursing his lips in a curious way, as though fearing that a normal smile would somehow rob him of his dignity.

'You think you recognize me from the VR – right, Charlie? That was just Dr Flemyng's little joke. She morphed a semi-lookalike – not quite the same thing. Just another test of the acuity of your recognition. You recognize Dr Flemyng, I know.'

There were at least half a dozen people standing around where Charlie lay like a patient in an operating theatre. They were all men and he knew none of them. But standing furthest away was Kathy, or Dr Flemyng as he had now accustomed himself to thinking of her. Their eyes met, but she made no acknowledgement of him. There was something blank and, he thought, defeated in her gaze.

'You do recognize her, Charlie, don't you? Tell me.'

'Of course I do,' Charlie said without thinking. Only then did he realize what had happened. He had spoken. His voice had formed words – wonderful, liberating words.

He looked down at himself. There was no silvery spacesuit this time, no cables and no helmet. Instead he wore something that looked like a hospital smock from which his feet and arms protruded. They were hairless and human.

The man who had spoken was holding something up. Charlie turned his head and saw it was a mirror. In it was his reflection. He was himself again. He was a man.

'It's you, Charlie. This is who you really are.'

'But how . . . why . . . why all that . . .?'

He didn't know what name to give to what he was trying to ask about, and his voice tailed off feebly.

The man with the mirror handed it to a colleague and leaned over Charlie like a consultant explaining to a patient the treatment he has just undergone or is about to undergo.

'All in good time, Charlie. There's still more going on here than quite meets the eye, so try to relax, and all will become clear eventually. My name's Latimer West, by the way. Dr Latimer West.'

Charlie made a move to sit up, but felt himself restrained by something under the smock. West held up a warning hand.

'Patience, Charlie. You're attached – not for restraint. It's your support system. You've been here for a couple of days, and that means intravenous drips and bodily evacuation systems. But you're in perfectly good shape. You'll find you haven't lost any muscle tone.'

Two technicians quickly went to work. In a moment the drips that were in him were removed, as was the streamlined arrangement clamped around his lower parts, like something between a chastity belt and a child's nappy.

'The scenario you've just been through was almost real time,' West was saying. 'We foreshortened some of the sleep periods, which saved a day. All the same, you've been stretched out here for quite a spell. We tried to make you as comfortable as possible.'

Charlie looked at him from beneath lowered eyebrows. 'Okay,' he said, with a touch of menace in his voice now, 'if that was virtual reality, show me how you did it.'

West looked over at Susan and beckoned her forwards. She approached, Charlie thought, like an automaton, her face devoid of expression and with a listlessness in the way she moved.

'Show him, Dr Flemyng. Show him how we make this work.'

Charlie searched her face, but she avoided his gaze and reached behind him for something. She produced a curious-looking forked instrument attached to a cable. The forks, five of them, were slim and black, curved in a way that would make them fit easily on the human head. She attached it now to Charlie's head. The pressure was so light he barely felt it there.

'It bypasses all your sensory faculties,' she said, still avoiding his gaze. 'All we have to do is switch it on and the effect is instantaneous.'

'Show me,' he said.

She looked directly at him for the first time. 'Are you sure you're ready? It's quite a shock.'

He nodded curtly, not bothering to observe that no shock could be worse than some of the things he had already endured.

'All right – brace yourself.'

She reached for a control panel, pressed two switches, then a third. There was a strangely silent explosion inside Charlie's head. It sprang from the intangible centre of his consciousness and fireballed out to encompass his entire universe. He was back, instantaneously, in the body of a chimpanzee, roaring with pain as his opponent's teeth sank into his side. Spinning around, he grabbed the other chimp's arm and threw him flat on his back. He began kicking him, but several other males now began attacking Charlie from behind with bites and punches. They didn't know how to fight and he chased them off easily, but that gave his first opponent time to escape and shin up one of the three tall oaks that had been stripped of all greenery and transformed by constant use into natural climbing frames.

He was about to chase the terrified chimpanzee up the first of the trees, when he stopped. The sense of déjà vu was overpowering. What was happening was real. There was no way he could doubt that. The feel, the smell, the sound of everything, this was neither dream nor hallucination, but reality.

Yet he knew that it was not reality, because it had happened before – just like this. The same incident, the same details. Even, now that he stopped to think about it, the same strange sense of detachment from what was going on. He remembered that last time, in the middle of the fight in that tree he was looking up at now, the thought had suddenly crossed his mind that perhaps he was a figure in a computer game. Then his concentration had gone and he had been hurt.

'Aaaaghhh!!!'

Charlie was hit from behind by what felt like a brick wall coming down on him. His concentration had gone again, but this time it had happened on the ground and not, like last time, up in the tree. Three powerful males, he realized, had come at him from behind and were now kicking and pummelling him with all their strength. Vaguely he saw the fourth one coming down from the tree to join in the entertainment.

Charlie struggled to fight back, to get to his feet, but they were too many and too heavy. This was just as real as before, just as real as anything that had ever happened to him – but worse. This time he was going to lose. This time, if no one intervened, he knew he was going to die or be left a crippled wreck.

As abruptly as it started, it was over. He was returned to his previous surroundings with an abruptness that was almost more breathtaking than the beating he'd been suffering. The woman Charlie knew as Dr Flemyng was withdrawing her hand from the switch she had just pressed.

'As you see, Charlie,' West was saying, 'the programme is variable according to the feedback from you.'

Charlie found himself breathless, his heart beating fast – which was ridiculous, he told himself, because he hadn't been doing anything, just lying here with all these artificial thoughts running through his head.

'I'd no idea VR was that good.'

West gave another of his little smirks. 'It's not something we'd want the whole world to know about. There are many things we don't want the whole world to know about.'

'But what about . . . what about my . . .?'

Charlie broke off and shook his head, able neither to frame the question nor come to terms with the reality he was beginning to perceive behind it.

'What about the rest of your life, Charlie? Is that what you're asking?'

Charlie nodded. Yes, West was right – that was what he wanted to know.

'Your childhood, everything until the time you went to the Farm . . .'

West paused, preparing Charlie for the enormity of what he was about to learn.

'Show him, Dr Flemyng.'

Still avoiding Charlie's eyes, she pressed another switch.

The noise almost burst his ear drums. A clattering roar of steel combined with the throb of massive diesel engines. He knew at once where he was. It had been exactly like this – the rail yard, the freight train that he and Kathy were racing to board, and the two cops coming after them.

He grabbed a handle, swung his feet up and forced open the wagon door. Then he reached down for Kathy, holding out a hand to pull her up before she fell or simply gave up trying to keep pace with the train's gathering speed. He saw her face plainly as she looked up at him – pale, perspiring, desperate – as she tried to reach his outstretched hand. He remembered in that moment that once, at some point in the future, he had been unable to recall her face, Kathy's face. But now it was as much a part of the natural world around him as anything else, something he could never conceivably forget: Kathy, little more than a child, simply dressed, frightened, trusting in him . . .

The cop's night stick cracked down on his fingers with a savagery that must have broken bones. It was the hand hanging on to the freight wagon door. He didn't so much let go as feel the hand cease to function – that was just how it had been, and how it was now.

And yet, last time, he had still put up a fight – a fight which he supposed he was about to have again.

He fell hard on the cindered earth, only inches from the thunderous clanking of the rolling wheels, in spite of which he could still hear Kathy's screams . . .

Then a sudden silence cut through the whole thing like a knife. He was back on the operating table, the same faces looking down at him, including Kathy – transformed once again into Dr Flemyng – her expression and everything about her still strangely muted.

Unable to contain his frustration and confusion any longer, Charlie gave a roar of outrage and reached for his chief tormentor, the man who'd said his name was West.

42

Control followed the two guards and waited as one of them unlocked the heavy steel door. He nodded to confirm what he had told them already, that he was to be left alone. Then he stepped into the cell and heard the door shut behind him.

The cell was of reasonable size, far bigger than a police cell, at least fifteen feet square. It was painted white, with a table, chair, washbasin, lavatory and a single bunk attached to the wall. Charlie, wearing a tracksuit and running shoes, was sitting on the edge of this when the door opened. He got to his feet when he saw who his visitor was.

'Good morning, Charlie,' Control said.

'Good morning, sir,' Charlie replied stiffly.

'Sit down, relax. Tell me what's been going on.'

As he spoke, Control pulled the chair around so that he could face Charlie, who resumed his place on the edge of the bunk.

'Isn't it about time *you* told *me* what's been going on?' Charlie replied with a note of sullen defiance that he didn't normally display in Control's presence.

Control regarded him from beneath slightly hooded eyes. There was a trace of something playing at the corners of his mouth, not a smile so much as an acknowledgement of the mood he found Charlie to be in.

'I'll ask the questions, Charlie, and you'll answer them. Is that clear?'

He paused, requiring an answer before he went on.

'Yes, sir,' Charlie murmured, resentful but obedient.

'I'm told that you attacked Dr West.'

'I wouldn't say attacked. I guess I grabbed his collar without really thinking what I was doing.'

'And . . .?'

'I blacked out, and woke up here.'

Control nodded, as though Charlie's words confirmed what he already knew, and he just wanted to check Charlie's version. He reached into one of the pockets of his jacket and produced a small black object.

'Someone used one of these on you.'

Charlie recognized the object at once. It was no more than two inches long, a little more than an inch wide and about half a centimetre thick.

'Kathy had one of those things that night in her apartment. What is it?'

'You have something planted in here, Charlie,' Control said, vaguely indicating an area somewhere on his own chest. 'It stops you dead in response to a signal from this.'

Charlie's hand involuntarily rose to the upper part of his body, as though feeling for the thing that Control had described there.

'Of course,' Control continued, still displaying the little black object on his palm, 'not many people have access to one of these – for obvious reasons.'

'That guy down town had one,' Charlie said, thinking back to the image of marijuana shirt standing in the traffic and pointing something at him. 'At least I think he did. He pulled something on me and I blacked out in the back of the cab I was in, but not for long. There was a truck got in the way, maybe cut the signal.'

Control nodded. 'I gather that's what happened. That was a bad business, Charlie,' he said, more serious now, 'you going rogue like that.'

'Rogue?'

'What else would you call it?'

Charlie shrugged. He didn't, when he came to think of it, have an alternative word for what he'd done.

'We knew you'd lied to us, Charlie. You told us you'd never seen that woman at the beach before. Of course the truth was you hadn't, but you *thought* you had. The proof was that you went looking for her the first chance you got. It showed us we'd successfully planted the memory of her, which was good, but it turned out the memory was so powerful that you became more loyal to her than you were to us, which wasn't so good. We need to be one hundred per cent sure of you, Charlie, if you're going to go on being of use to us.'

Charlie looked at him with a distrust bordering on hostility. 'Where are we? Still in that place I followed Fry to?'

'That's where we are, and where you're going to stay – until we're satisfied you're back on track.'

'Back on track?' Charlie echoed. 'How is all that monkey stuff you put me through supposed to get me back on track?'

Control shifted slightly on his chair and crossed one ankle over the other knee. He wasn't a young man, but he still had some of the easy-moving ranginess of an athlete.

'Charlie, let me tell you something about yourself. You remember that story you heard when you thought you were a chimpanzee, about how we were trying to create a kind of super-agent, faster and stronger than any man on earth. Well, it's not just a theory, Charlie. Not even a plan. It's an achievement. And you're it. You're the prototype. On an operational level you've scored high, even better than we dared hope. I don't have to tell you what you've done and what you're capable of doing. You've carried out some difficult and dangerous assignments, and we're very aware of that.'

Charlie stared at him. 'Are you telling me,' he asked after a longish moment, 'that I'm a chimpanzee?'

'That's what I'm telling you, Charlie. Mutated, but still a chimpanzee.'

'I don't believe you.'

Control gave a faintly tired smile. 'That whole virtual reality programme – the "monkey thing" as you call it – wouldn't have worked with anybody else, at least not so well. It depended on your having the genetic predisposition to buy into the experience that the scenario offered.'

'I still don't see the point . . .'

'The point,' Control said, interrupting him, 'was to find out which you felt yourself to be. Stripped of external reinforcement – your human self-image, your lifestyle – what would you perceive yourself as in your own mind?' He paused, regarding Charlie for a moment with a look that was almost affectionate. 'Interestingly, you never let go the idea that you were human, did you?'

Charlie nodded. 'No, I guess not.'

He was acutely aware that Control, despite his relaxed appearance, still held the small black object, the 'zapper', in one hand. No doubt the guards had theirs too. Charlie knew that physical power was no use to him here.

'I need some proof. Before I believe what you say, that

I'm a chimpanzee, you're going to have to prove it to me.'

Control looked at him a while, still with a certain odd affection, but also as though he was measuring him in some way. Then he made a decision.

'Charlie, there's somebody I think you should meet. Come with me.'

He got to his feet, rapped on the door to have it opened, then beckoned Charlie to follow him.

43

They walked down a long windowless corridor. Charlie suspected they were underground, but there was nothing to indicate how far below the surface. Nor was there, for that matter, anything to suggest whether it was day or night.

'I think it's time you met your parents, Charlie,' Control said.

The idea shocked Charlie more than anything he could have imagined, even at this stage of his displacement from reality. It offended him in a way that he found surprising. 'Parents? I have no parents,' he said sharply.

'Oh, yes, you do. Your parents are alive and well.'

They turned into another corridor, then Control pushed open a door with a small glass panel in it. The room they entered was unlit, though Charlie could make out the bars of a cage on one side. He heard something move and saw a dark form rise from the cage floor. Then Control found the light switch he'd been looking for and turned on a couple of overhead strips. Charlie found himself looking through the bars at two full-grown chimpanzees.

'This is the real thing, Charlie, not VR,' Control said, warning him, 'so be careful you don't get your hand bitten off – they're not going to recognize you any more than you recognize them.'

Charlie approached the cage slowly, not taking his eyes off the two creatures in it. They gazed back at him uncertainly. Something that he didn't understand filled him with an emotion he hadn't felt before. Perhaps, he thought, it was the improbability of what he was being asked to believe. Or perhaps it was the emotive power of the word 'parent' to someone for whom it had never had concrete meaning before. Or perhaps, somewhere at the back of his mind, there was a recognition that this was the truth, and these creatures were his flesh and blood.

The two chimps moved away from him at first, showing signs more of distrust than open hostility. Then, despite the agitated, anxious chatterings of her mate, the female edged forward a few steps to get a better look at him. She tipped her head slightly to one side as though something about this human-like stranger seemed to find an echo in her memory. There was an intelligence as well as an intense curiosity in her gaze. Her eyes locked with Charlie's and she came right up to the bars, wrapping her long black fingers around them.

Charlie too drew closer, and their mutual gaze remained unbroken. Very slowly she freed one of her hands and held it out to him. It was a tentative gesture, not a threatening one, and when he didn't back away she began, very gently, to stroke the smooth side of his face with the hard skin of her hand. Charlie heard a soft intake of breath from Control behind him.

'Isn't that interesting! I can't believe she recognizes you, and yet . . . just look at that.'

It was some moments before Charlie turned his gaze back to Control. When he did, there were tears in his eyes. 'What have you done?' he asked in a voice that was little more than a whisper. 'What have you done?'

'Something that evolution wouldn't have accomplished in a million years, left to itself,' Control replied calmly. 'You're custom-built, Charlie, a hero for our time. The trouble with James Bond and all the rest of them is they only exist in books and movies. We need them here and now, in the real world, doing what we ordinary mortals can't.'

'But not asking questions. Just following orders, not thinking too much – right?'

Control tipped his head to one side in an amiable and unashamed acknowledgement of the charge. 'Right, Charlie. We want you thinking, but only up to a point. Defining that point is turning out to be quite tricky. You've already gone a step or two beyond what would have been ideal.'

Charlie looked at him for a moment, thinking how little he knew this man. Perhaps all men. Then he asked, 'Am I the only one?'

'For now. As I told you, you're the prototype. It's early days.'

The cage and its occupants had been forgotten for the time being. Charlie had turned away, but not stepped back. Suddenly, without warning, the male – his father, if Control was to be believed – elbowed the female aside and aimed a vicious blow at Charlie's head. Only some inhumanly swift reflex saved him from injury, and he realized in that instant that Control had spoken the truth: he wasn't human; he couldn't be. He spun away, more shaken by what he had just learned about himself than by the ferocity of the attack.

The male chimp, sensing that he'd won some kind of victory, began to leap and chatter around the cage, then took to swinging on the bars and shaking them with macho glee.

Charlie watched him with a strange and awful fascination, then he heard Control behind him. 'Come on, Charlie,' he said, and there was a hint of sympathy in his voice now, 'I think you've seen enough. Let's go.'

Five minutes later they were back in Charlie's cell, seated as before.

'How long are you going to keep me here?' Charlie asked.

'Not long, I hope. I've just got to persuade certain people that you'll behave reasonably if we let you out. I'm sure you understand.'

'As long as you've got that zapper I don't have much choice, do I?'

Control gave another of his faintly wan smiles and crossed his legs in his habitual way, ankle on adjacent knee. 'No, you don't. But we'd rather your good behaviour was voluntary. You understand that, don't you?'

Charlie got to his feet and gave a bitter laugh. 'Understand!' He began pacing back and forth, all the time running a hand through his hair as though the movement would somehow help clear his mind. 'You're telling me my whole childhood never happened – the orphanage, none of it. Until the Farm.'

'That's right, Charlie.'

'But where *was* I all that time?'

'You were in a lab. In this building, as a matter of fact. In a specially designed harness developed from something invented over half a century ago by an American psychologist, B. F. Skinner. It allowed you to grow and develop physically quite normally – in fact rather better than normally. At the same time, using the VR techniques you're now familiar with, we gave you a carefully scripted life experience that primed you for the future we had planned for you. A team of psychologists worked on every detail.'

'To create a psychopath.'

'To create *you*, Charlie. Do you think of yourself as a psychopath?'

'I don't know what I think. I'm not even sure any more if I think at all.'

'Oh, you think all right. There's never been any question about that. You're a highly intelligent individual. The only problem we encountered was with your visual memory. We'd planted information – people, places and events – but we couldn't plant the pictures to go with them. That was a problem we had to overcome – not because it was essential in your case, you were already up and running – but because we knew we'd need to do it in the future. As I told you, you're our prototype.'

Charlie stopped pacing and turned to look at Control, who sat back looking up at him. Control had, Charlie noticed, one hand hooked loosely on his ankle, and the other in his pocket where the zapper was.

'Dr Flemyng had been developing some very interesting techniques in the treatment of brain-damaged patients,' Control continued in the same amiable, matter-of-fact tone he'd been using all along, 'techniques that we'd found considerable application for over several years. Eventually we persuaded her to collaborate with us more closely. It was Dr Flemyng who gave a face to your memory of Kathy. That was a big step forward.'

Charlie looked puzzled. 'But she gave Kathy her own face? Why?'

Control shrugged. 'That was her decision. Kathy was

obviously someone you'd have to meet, and I daresay Dr Flemyng thought she could observe your responses herself better than anyone else could.'

Charlie rubbed a hand over the side of his face and around the back of his neck, as though having cleared his brain he was now trying to absorb what he was hearing. Control shifted slightly on his chair, lifting his ankle from his knee and re-crossing his legs knee over knee. His hand, however, remained in the pocket of his jacket.

'What we hadn't anticipated,' Control continued, 'was your switch of loyalties. But even that furnished useful information. We knew you functioned on an operational level with great reliability. The question was, how far could that reliability be pushed before it buckled? We knew you wouldn't crack under physical torture – at least not until long after any human agent would have cracked. But we didn't know how you'd resist emotional pressure.'

Charlie was pacing again, pacing and turning, still running a hand over his head and neck.

'But she came back.'

Control frowned, puzzled. 'Came back? How d'you mean came back?'

'Kathy. Dr Flemyng. When I was wired up to think I was a chimpanzee, she came back. She talked to me, explained what was happening as if . . .'

He broke off. Control was watching him closely, waiting for him to put the pieces together. Charlie began to nod his head as the picture emerged.

'When I was in the cage, she was part of the VR process . . .'

Control smiled his approval as Charlie reached the right conclusion.

'Authenticity, Charlie. Her image was the link between

your two worlds. She was the same in both – except that in one she was real, in the other virtual.'

Charlie sat down on the edge of his bunk again and leaned forward with his head in his hands. 'I think I'm going crazy.'

'You're not crazy, Charlie. You're just learning how the world works. What *can* be done *will* be done. People argue over should and shouldn't, but it makes no difference. If it *can* be done, it *will*.'

Charlie was silent for a moment, then said, 'Tell me – those women who were always around? Did you arrange all that, too?'

Control gave a qualified nod of his head. 'Most of them were on the payroll. They didn't know anything about you – you were just another client.'

'*Most* of them?'

A faint smile crossed Control's face again. 'To your credit, quite a few were volunteers you picked up for yourself. You're a good-looking fellow, Charlie – take a look in the mirror. A lot of men would like to look like you.'

There was a small mirror, unbreakable, set into the wall above the washbasin, but Charlie didn't even glance at it. Vanity on that level was something that had passed him by. Instead, he remained focused on Control, struggling to assemble the fragments of his broken universe into some kind of order.

'So why do I get the feeling, despite everything you've said, that Dr Flemyng isn't really part of all this?'

Control looked back at him, his face lighting up with the kind of interest that Charlie had noticed from time to time whenever he said something that the other man hadn't anticipated.

'Is that the impression you get?' Control asked.

'The impression that she's doing this reluctantly? Yes, absolutely.'

'That's very sharp of you, Charlie. You read body language better than almost any human being I know. That's one of the things we've discovered about chimpanzees – this right-brain intuitiveness.'

'So I'm right?'

Control sighed and got to his feet. Charlie watched as he walked over to the door and knocked for it to be opened. Obviously the interview was at an end.

'Dr Flemyng is a very brilliant and dedicated woman,' Control said, turning back to look at Charlie again. 'She has her reasons for doing what she's doing.'

With that, he stepped into the corridor and the door banged shut behind him.

44

Outside Charlie's cell was a holding area, and beyond that another gate operated by a guard on the far side. Control stepped through and into an area where three more guards lounged on comfortable chairs, played cards, drank coffee and watched television. On a separate screen was an image of Charlie's cell, viewed from a camera in the ceiling. Control paused to look, and saw Charlie standing perfectly still, apparently staring into space.

Latimer West stood in a doorway on the far side of the room. He waited for Control to acknowledge him with a patient deference that left no doubt who was the senior of the two men. When Control finally turned away from the monitor with its image of Charlie, West moved aside to let him pass through the door, then fell in step alongside him.

'Well, sir,' he said after they'd walked a little way, 'what d'you think?'

'He's suffering, Latimer. More than I'd ever thought he could. The trouble is, he's too damned intelligent.'

'I agree. It's a matter of fine tuning. It's hard getting it exactly right, though when we do we'll be able to reproduce the process indefinitely.'

They walked on a little further.

'He's no use operationally in this state of mind,'

Control said, a note of impatience creeping into his voice. 'I couldn't trust either his concentration or his obedience to orders. What's more, he knows too much now.'

Control let the last sentence hang in the air, its resonance undefined but fully understood.

They reached a single set of elevator doors. West touched a button and they opened at once. The interior was plain grey with no mirrors or decoration of any kind. West touched another button and they began to glide soundlessly and smoothly upwards.

'So the question is,' Control went on, 'what do we do with him now?'

West gave a non-committal shrug. 'As you say, he's no longer of operational value. Scientifically, however, there's still a good deal to be learned from him.'

Control looked sideways at the shorter man. 'You mean you want to experiment on him?'

'I have a few things in mind I'd like to try. After all,' he added, seeing Control's uncertain expression, 'our options are limited. We can't turn him loose, so we have to keep him caged, or put him down. Either that, or use him in the lab. Strictly speaking, he's still a lab animal.'

Control took a deep breath, then exhaled it in a long sigh. 'I suppose you're right. If there's something left to learn, we have an obligation to learn it.'

West paused a moment before saying any more. He was gauging how frankly he could express the thought that was uppermost in his mind. He broached it cautiously. 'Dr Flemyng's cooperation would be of the greatest value, if it could be arranged. I fear, however, I have very little chance myself of persuading her to work with us any further than she has already.'

Control cleared his throat, tacitly acknowledging that

the problem of Dr Flemyng was a thorny one. 'It's still my greatest regret,' he said, 'that we had to involve her directly in this at all.'

'I couldn't agree with you more,' West said quickly. 'However, as you admitted yourself, we had little choice given the circumstances confronting us, and bearing in mind what she was proposing to do.'

Control made no reply, just stood waiting for the doors to open as the elevator slowed to a stop. The two men stepped out into a bright corridor running the whole length of a slightly curved building. The outer wall was made entirely of tinted glass, yielding an impressive view over the Irvine Spectrum. The sun was low in the east; it was early morning.

They stopped at one of several doors after walking about thirty yards. West turned to his superior. 'Will you talk to Dr Flemyng now, sir? As we discussed?'

Control nodded gravely. This was not a task he relished.

West opened the door, but did not go through it. Instead he pointed out the way that Control should go. 'Down there as far as you can, left, then you'll see a blue door. I'll be in my office if you need me. Good luck, sir.'

Control gave a taciturn nod, and started walking. A few moments later he stood outside the blue door, hesitating before opening it. He finally turned the handle and stepped into a conference room. There was a long table in the centre, chairs all around, modern art on the walls. The entire far wall was, like the corridor he'd just left, of tinted glass. The room was empty, except for Susan, standing with her back to him, looking out at the view. When she heard the door, she turned.

Her eyes widened in astonishment, and she gave a gasp

of surprise and happiness. She ran to him and threw her arms around him, laughing and crying with relief.

'Daddy! Oh thank God, you're alive! I thought you were . . . I thought they'd . . .'

Amery Hyde held her tight and stroked her hair.

'It's all right, my darling. It's all right. Everything's going to be fine.'

Part Four

45

They sat at a corner of the long table, holding hands.

'I don't think they ever intended killing me,' Amery Hyde was saying, 'or Christopher. They just had to find some way of keeping you quiet, and threatening the two of us was the only way of doing it.'

'But they would have killed you if they'd had to. These people wouldn't stop at anything.'

'Maybe. All I know is they haven't killed any of us yet, and they don't seem to want to if they can possibly avoid it.'

She looked at him in an oddly enquiring way. 'Is that really the impression you get?'

Amery realized he had to be careful, but then carefulness to him was the habit of a lifetime. He liked to think of it as respect for the feelings and sensibilities of others. Not everyone, his daughter included, was ready to face up to the harsh realities of life. West had accused her, he knew, of living in an ivory tower, and in Amery's opinion there was some truth in the charge. Yet he would do everything in his power, as he was doing now, to protect her from being forced out of her protected and unreal world before she was ready. Some people, he knew, would never and could never be ready for that level of encounter with reality. It was possible, he had long since acknowledged to himself, that his daughter, despite all her brilliance, was one of them.

But then he started to realize something else as he listened to her speaking. He began to see that some kind of change was coming over her, some shifting of perspective; and for the first time in many weeks he allowed himself to hope that everything he had fought so hard for – and sometimes, he had feared, hopelessly – was now within his grasp.

Susan spoke quietly but with an urgency that seemed to come from long and deep reflection. The decision she had reached was simply stated; more importantly, she was anxious that her father should understand the process that had brought her to it.

Amery listened gravely, taking his eyes from hers only to nod from time to time in solemn agreement.

'I haven't changed my mind about Latimer West,' she told him, 'and I don't take back anything I've said about him or the foundation. And yet, now that I've had time to think about it, I have to admit there's some truth in some of the things he said, and some justification for what they've done. It's true that what *can* be done *will* be done. It's inevitable, a law of nature, and neither right nor wrong has much to do with it. The moral argument in the end is just a commentary. It doesn't control the process, or even influence it much. I can see now that this whole programme would have gone ahead with or without me. It's just that I was the one who happened to be there, whose work came along at the right time. Otherwise there would have been somebody else.'

She paused, lifting her eyes to meet her father's gaze, faltering slightly before saying what she had to say next. Amery knew how much she cared about what he thought.

This was the kind of moment in which he wondered at his ability to play the game he had been playing all his adult life, a life spent in the most secret service of his country at the highest levels. He had done many things which had troubled him, not least the fact that he had never been able to be entirely open either with his wife before her death or with his daughter now. He had loved them both as much as any man had loved his family; that was his profound conviction. He had never allowed the secrecy his work imposed on him to drive a wedge between them, to compromise in any way the natural intimacy of man and wife or father and daughter. Yet he had never been sure how his wife would have reacted had she known the truth; and he had always known with certainty that Susan would not have understood. He didn't know why, but she'd had an instinctive distrust of authority all her life. It wasn't that she was any kind of anarchist or natural rebel; just that she had always accepted as a natural truth the dictum that power corrupts, and must therefore be distrusted and checked at every opportunity. Amery had always respected her views and rarely argued with her. In fact, his own attitudes were generally liberal, but he was also a realist who knew that freedom had to be protected, and sometimes difficult and even ugly things had to be done in the course of maintaining that protection. On the whole, however, he felt that his deception of his daughter – not so much outright lies as truths left untold – was justified. His duty as a father was to play the role she needed him to play; and that he did with all his heart.

'There was something else West said,' Susan's voice trembled slightly as she spoke, 'something I hate him for. Hate him because it's true. But he was right when he said there was a part of me, despite all my objections, that was just a little bit excited by all this – as a scientist.'

'Well, you *are* a scientist, so why shouldn't that be true?'

'But thinking and doing are different things. Nobody in their right mind judges people on what they think. It's what we do about it that matters. And I'm collaborating with the people who murdered my husband.'

'You're saving your son's life.'

'Yours, too. And I'd do it again to save either of you. But what I mean is . . .'

She paused again, trying to find the words for something she seemed only partially to understand.

'. . . What I mean is, that's not my only reason. Not any more. I've also become involved in this research. Intellectually. I'm excited by it.'

She looked at him, her eyes searching his for help. 'Is that wrong? Is that how Mengele felt when he was experimenting on those children in the death camps?'

Amery answered her sharply, almost surprised by his own anger. 'Stop that. There's no comparison, and you know it.'

'But you can understand what I mean, can't you, Daddy?'

He tightened his hands gently over hers. 'You're doing what you have to. For the time being you mustn't try to think any further than that. Later, when we're through all this, we'll talk about the rest.'

And talk they would, at length. If he had understood correctly what she was trying to say, she was coming around to seeing things in a way that would make his life much easier and less painful. He would never be able to tell her the whole truth; there were too many years of lies and unspeakable secrets. He would never be able to tell her that, even though he didn't order her husband's death, he was a part of the shadowy establishment that did. He would never be able to tell her that the plan to kidnap her son and force her into collaborating with her husband's killers had been his plan; or that the dreadful moment when she thought that he, Amery, had been killed because of her reckless disobedience had been his idea. He would never be able to tell her because she would never be able to forgive him, even though the alternative, proposed by people more powerful and uncompromising than himself, had been to have her killed before she did them the kind of damage that she threatened to. He had saved her life, but it had been a cruel kind of mercy, one for which he expected no thanks. All he hoped for was that she be spared and allowed to build a life for herself and Christopher that was not too far from the one they had enjoyed before. And that would be possible only if she showed some sign of willingness to view events in terms less purely black and white than she had formerly done.

If Amery was not mistaken, the first signs of such a willingness had been apparent in the words she had just spoken. For the first time in many weeks, he found himself facing the future with more than simply fear.

'D'you think she knew the place was miked?'

'It would be a fair assumption – certainly, one that I'd make in her place.'

'All right, let's suppose she knew. How much of what she's saying can we believe?'

All eyes in the room turned on Amery Hyde. He didn't know why they imagined he knew more than the rest of them, and yet he understood why they asked. He was her father; he was supposed to know how her mind worked, to see at once when she was telling the truth and when she wasn't. He cleared his throat, and immediately cursed himself silently for the mistake: it was a sign of uncertainty, an admission that he was far from sure of what he was saying.

'I believe,' he began, 'that she was telling the truth. After all, what motive would she have for lying? She wants her life back, and her son's, and she'll make whatever compromise she has to in order to accomplish that.'

He left it there. Always better with these people to say less rather than too much. It was rare that Amery Hyde felt himself intimidated, but in the company of this group the feeling was inescapable. There were five of them, ranging in age from thirty-something to early seventies. Their appearances differed equally widely. One looked like a lawyer; another like a university professor in crumpled tweeds and with unruly red hair; a third, the one in his seventies, had the mandarin demeanour of a diplomat, and acted loosely as chairman of the proceedings. The fourth man was in his mid- to late-forties and struck Amery as a civil servant whose task, though not in any way to lead the discussion, was to sum up its consensus.

The fifth member, the only woman, was a mystery to Amery Hyde. She could have been a philosopher, he suspected, from the detached precision of her questions; but with her broad rosy-cheeked face and strangely hovering smile, she resembled the kind of scoutmistress you might encounter on a mountain hike with a couple of equally robust friends.

Amery didn't know anything about them individually, only that they were unelected and answerable to nobody, and therefore their power was infinite. They were the people who thought the unthinkable, then decided what to do about it. Their counterparts existed in all societies, always had and always would, though no society would ever openly acknowledge them.

'And yours.'

It was the woman who had spoken. Amery looked at her, taken by surprise after a long silence so unexpectedly broken.

'Your life,' she said, smiling in her strange, almost orientally inscrutable way. 'Your life, too.'

'Yes, of course. That's part of it from her point of view. My life, too.'

The woman turned to the lawyer type on her left, then to the mandarin diplomat on her right. Whatever passed unspoken between them seemed to satisfy the three of them. The other two made their agreement felt by remaining silent.

'Very well,' said the diplomat, 'let's proceed for the time being on that basis. We shall rely on you, Mr Hyde, to alert us to any change in the situation that you might become aware of. I'm sure you'll agree that's the best course open to all of us for the time being.'

The words were polite, almost anodyne. There was nothing in the manner of their delivery to imply a threat. But, as Amery knew, people with real power never made threats.

They didn't need to.

46

There were two guards in the lab in addition to Charlie and Dr Flemyng. They sat in separate corners, each holding one of the small black objects that would render Charlie instantly unconscious in response to the slightest pressure. Dr Flemyng also had one, Charlie knew, but she was too preoccupied with the equipment in front of her to use it fast enough in an emergency. So the guards sat there like youths in some video game arcade, their eyes glued to the image before them, waiting to jab the button when their cue came up.

'Don't give me that accusing stare, Charlie,' Dr Flemyng said.

Charlie blinked. He hadn't been aware of looking at her in any particular way. He was just tamely going through the motions, doing what she said because he had no choice, turning this way then that, holding his breath as a shiny metal tube – some kind of scanner, he supposed – moved over him and a helmet-like object closed over his head with an electronic buzz that made his skull tingle.

'All right, Charlie,' she said after about five minutes, 'that was just a test; we'll get into the real thing in a moment. I've never done this before – in fact nobody has, so I've no idea if it'll work or not.'

'Shouldn't you get yourself a back-up lab rat in case you kill this one off by mistake?'

He was gratified by the look of anger she flashed him in response to the cold cynicism in his voice.

'Don't worry, Charlie, I'm not going to kill you off – you're too useful for that. Now just lie back while I attach these electrodes. They're the same as before, so there's nothing to worry about.'

'Hey, I'm past worrying. In fact I'm way past panic. Nothing you do from now on is going to worry me one bit.'

It was just bravado, of course. He could see in her face that she knew it was, but she made no comment. He almost liked her for that. Funny, he reflected, to think of almost liking someone he'd once loved, or thought he'd loved.

She reached somewhere behind his head and produced the five-forked device that she'd used earlier to create the extraordinary virtual reality experiences he'd undergone. She slipped it on his head, made a few minor adjustments, then stepped back.

'I'm not going to tell you what's going to happen, Charlie, except that it's going to be different from last time. I want your responses to be spontaneous and not conditioned by expectation. It'll take a while and you may feel a little strange at first. All right, here goes. I'm pressing the switch . . . now.'

Charlie watched her hand go to the control panel, and blackness enveloped him.

It was impossible to know, when he opened his eyes, how long his unconsciousness had lasted. He looked around, and found himself back in the cell that had been his home since his attack on Latimer West. He supposed it was night because the lights were turned low, leaving just enough illumination for him to find his way to the bathroom if he needed it. A switch glowed on the wall within easy reach. If he wanted to read or move around or find the remote control for the TV set they had installed for him, all he had to do was press it. But he didn't move. He lay in the near-dark, gazing up at the ceiling camera that he knew observed his every move.

Then he heard something. It sounded like the lock on his cell door, followed by the movement of a well-oiled steel hinge. He sat up. A shadowy figure approached the bunk where he lay. He recognized Susan Flemyng. She put a finger to her lips to silence him when he opened his mouth.

'Get dressed, Charlie,' she whispered. 'Quickly, we haven't much time.'

He didn't move. 'What's going on?' he said. 'What happened? Did somebody zap me again?'

'Nobody zapped you, Charlie. The experiment never happened. If it had it would have more than likely fried your brains, and I wasn't prepared to risk that. But I had to go through the motions for the benefit of those goons in the corner, and also because the whole place was bugged. Every word I said to you was being recorded.'

'What about now? Are you saying it's different here?'

Once again his eyes went up to the camera in the ceiling. She followed his gaze, understanding his concern.

'Don't worry, nobody's watching us now. We're being recorded, but it'll be too late by the time anybody looks at the tape.'

'Too late for what? How d'you know nobody's watching? What's this all about?'

'Later, Charlie. And in case you get impatient, just remember that I've still got this.'

He didn't have to look at what she was holding; he already knew. He held up his hands in mock surrender. 'I'm not making any trouble. Just tell me what you want, I'm following orders.'

'I want you to come with me and do exactly as I say.'

'That's what I'm doing.'

She didn't turn her back as he pulled on his clothes, so instead he turned his. When he was dressed, she nodded her head for him to precede her out of the door. He stepped into the narrow holding area, then through to the room where three guards were on duty twenty-four hours a day. They were there now – all three fast asleep, two slumped in their chairs, a third draped face down across a desk where he had obviously been reaching for a phone when he lost consciousness.

'I stopped by for a cup of coffee,' she said, 'and offered to make a fresh pot.'

Three paper cups lay on the floor, the remains of their contents soaking into the plain grey carpet. Charlie turned a questioning gaze on Susan, and saw her looking back at him with the hint of a smile on her lips. 'Of course, I didn't have time to drink any myself.'

She pulled open a door on the far side. 'Go ahead,' she said, pointing down the corridor. 'I'll follow you.'

After a few yards she told him to stop and open the door on his right. He did so. Concrete steps led down into darkness. 'There's a light switch on your left,' she said. 'Press it.'

The stairwell flooded with light. Charlie started down and she followed. They entered a basement complex with heating ducts running along the low ceiling and thick bunches of electric cable on the walls. Susan had obviously reconnoitred the area well and issued crisp instructions to turn this way and that as they threaded their way through the maze of subterranean tunnels. Eventually she said, 'Stop. That door in front of you leads to some more stairs that will take us to ground level. When we reach it we'll very likely run into one or more guards before we arrive at the place I want to get to. None of them have zappers because they're only issued to people who have close contact with you. But they're all armed and they'll shoot if they have to. Be careful, do what you have to, but don't kill anybody. They're just ordinary men doing the job they're paid for, and none of them knows the full story of what's going on here. D'you understand me?'

Charlie turned to look at her and nodded solemnly. 'I understand,' he said, 'but before we go any further you're going to have to answer one question or I'm not moving.'

Her face hardened with annoyance, but after a moment she said, 'All right, what d'you want to know?'

'I want to know why you're doing this. What's the game?'

'It's not a game, Charlie. I never wanted to be part of this project. I've been forced into it; and I don't like that.'

'So that's why you're helping me escape?'

'That's why I'm helping you escape. But there's a condition.'

'What condition?'

'I want you to help me.'

He frowned. 'Help you how?'

'My son and my father are being held hostage to guarantee my good behaviour. I want you to free them.'

'Where are they?'

'Until today my son's been kept on a ranch, too far

270

away from here to do anything about it. My father's had a little more freedom, but they'd have killed him if they had to.'

'You said until today – your son.'

'I've made a deal with them. I convinced them I would go on cooperating voluntarily if they let all three of us return to some semblance of normal life. They believed me enough to let my father fly up to the ranch and bring my son back here to visit. They're in a hotel only fifteen minutes away. I spent an hour with them this afternoon. They're not heavily guarded. You can get them out of there, Charlie. It's their only chance.' She fell silent, searching his face for some response. 'That's it. Will you help me?'

He looked at her steadily for a while, then said, 'It doesn't look to me as though I have a whole lot of choice, not if I want to get out of here. Okay, let's go.'

She didn't respond right away. Something in her eyes said she wasn't satisfied with his answer and was wondering whether to press for something better, but in the end she let it pass. 'All right,' she said, 'go ahead, through that door.'

They went through the door facing them, up another flight of steps and reached a set of double doors with horizontal push-bars. 'Careful,' she said, 'we could walk right into a security patrol.'

Charlie looked over his shoulder and pointed to a switch on the wall behind her. 'Put that light out,' he said. She did so, then he pushed open one of the doors. Susan winced at the sound it made, but Charlie slipped through quickly and motioned her to follow him.

They found themselves standing in the angle of a concrete path bordering an L-shaped, featureless brick wall. On the other side of the path was a hedge of chest-high shrubs. The night was dark with a high cloud covering, and although the grounds were well lit no direct light fell where they were standing.

'This way,' she whispered, pointing to the right. 'And remember, there are foot patrols as well as mobile.'

'Don't worry,' he said, 'I've been trained for this.'

'I know what you've been trained for, Charlie. That's why I said go easy on these men.'

'Just stay close.'

'Oh, I will.'

The light grew stronger as they approached the corner. Charlie waved a hand for her to get down below the level of the shrubs. They stayed like that as Charlie listened for sounds of movement, then he manoeuvred himself this way and that to get as clear a view as he could of their surroundings.

A door banged somewhere close by. Susan gasped. Charlie again held up his hand for her to remain still. They watched as, a few yards away, a guard appeared, leaned against the wall and lit a cigarette. He inhaled gratefully a couple of times, then strolled off away from them.

'Which way do we go from here?' Charlie whispered.

Susan pointed to a building about fifty yards away on the far side of an open stretch of grass. 'See that glass door? We have to go in there, then down to the parking lot. I've got a car ready.'

Charlie's glance swept across the area, which was overlooked by a further building with a wall made almost entirely of tinted glass. Lights were on in many of the offices and rooms, though he could see no movement in any of them.

'Come on,' he said, slipping his hand under her elbow, 'keep your eyes down as though we're talking. Don't look as if you're afraid of being seen.'

They strode briskly over the grass, miming a conversation as they went. No one called out or questioned them. They reached the glass doors, Charlie pushed them open, and Susan led the way past the elevator and to the stairs. They went down one flight leading to a fire-hinged door. Charlie pushed it open, and they found themselves in the underground parking lot.

'Over here,' she said, instinctively talking in a whisper. Charlie followed her. The car she led him to was a dark blue Honda. 'I don't have a key, you'll have to break in and start it somehow – but I'm sure your training covered that.'

He reached for the handle of the driver's door and tried it. The car was unlocked. 'Lesson one,' he said, giving her a wry smile, 'never overlook the obvious.'

'That's good. Now tell me the key's in the ignition.'

He looked. It wasn't. 'The easiest way to do this is if I open the hood,' he said, finding the catch. Then he went around to the front of the car and leaned into the motor.

A sound across the floor made her gasp audibly and turn. A door had opened and swung shut, like the one they had just come through. There was nothing to see, but footsteps began echoing off the concrete walls. Charlie didn't move, but kept his head low, peering through the crack between the raised hood and the car's bodywork. A guard came into view, jiggling car keys in his hand and whistling softly as he looked forward to going home at the end of his shift. Then he saw them and stopped.

'Some problem here? Need any help?'

'No . . . no, thank you,' Susan said. 'We're fine, thank you.'

Charlie could hear her trying to keep her voice steady. She wasn't doing too good a job of it. He saw the guard frown, suspicious now.

'Wait a second . . . aren't you Dr Flemyng?'

'There's really no problem here,' Susan said, sounding even more nervous. 'We've taken care of it. Thank you.'

The guard was already walking towards them. His keys were back in his pocket, leaving his hands free. His right, Charlie noted, was dangerously near the .38 on his hip. He didn't have a face Charlie recognized, so he hadn't been one of the detail looking after him, which meant he probably wasn't armed with a zapper. That was a chance Charlie was going to have to take.

'As a matter of fact, I'd be glad if you'd take a look,' Charlie said from under the hood. 'I'm not sure I can figure this thing out.'

The guard approached, making a circling movement to see who this man was before getting too close. Charlie waited until he heard the footsteps stop, then turned.

Although Charlie didn't recall ever seeing this man before, the guard obviously recognized him. His eyes widened and his hand went for his gun. Charlie covered the space between them before it was out of its holster, knocking the man cold with a sharp jab to the solar plexus and another to the side of his neck. He even had time to catch him before he hit the floor.

'Don't kill him!' Susan was repeating. 'Don't kill him! You don't have to kill him!'

'I haven't killed him,' Charlie said. 'He'll be fine in a few minutes.'

'We need more than a few minutes.'

Charlie slipped his hands under the guard's armpits and dragged him across the floor. He was a big man, but Charlie handled him as though he weighed no more than a child. They found a closet filled with buckets and mops and other cleaning stuff. Charlie tied him up and gagged him with a length of old towelling. Then Susan told Charlie to take the guard's gun and give it to her, which he did. She slipped it into the pocket of her coat with a look that challenged him to ask her why she wanted it. He didn't say anything.

It took only a moment to start the car. She told him it belonged to one of Latimer West's female assistants who often worked late. She said she thought the young woman and West were having an affair. Charlie climbed into the trunk while Susan tied her hair back and put on glasses, saying that to a casual glance from the guards at the gate she would look sufficiently like West's mistress for them to wave her through unchallenged.

Charlie held his breath in the darkness as she drove. He felt the car slow at the gate and heard voices, then they picked up speed and were through. Ten minutes later they came to a stop. Susan opened the trunk and let him out.

They were in the parking lot of a Holiday Inn or some similar hotel, under the sodium glare of overhead lighting. There was nobody around, just rows of parked cars and the hum of traffic from the nearby road. Charlie stretched, flexing his shoulders, and saw Susan take another step back, keeping a safe distance between them. She kept her hands in the pockets of her coat, and he had no doubt that in one she held the zapper and in the other the gun. He looked at her, waiting for her to tell him what came next.

'You didn't give me a proper answer back there about that bargain I proposed,' she said, 'so I'm going to ask you one more time. Will you help me?'

He gave a slight shrug, almost of indifference. 'I told you, I don't have much choice, do I?'

'You have all the choice in the world, Charlie. If you're not prepared to help me willingly, then you're no good to me. So what's it to be?'

He almost laughed in her face. What was this shit? Who did she think she was kidding? 'And if I refuse, then what? You zap me and take me back?'

She shook her head. 'What good would that do me? I can hardly go back there myself now, can I?'

He shrugged again. 'Okay, so you won't take me back. You can knock me out, put a bullet through me – either way, we're hardly having an equal discussion here.'

'That's just what we're having. I'll say it again – either you help me willingly, or you're free to go. Just walk away. I won't do anything to stop you. You've got me this far, and if that's it for you – fine. I'll take it from here on my own. After all, I've got a gun now.'

Charlie's eyes narrowed suspiciously. 'Are you as crazy as you sound? Are you saying that if I walk away, you'll let me?'

'That's exactly what I'm saying.'

He looked at her a moment longer. This, he knew, he had to prove for himself.

'Okay,' he said, as casually as he could, 'then I'll walk.' He turned and started across the lot and towards the road beyond.

As he walked, his footsteps echoed with a strangely heightened clarity against the background murmur of the urban night. He was waiting for the moment when it all went blank, or a shot was fired and there would be a sudden sting of pain in his back. Yet he went on walking, and still nothing happened. When he reached the road, he stopped and looked back. He could see her in the distance, a solitary figure in the hazy artificial light, still standing where he'd left her. She seemed to be watching him, but he couldn't make out the expression on her face. They stood like that for some time, each daring the other to make the first move. In the end she turned away and started for the hotel.

He knew what she was going to do. There was a determination in her walk which convinced him that what she had said about going in there alone was no empty boast. But it was madness. He had to stop her. She would die, or worse, and he would be responsible.

Except that he wouldn't be. He wasn't responsible at all. It was her decision, not his. He hadn't pushed her into any of it. How could he even be sure she'd told him the truth about her son and her father? It would be the first time she'd told him the truth about anything.

So what was her game this time? And did he even care? Shouldn't he just grab his freedom while it was there?

But freedom meant being able to do what he wanted, not what he had to or thought he should. So what was it that he wanted now? He knew as soon as he asked himself the question that he wanted to go after her. He wanted to keep the promise he'd made to help her. The only thing that held him back was the mystery of why this was so. Surely the feeling was no more than a legacy of the conditioning they'd put him through. Why could he not accept that nothing he'd ever felt for her, or imagined that she'd felt for him, was real?

Yet surely what he felt was real. A feeling, any emotion, whether love, hate or fear, was by definition real, wasn't it? The reasons behind it could be questioned and found wanting, but not the feeling itself. So should he act on what he felt, or on what he suspected were the flawed reasons behind that feeling?

He never resolved the dilemma. He just began running. When she heard his footsteps she stopped walking and turned. She made no attempt this time to keep a safe distance between them. She looked up at him, her face open and expectant, waiting for him to speak.

'I had to be sure,' he said. 'It was no good unless I knew you meant it.'

Her expression didn't change, but he thought he detected a relaxing of the muscles, a kind of relief. Or maybe he imagined it. She gave the slightest of nods in acknowledgement, and said simply, 'Thank you, Charlie.'

He looked up at the anonymous façade of the hotel with its matching symmetrical balconies outside every room. 'Your son and your father – which floor are they on?'

'The seventh.'

'How many people with them?'

'I don't know.'

'There'll be a small army when they realize we've escaped.'

Susan glanced at her watch. 'We've only been gone twenty minutes. It could be they don't know yet.'

'Well, they will soon. We need to move.' His eyes locked on hers. 'I'm with you. Only I have a condition, too.'

'What is it?'

'I'll feel a whole lot happier with that zapper in my pocket instead of yours.'

She hesitated fractionally, then reached into her coat. 'Here. You're welcome to it.' She held it out to him. 'Though it won't do you any good.'

'I'm more concerned about it not doing me any harm.' He took it delicately from her outstretched hand.

'It won't do you any harm, either. Try it.'

He looked puzzled, his gaze shifting from the tiny object in his palm to her, then back again. 'What d'you mean?'

'Go ahead – press it.'

He gazed at her, incredulous. She gave a little smile of reassurance. 'Trust me. Nothing's going to happen. I wouldn't want you to pass out cold just now, would I?'

Gingerly, he closed his thumb and forefinger over the small black rectangle, then squeezed. No curtain of blackness descended. It was just as she had said: nothing happened.

Except he suddenly became aware that *something* was happening, something else, something quite different from anything he had anticipated. When he looked at Susan he had to lift his gaze, then keep on lifting it. Because she was levitating right there in front of him, hanging in the air – two yards, now three – above the black tarmac of the parking lot.

His mouth fell open in speechless disbelief. Somewhere in the background two people walked to their car and got in without so much as a glance at the impossible phenomenon taking place in front of them. Their indifference, the sound of their car starting up, the sweep of its headlights over the whole scene, all served only to heighten his numbed sense of unreality.

But then of course he realized what this was, and gave a low groan of resigned understanding. He closed his eyes. When he opened them the scene was unchanged; the car's tail lights were disappearing in the distance, and Susan still hung in the air looking down at him.

'I'm sorry, Charlie,' she said, and there was a note of genuine apology in her voice, 'but I had to be sure. And this is the only kind of communication we can have that they don't know how to bug. When you come out of it, just say you don't remember anything. I'm going to help you escape, and you're going to help me get my son and father back, though not quite like this. But we'll do it. And then we'll put the sons of bitches who are behind all this where they belong.'

He wasn't sure whether he opened his eyes or whether they'd been open all the time. At any rate, he found himself back in the lab with Susan in the act of removing the five-point device from his head. Then she took a similar one off her own head. So that was how it's done, he thought: a two-way link.

As before, the two guards sat in their separate corners. He glanced at the clock on the wall to his right. Less than half an hour had passed. Interesting, he thought: the whole illusion had taken place in real time – assuming that the clock was accurate and wasn't just another part of the set-up.

'All right, Charlie,' Susan said brightly, 'd'you remember me?'

He looked puzzled. 'Of course I remember you.'

She made a little sound through her nose, as though this wasn't the answer she had wanted. 'Hmm. D'you remember anything of what just happened?'

Their eyes met briefly. Charlie played along, looking puzzled. 'What d'you mean what happened? Nothing happened. You just put that thing on my head, now you've taken it off.'

She didn't reply, just looked annoyed. It was an act, he supposed.

'Okay, you can take him back,' she said to the guards. 'Looks like I've got more work to do.'

47

Susan didn't like lying to her father, but she had no choice. In fact it was less an outright lie than an economy with the truth. She knew that every word they spoke in the building was going to be recorded and listened to; even outside in the grounds she couldn't be sure there wasn't a directional mike following them. So she told him again, as she'd told him repeatedly, that her way of thinking had changed. She was ready to compromise now, even to participate voluntarily in the programme. At first she'd been a little disconcerted at the way he'd gone along with and encouraged her in this change of heart, but then she realized he was thinking only of what was best for her and Christopher. Anything that kept them alive and allowed them to lead at least some kind of normal life was fine with him. Amery Hyde was a pragmatist as well as a man of principle, and she loved him for it.

At any rate, she figured that if she could fool her father then she could fool Latimer West and the rest of them, whoever and wherever they were. All she wanted was to lull their suspicions of her, to persuade them that she wasn't actively working against them any longer. None-theless, despite all their vague promises, no decision had been made about actually letting her and Christopher return home, and she felt increasingly in her heart that it was never going to happen. Putting herself in West's shoes and those of the people behind him, she knew that the risk of letting her go free with what she knew would be too great. The likeliest course she could imagine was that they would get all the work out of her that they could, then kill her. They would have to kill her father too, of course.

But Christopher? She found it hard to believe that even these people would cold-bloodedly murder an innocent child. It was the *threat* of murder that was compelling. They knew they could depend on her so long as Christopher was in their power, but that was a situation that she intended to change – with Charlie's help. And if she failed, if she and maybe even Charlie died, then they would no longer have any reason to kill Christopher, or her father for that matter. That was her last hope.

It was Thursday, the day of her trial run with Charlie. She worked late that night, programming and re-programming the giant computer that both generated the VR environment and also controlled the lab equipment used in the current set of memory experiments she was supposedly performing on Charlie. Nobody checking her work would have had the first suspicion of what she was actually doing. It was the one weakness in their hold over her – the fact that she was the expert and they weren't. When she was doing what only she knew how to do, they were in her hands. The only way they could check on her was by getting another expert to watch her every move. But they didn't have another expert, not one as good as her who could operate on the same level. If they did, they wouldn't have needed her in the first place.

She looked at her watch as she finished working and

sat back from the keyboard. It was just after three a.m. In six hours she would be back in the lab with Charlie, feeding the programme she had just written into his brain. It would tell him that she was flying up to the ranch on Saturday morning to spend the weekend there with Christopher and her father.

It would also tell him, now she was as sure as she could ever be of his dependability, how he was going to get out of this place and join them.

'Chuang Tzu was a Chinese sage who lived two and a half thousand years ago. He told once of how he dreamt he was a butterfly, and didn't know when he awoke if he was a man who had dreamt he was a butterfly, or a butterfly who now dreamt he was a man. People have been telling that story ever since, because it represents something that mankind has always known instinctively – that we can never be sure whether the outside world corresponds to the picture of it that we have in our head. We can't even be sure that the outside world is actually there. For all we know, we could be imagining it. We can't *prove* it either way. And in the end it doesn't matter. It makes no difference because the things we experience are the same whether they're coming *to* us or coming *from* us. They're there, and that's all that matters.'

Charlie shifted his weight from one foot to the other, listening closely.

'The important thing to grasp, Charlie, is that *all* reality is virtual reality. It's the only kind of reality there is.'

She held up a red rose. He didn't know where it had come from, it just appeared in her hand. But he was used to those tricks by now.

'You don't suppose this rose is actually red, do you?'

He'd got the hang of rhetorical questions, too. She was making a point, and he didn't interrupt with an answer.

'Colour, like everything else, is in your mind. Light impacts on the nerves behind your eyes and sends a series of electric impulses to your brain, which sorts them out into shape, size, depth of focus and colour. But all of that's just your internal picture of what's out there, and you've no guarantee that your camera isn't playing tricks on you – like now.'

They were standing on the moon – or, more precisely, a very convincing simulation of it. They were not wearing spacesuits, and gravity was operating – or *appeared* to be operating – as on earth. That, however, was easily adjusted; he'd already spent several enjoyable moments leaping thirty feet into the air (air?) and drifting gently back down.

'Okay, Charlie,' she'd said, 'that's enough theory. The point is just to let you know we're in VR, but there's no way you can be sure of that unless something impossible happens.'

'If you shot me with a VR bullet, would I die?'

'I could make you think you had.'

He remembered when he thought he'd been going to drown, and believed her.

'The way you're going to escape from captivity, Charlie,' she continued, 'isn't through me slipping a mickey into the guards' coffee. For one thing, that would prove that you and I were working together, which isn't what I want them to think – at least not so quickly. So what I've done is knock out the receiver in your chest. I've been trying for a while, using that big scanner, but only managed it yesterday. That means you can't be zapped any more. I've zapped you several times in the last twenty-four hours, and you haven't even noticed.'

Charlie felt his heart beat faster. That, he knew, was no virtual reaction; that was for real, and forget all the fancy definitions of 'real' she'd been giving him.

'Easy,' she said, 'don't get excited. I'm reading your responses and they're going off the graph. Everything I say to you now is on the assumption that you're going to keep your promise to help me if I get you out of here. One thing I still can't do, Charlie, despite all this technology, is read your mind. My only knowledge of what you think comes from what you choose to tell me. Whether I hear it from your lips or read it from your brain activity makes no difference. Maybe we'll get beyond that soon, but so far we haven't.'

'Trust me.'

'I do, Charlie. Hadn't you noticed?'

He looked at her, standing just a few feet from him in that wholly convincing and yet unreal lunar landscape, and wondered whether the pensive smile he saw on her face meant anything. Was it just a computer-generated appropriate response? Or was it in some way wired into her real feelings? Was anything real going on between the two of them, or were they just lobbing words at one another from behind their electronic masks? And anyway, what was the difference between an electronic mask and one made of flesh and bone?

'Now,' she said, suddenly businesslike, 'let's get down to details . . .'

The transition was seamless, but still took his breath away. From standing on the moon with a distant and spectacular view of planet earth, he found himself on a rocky hillside beneath a blue and white sky, overlooking a forest of aspen and pine trees and a lake.

'This is a simulation from memory and guesswork. I don't have access to maps or photography, so this is computer-enhanced recall. It looks real, but it's not a hundred per cent accurate. However, it'll give you all the key reference points to look out for.'

They began walking downhill, Susan pointing out various landmarks to help him get his bearings. 'I've only seen all this from the air when I've flown in,' she said, 'but there's a highway down there to the south – let's take a look.'

The world around them dissolved and re-formed into a six-lane highway. They were standing on the central divide with vehicles moving past them in both directions. Charlie reacted instinctively, grabbing her in preparation for a leap to safety. 'It's all right, Charlie,' she said, 'we're not here to play with the traffic. *This* is what we're here for. Hold on to your stomach.'

He couldn't be sure whether the ground was lowered or they were lifted. All he knew was that his perspective changed with startling speed to a dizzying bird's-eye view of the highway and its surrounding tree-covered, mountainous terrain. He gulped and, even though he knew that in reality he hadn't moved, he felt his stomach turn.

'Sorry if that was a little fast,' Susan said as she floated beside him in the air, 'but you need to get the layout of the place. This is how I see it when I fly in.'

They began travelling at the speed of an aircraft preparing to land, except there was no aircraft, no window to peer out of, just empty space beneath them as they flew like Peter Pan and Wendy suspended from invisible wires.

'There's the ranch,' she said, pointing ahead to a

sprawl of buildings. 'We'll stop a moment for you to get your bearings.'

They froze in mid-air, then revolved slowly, Susan pointing out the things he needed to be aware of. There was a slip road from the highway that wound up through trees, emerging not far from one part of the ranch's boundary fence.

'As far as I know,' she said, 'that's the only made-up road that goes up there. But there's a couple of tracks I've spotted from the air.'

They moved around – or, rather, the world beneath them shifted. There was only one track that looked as though it could take a vehicle. It emerged from a thick cluster of trees along another side of the boundary fence, then descended sharply until it reached a minor road that eventually joined the main highway.

'Over there,' she said, pointing in another direction, 'you can see the landing strip.'

He looked. At one end of it an executive jet was parked like a toy plane. Not far from it was an equally toy-like helicopter. After that they drifted to a point right above the main buildings, with the pool, the tennis court, the barns and stables off to one side.

'Okay,' she said when he'd absorbed everything he could from that angle, 'now let's go down and take a walk around.'

Once again the world around them dissolved and re-formed into a new perspective. Charlie was getting used to these strange jump-cuts through time and space: it was like being inside a film instead of simply watching one. They found themselves outside a long two-storey building with a verandah running around two sides. 'These are the main living quarters,' Susan told him. 'We'll make it a

288

quick tour, because you probably won't need to know too much of this.'

They moved through the rooms not at walking pace but like a video on medium fast-forward. At these speeds Charlie had no sense of being there; he was a disembodied observer passing through. But on the two or three occasions when they stopped to check some detail, things returned to normal.

'Normal.' He laughed inwardly when he thought about the word. Then he laughed again when he wondered what he meant by 'inwardly'. Where exactly was that? Could you travel inwardly for ever? Could you implode? Were we black holes, was that it? Or was he the only one who felt like that – the mutant?

His thoughts were interrupted by her voice – or, he corrected himself, the thought of her voice. 'I want to show you Christopher,' she said, 'so you'll know what he looks like.'

They whizzed forward a few yards and came to a stop on the porch of the main building, looking out over an empty patch of ground. Suddenly a child riding a horse materialized out of nowhere about fifty yards away. A young man seemed to be giving him instruction, then helped him down as though the lesson was over. The child started running towards them, arms outstretched, excited to see them. It was a strange feeling for Charlie to have this unknown child running towards him, as though he, Charlie, were a parent or beloved friend. He felt a surge of unease, wondering how to react if the child leapt into his arms as he seemed about to do; but at the last second the image froze.

'It's not a perfect likeness,' Susan said. 'I had to morph him from a photograph. But that's Christopher.'

Charlie gazed at him a moment, fixing the delicate small features in his memory.

'And then of course there's my father,' she said. 'You'll need to know what he looks like, too.'

There was the sound of a door opening behind him. Charlie turned, and felt as though the breath had been kicked out of him. The tall silver-haired man who stood framed against a dark interior, a faint smile on his lips and his eyes fixed unblinkingly on Charlie's, was Control.

'This is my father. His name's Amery Hyde,' Susan was saying. 'I've morphed him from an old picture I had in my purse. That's why he looks a little like a waxwork. But at least you'll know him when you see him again – okay, Charlie?'

She looked at him, waiting for some response. But Charlie felt paralysed, barely able to breathe. For an insane moment he thought he was going to pass out, or even die right there, expire within this electronic universe and become vaporized into some abstract host of random impulses.

'Charlie?' he heard Susan say. There seemed to be an edge of concern in her voice, though whether this was real or just some other part of the simulated universe that he was in, or even just the product of his own imagination, he couldn't say. He couldn't say anything at the moment. He wasn't even sure that he could think. Not only words failed him but thoughts too.

'Charlie, are you all right? I'm registering a very odd response in you.'

With an effort he tore his gaze from the frozen image of Control and focused on the animated one of Susan.

'What is it, Charlie? What's wrong?'

'What's wrong?' he repeated incredulously. His voice

seemed to undulate through different levels, as though his head had become an echo chamber. 'Don't you know who this is?'

'I told you – he's my father.'

Charlie looked again at the tall patrician figure in the doorway. 'Is this some kind of test?' he asked.

'It's no test. Why?'

He didn't answer. Without looking at her he could feel the intensity of her scrutiny.

'Charlie?'

Still he didn't respond. His mind was racing.

'Charlie,' she repeated, more insistently, 'tell me what's going on in your head. I need to know what this is about.'

'This is the man I call Control,' he said.

It was she who fell silent now. He turned to regard the image next to him. She was motionless, her face without expression. Yet there was something stricken in her stillness. Either that or he was reading the emotion directly from her brain through their link-up in the lab.

'You're mistaken,' she said eventually, and there was a strange tone to her voice, her electronic, artificial voice, that he hadn't heard before and was unsure how to interpret. 'You must be mistaken.'

'I don't believe I am.'

48

They were back in the lab almost at once. Their time was up, the programme at its end. The guards were in their usual corner and Susan was removing Charlie's headset, which she put down alongside the one she had just taken off herself. She was tense. He could see it in her face and feel it between them.

'All right, Charlie,' she said, 'how much of what just happened do you remember?'

He remembered everything, of course, as she well knew. This question, and the answer they'd rehearsed, was for the benefit of the recording devices around them. She wanted everyone to think that the experiments she was performing on him were beginning to work. She had told them she was perfecting a method of planting and deleting memories at will; ultimately, she said, she was going to be able to programme his brain as easily as a computer.

Charlie frowned, sticking to the scenario they'd agreed. 'Not much,' he said. 'In fact, now you ask, I don't remember anything. Have I been asleep?'

She didn't reply directly, just as she'd told him she wouldn't.

'Do you remember me?' she asked. 'Do you remember who I am?'

He pretended to study her face, as though surprised by the question. 'No,' he said. 'Am I supposed to? I don't think I've ever seen you before.'

She nodded briefly as though it was the answer she wanted. 'You can take him back now,' she said, and the guards got to their feet and motioned Charlie to do the same.

His eyes held hers for a moment longer, and each knew what the other was thinking. Was he lying, or just plain wrong? Or was she genuinely unaware of who this man she called her father really was?

The senior of the two guards ordered Charlie to get moving. On the walk back to his cell he was sorely tempted to test her claim that she'd neutralized that implant in his chest. The urge to give these two goons the surprise of their lives was almost overwhelming. He could have busted out of the place right there and then – if what she'd told him was the truth. Either way, there was little to lose and everything to gain. If she'd lied and the implant wasn't neutralized, the worst that could happen was he'd be unconscious for a while; if she'd told the truth, he'd be free.

All the same, he decided to play a long game, longer at any rate than taking those two guys apart for the fun of it. He remembered how Susan had warned him against violence, and she was right. When all this was over, he wanted people to regard him as more than just a mindless killing machine. He had killed – often – but it had never afforded him any special satisfaction. It was just what he had been trained for. What he had been created for.

It was strange to think that all those powerful forces that had made him what he was – the painful childhood, the beatings and the anger – had turned out to be mere illusions. But why did he say 'mere'? That was something else Susan had said: in the end you have to drop the 'virtual' off reality, because it doesn't make any difference.

Knowing he was a mutant, though – neither wholly chimpanzee nor wholly man – that made a difference. Strangely enough, he felt, if anything, less alienated from humanity than before. Now he knew that the world he lived in was his alone; it could not be shared with others of his kind because there were none. Realizing this had changed the way he felt about humanity. He felt less superior now, less special. Just different.

Where, he wondered, would that lead him?

Susan, too, slept little that night. She needed desperately to get up and pace, pour a drink, take up smoking – anything to soothe the din of doubt and questions in her mind. But she was afraid of the invisible cameras and listening devices that she felt sure were planted everywhere. She couldn't afford to give away her anxiety so obviously.

Was Charlie playing mind games with her? Was it some kind of revenge? That was at least as likely as the idea that her father was who Charlie claimed he was. That, surely, was the only impossibility.

Wasn't it?

Lying in the dark, she thought back over her life and her father's role in it. He had been a dominant influence, although sometimes a distant one. His needs had always taken precedence in their family, and the direction their lives had gone in had always been, if not dictated, at least decided by him. But they had been a happy family. Her early memories of him were vague compared with those of her mother. She later understood that he had been working very hard in those days, building a career that had risen fast through the state department, then on to a string of government appointments, consultancies and visiting professorships. But he had always had time for her when she needed him, and had encouraged her from childhood to ask questions and think for herself. When she'd begun to show intellectual promise and talked about becoming a doctor, he had again encouraged her. She hadn't needed his help to get into the best schools; her own abilities had been enough. But when it came to getting grants and making contacts, it hadn't hurt to have a father so influentially placed as Amery Hyde. Her father, it had always struck her, seemed not so much to know everybody as to know someone who knew them.

She remembered with a brief moment of discomfort that he'd checked out the people behind the Pilgrim Foundation for her – and pronounced them decent philanthropic individuals in whom she could safely place her trust. It would have been easy for him to lie to her, knowing that she would accept whatever he said. Just as quickly she reproached herself for the unworthiness of such a thought and the suspicion it conceded. Some part of her was judging her father guilty before she'd even heard the evidence. What was wrong with her?

It was true that there had always been a sense of distance about him; he was an intensely private man. But his opinions, when he'd voiced them, had been sensible and moderate. He was no extremist. She had always understood there were things he could not talk about, secrets he had to keep; she had taken that for granted. But could these secrets have been of the kind implied by Charlie's claim? Could her father be capable of that kind of deception, let alone the ruthlessness that made it necessary?

Her mind lurched away, like a force repelled by its opposite, from the contemplation of such thoughts. But they wouldn't go away.

She thought back on how, after Charlie's claim that her father was Control, her first instinct had been to call off the whole escape plan. The idea had thrown a wrench in the works, and she didn't know how to deal with it. She felt off-balance, her resolution fatally undermined.

It was Charlie who'd said no, this was his decision now. It was Charlie who wanted answers, and he would only get them by going through with her plan.

She could stop him, of course, but she could do it only by making a confession to West of what she'd been planning. As Charlie had told her, he didn't think she would do that.

He was right of course.

49

The weekend began for Susan on the following afternoon, which was Friday. She was flown up to the ranch in the executive jet, arriving in time for supper with Christopher, after which they played a few games and then watched television.

Her father was due to arrive in the morning, taking a scheduled flight from Washington where he'd been on business for the last few days. The increasing ease with which he seemed to have returned to normal life was just another factor in the gnawing and terrible suspicion she found herself harbouring about him. To get away from it she forced her mind to other things, especially the plan on which she and Charlie had agreed, and which now more than ever she could not afford to give any hint of to her father.

On Saturday she rose early after a second sleepless night. She looked out of her window on to a crisp Fall morning. It struck her that the main difference between the simulation she'd run for Charlie and the real thing was the colour of the leaves; she'd forgotten how fast the seasons turned. But that, she told herself, wouldn't cause him any problems – always supposing he got this far. Of course, it was still possible that he would reconsider his position and just walk away. If that happened, she might never know the truth about her father, and maybe that would be a blessing.

But in her heart she knew that a question such as this, once posed, would brook neither evasion nor subterfuge. It was, frankly, a relief that the decision to challenge her father's truthfulness, and with it a dauntingly huge part of her own life's authenticity, was now in Charlie's hands instead of hers.

She had a quick breakfast with Christopher, after which she had promised to go riding with him. Her protest that she was years out of practice had met with his insistence that she try out the sweet-natured old horse that Michael had selected for her. And besides, Michael would be coming with them, so what could go wrong? Her main fear (that things would start to happen when she and Christopher were too far from the ranch itself) had to remain unspoken; but she made a quick calculation of the earliest time Charlie could get to them, assuming all went to plan, and decided that a brisk early ride would present no problem.

Buzz had to be persuaded to stay indoors. He'd been reluctant to obey, but a quick trip to Mrs Hathaway's kitchen for a bone had taken care of that. The ride was pleasant, the air clean and bracing. Susan enjoyed the experience more than she had anticipated, grateful for the distraction from her preoccupation with what might happen in the next few hours. It was a relief not to have to talk much, aside from telling Christopher that, yes, this had been a great idea; and yes, the horse was just as good natured and easy to handle as Michael had promised; and yes, Christopher's own horsemanship was even better now than the last time she'd seen him mounted. She found herself laughing out loud more than once, forgetting for a brief moment the threat that hung over them.

Michael rode with them, keeping a respectful distance and on the whole not speaking unless he was spoken to. Nonetheless, she had the impression of being accompanied by an armed guard, even though he carried no weapon that she could see; but somehow his demeanour, the watchfulness she sensed in his pale blue boyish eyes, the phone strapped to his waist like a handgun, all combined to remind her that, despite the easy superficial atmosphere of this place, she and Christopher were prisoners.

A clattering sound broke the silence. In the distance the helicopter rose above the trees, hung suspended for a moment, then tilted and moved off in the direction of the airport.

'That's Joe going to pick up Grandpa,' Christopher told her with the authority of someone who knew the ropes around here. He waved at the departing chopper.

Susan, too, watched it out of sight, as though in some strange way it carried all her hopes – not just of escape, but of understanding certain mysteries so intimate that, until now, she had never suspected their existence.

Latimer West was finishing breakfast in his private apartment. It was behind the office where he had frequently interviewed, argued with and, more recently, reached a kind of understanding with Susan Flemyng. The apartment, like his office, was comfortable and spacious, a penthouse running two thirds the length of the main building with a wide terrace on two sides.

The first sign of trouble came when he heard voices

below, men shouting in confusion. Then an alarm went off. West got up from his chair, wiping his mouth fastidiously on the corner of his white linen napkin, and slid open the glass doors to his terrace. Looking down, he saw guards running. A security patrol car raced around a corner and screeched to a halt. More men piled out. Before he could discover what was happening, a phone started ringing in his apartment. He went back in to answer it, leaving the glass doors open.

The call was from Morris, the chief of security. 'Monk's broken out, got over the fence before we could do anything.'

West felt a prickly chill run down his back. 'How, for Christ's sakes? How could he possibly break out?' His voice was suddenly an octave higher than usual, his heart beating fast.

'They were escorting him to the gym for his morning workout. Three guards with him, two in the corridor. There's a semi-blindspot down there, but we got part of it on video. He just took 'em all out faster than you could count. Nobody dead, but a few broken bones.'

'Five of them? Why didn't anybody stop him?'

'Some malfunction in the electronic restraint system. I've spoken to a couple of them – they zapped him repeatedly, but he didn't respond.'

'They had guns, for God's sake!'

'The way that guy moves, nobody gets time to both pull the gun and fire a shot.'

'Then you should have had *ten* men down there! This is inexcusable!'

West was shrieking now. The security chief continued his report in a monotone, professionally impervious to

300

his boss's anger, which was proof only that West feared being held responsible by higher powers for this situation.

'He took two guns and a clip of ammunition, shot out three security cameras, which is how we lost him. But we found where he went over the fence, because he dropped one of the guns.'

'How long's he been gone?'

'Three minutes – nearly four.'

West groaned miserably.

The chief continued. 'We have all available vehicles and men covering the surrounding area. I need your okay to call the police department.'

'Not yet. I have to get clearance. I'll get back to you if we want the police involved.'

He hung up. Outside, through the open doors to his terrace, he could hear more voices and vehicles accelerating away. Then there was silence. West sat for a moment with his head in his hands, struggling to come to terms with the enormity of this blunder, wondering how to report it to his superiors in a way that exonerated him, or at least minimized his responsibility.

Then he felt something on his shoulder, just the lightest of touches, hardly more than a passing gust of air. Except it didn't pass but stayed where it was. West's veins froze as Charlie's voice came from right behind his ear.

'All right, just stay calm, and let me tell you what we're going to do . . .'

Amery Hyde was in the helicopter about ten minutes from the ranch when his mobile phone rang. His pilot, Joe, couldn't hear the conversation through the clatter of the motor and the radio headset that he wore. But he didn't miss the way the colour drained from the older man's face. There was no doubt that this was bad news.

Barney Cole, as the oldest and slowest member of the security team, had not been included in any of the groups out scouting for Charlie. They'd left him on gate duty because somebody had to be there, though with Charlie gone there was less need for the usual rigorous checks on every vehicle. When Barney got the call from Dr West himself saying he was heading for the airport and didn't wish to waste any time about it, he made damn sure that the gate was open ready. The car was through in a flash, West himself at the wheel giving him a wave of thanks.

Charlie got up from the floor after fifty yards or so. West felt the pressure of the gun against his right kidney lighten – not that he had any illusions that Charlie needed a gun to make him suffer very badly if he didn't do exactly what he was told.

'Okay so far. You're doing fine,' Charlie said, settling back in the passenger seat and buckling his seat belt. 'Just keep it up, and you might even come out of this alive. Even better, you might come out alive – and still able to walk, talk, see and hear.'

He saw West flinch, and had to make a serious effort to keep a smile of amusement off his face. It was so easy to frighten people. Of course, it helped if they knew that you could deliver on your threats. Empty threats were no use at all. But Charlie knew that everybody, including himself, was aware that his threats were real.

'You're in for a bigger surprise than you think when we get there, Charlie,' West said, the tremble in his voice betraying the defiance of his words.

'Not as big a one as Amery Hyde,' Charlie replied casually, with the hint of a smile.

It was a remark that made Latimer West's eyes almost pop out of his head.

50

Just as they began a gentle gallop, Michael's phone rang. He pulled his horse up as he took the call. Susan glanced back and saw his face muscles tighten. She had little doubt that the message concerned Charlie's escape, and that they would be ordered back to the ranch as part of a security clampdown.

At the same time the clatter of the returning helicopter became audible. Susan looked up and saw it in the distance, descending slowly into the trees. She would have given a lot to know whether Michael's call was coming from that chopper or elsewhere. As though cued by her suspicion, Michael waved at her to slow and turn around. She called over to Christopher, and they both cantered back to meet Michael, phone now reinstalled on his hip, his features solemn.

'I'm sorry, Chris – orders,' was all he said when Christopher protested this premature return.

'But why?'

'I can't tell you that, Chris, because I don't know. Auntie May says we gotta get back there right now, so that's what we're gonna have to do.'

Mrs Hathaway? Susan wondered. Or Amery Hyde? She closed her eyes to keep the pain of that suspicion at bay, but opened them when she heard Christopher appealing to her.

'Tell Michael, Mom. Tell him you don't want to go back yet.'

'Don't make a fuss, darling,' she said gently. 'If Mrs Hathaway says we have to go back, then I'm sure there's a good reason.'

'Better listen to your mom, Chris. Let's go.'

As they rode back, she watched Michael with an almost clinical interest. She'd sensed something in his reaction when Christopher started to argue that reminded her of a time she'd spent years back de-programming cult members. There had been a very specific personality associated with many of them – the same openness and surface charm she found in Michael, but once you challenged or crossed them in any way they immediately closed up. You could see it now in his face and the whole set of his body. People like him were programmed to obey. Like Charlie.

Except that Charlie wasn't exactly 'people'. Also he was proving to have a mind of his own, which was more than she could say for most cult members. Or, she suspected, for the strangely inhuman people who worked in this place.

Amery Hyde was waiting on the porch when Susan and Christopher dismounted. He looked tense, but made a show of giving a big hug to Christopher and promising to play various games with him later. Then he embraced Susan. She could feel the tension in his body, and hoped it would mask the tension in hers.

'Let's walk,' he said, indicating with a glance that he wanted to get out of Christopher's hearing. Luckily the dog had come bounding from the house to greet his young master's return, and the two of them were already involved in some play of their own.

'Something's happened,' Amery said, slipping a hand under his daughter's elbow, as though he was about to impart bad news and felt the need of physical contact. 'We're being moved out, as soon as the plane gets here.'

She looked him directly in the eyes for the first time. 'Moved out? Where to? Why?'

He met her gaze. 'I don't know. I wondered if you might have some idea.'

It was a surreal moment. Her mind was in turmoil and her heart beating so loud she thought he must hear it. She shook her head, and the gesture felt awkward and unnatural, as though she were onstage with hundreds of eyes watching her, freezing her into a state of tongue-tied embarrassment. Of course there was only one pair of eyes – her father's. But that was worse. He knew her too well. Any false move she made would be instantly seen through, any lie immediately transparent.

'I can't think of any reason,' she said, clearing her throat which was suddenly dry. 'None at all. Who told you about it?'

'The Hathaway woman, as soon as I got here.'

'Something must have happened. There was no talk of moving when we went out after breakfast. Didn't she give any reason?'

'No. Just that the plane's coming and we have to get on it.'

Susan shrugged and turned away, trying to look puzzled. She thought he'd seen through her. He must have. But she couldn't be sure. Just as she couldn't be sure that she'd really seen through him. Was hers the greatest betrayal of all? Were her insane suspicions of him the only treason between them?

To her surprise she felt a profound sense of relief when she saw the loose-limbed figure of Mrs Hathaway striding towards them. She hated this woman in a strange way, a way that could be explained only by her complete failure to understand her. She didn't believe she had ever in her life met someone whose inner reality was quite so opaque.

'I'm starting to get Christopher's things together,' the woman said, reaching them. 'I thought perhaps you'd . . .'

'Yes, of course. I'll come right away.'

Amery Hyde watched the two figures walk back to the house and disappear inside. He felt more than nervousness at the news he'd received from West about Charlie's escape; uppermost in his mind was the fear that his daughter was somehow involved. If so, he wasn't sure how far he could protect her. The only solution was that Charlie be found soon, and preferably killed. He had become too dangerous a liability to keep alive. The electronic implant that he and West had been assured was fail-safe, as good as a steel cage, had failed. Time to cut their losses. But first they had to find him.

He walked around a corner where he knew he could not be seen from the house. Something had been nagging at the back of his mind for the past few minutes, and he suddenly realized what it was. That man Schiller and his wretched magazine – what was it called? It didn't matter, the committee had it all on record. He'd passed on everything that Susan had told him when she'd had him send that card to Schiller. Her idea had been that Amery should find Schiller on that flight to Great Falls and tell him the whole story. The ruse might well have worked, had Amery not been obliged to betray his daughter's trust. But it had been for her own good. Everything had been for her own good, including the staging of Amery's disappearance afterwards as a punishment. Her relief at finding him still alive had marked the beginning of what he had thought was a genuine change of heart. Now he was no longer sure that he'd been right. He even suspected now that his daughter had seen through him and had begun to treat him as 'the enemy'.

She was wrong, of course. He never would be that. Not to her. If only she knew the lengths he had gone to, was still going to, for her protection.

He used the emergency number that he'd memorized. Even though it was Saturday, the man he wanted to speak to was on the line in seconds.

'It's about the escape,' Amery said. He was intending to suggest that Schiller be put under round-the-clock surveillance and his phones tapped. There was at least a fair chance that, if Susan was involved, she would have instructed Charlie to get in touch with him.

'What escape?'

' "Epsilon".'

Damn stupid code name, he'd always thought. Some Greek scholar on the committee had picked it because Charlie was technically the fifth generation of these mutants, and the first to be even partially successful. It wasn't as though the name 'Charlie Monk' would mean anything to anybody listening in. And anyway, even though this was a cellphone, the call was reliably scrambled by some very sophisticated microcircuitry.

'I have not been informed of this.' The words were clipped and wary, with an edge of distrust.

Amery felt himself go cold. This couldn't be.

'I don't understand.'

'Where are you?'

' "Tara", ' Amery said. Another damn silly piece of coding, obviously by a movie buff this time. ' "Everest" told me forty minutes ago that he'd informed you, and you had issued instructions for him to fly up here at once.'

'Everest' was West's code name – his own choice, Amery had always assumed.

'There has been no report from "Everest" or anyone else regarding "Epsilon".'

Amery was silent, his brain racing. Suddenly it all fell into place with a logic that was perfect.

'Are you there?' the voice said.

'I've got to check something,' Amery replied. 'I'll call you back.'

He cut the connection and immediately redialled. Seconds later he was in contact with John Wayne airport, establishing that West had taken off twenty-two minutes ago, in great haste and with only one pilot instead of the usual two.

Aside from that the only other person on the flight was an unidentified man travelling with West.

51

'But why do we have to go?'

Christopher's voice took on a plaintive whining note.

'Darling, I already told you, I don't know.'

'*Where* are we going?'

'I don't know that either.'

'Are we going home?'

'Not yet. Soon.'

She hadn't meant to say that – 'soon'. She shouldn't have. She'd never known she was superstitious, but now she felt she mustn't tempt fate.

'Are we coming back?'

'I don't know that, either. Let's just go along with things and see what happens, like Grandpa says. It might be fun.'

Fun? She'd staked everything on Charlie pulling this off. If he failed, the most she could hope for was that they'd never prove her involvement. Not that they'd need proof: this wasn't a court of law; suspicion would suffice.

But what could they do – kill her? She'd already made her decision that anything was better than just waiting to be used up and then disposed of. The big gamble was that they wouldn't hurt Christopher – or her father, if he was as innocent as she prayed he was. Perhaps it was a gamble that she didn't have the right to take. The thought had tortured her incessantly. Yet in the depth of her being she remained convinced it was their only chance.

'Buzz – come back! Buzz! Good boy, come back, come back . . .!'

Christopher's voice snapped her out of the vortex of her thoughts. She looked across the room in time to see him disappearing out of the door, running after the little dog who was making one of his periodic 'bids for freedom' as John used to call them laughingly. It was a game the animal loved to play with Christopher, a breathless chase of hide and seek around the house. Of course, like all dogs, he would sometimes choose the worst of all possible moments to start – when they were on the point of going out, for example, and had to get him into the car and were already late. But the little dog had never chosen, she decided as she sprinted down the corridor, a worse moment than this. If he disappeared now, Christopher would never leave without him – unless she physically forced him to, which was the last thing she wanted to do.

'Christopher, come back! We haven't time! Buzz!'

The dog disappeared around a corner and Christopher went after him, neither of them paying her the least attention. She tore after them, around another corner and down a longer passage. The dog had his nose to the floor now, following a scent. She could see an open door and daylight in the distance and prayed that something would happen before Buzz got there. But there were no miracles, nobody stepped out of the shadows, no gust of wind banged the door shut in the nick of time.

Suddenly they were outside, racing along the back of the house, then towards the stables and various outhouses, and beyond that a barn. Buzz made for a small

311

door on the side, which was closed. He jumped up and tried to push it open, without success. Then he realized that Christopher had almost caught up with him and was about to grab him, so he made a dash to the left. It was a bad move because his way was blocked after a few yards by a fence. Susan and Christopher closed in, and he was cornered. He gave up without a struggle, as he always did at the end of one of these games, content to have had some fun but not wanting anybody to be really mad at him.

Susan bundled him up in her arms, insisting, despite Christopher's protests, on carrying the dog herself. Then she saw something, just a glimpse, a brief image passing a dusty window further back in the wall of the barn. It was her father. He hadn't seen her, she was sure of that. He seemed to be talking animatedly, waving his hands. She couldn't see who was with him, but she knew at once that something was wrong – in the sense that this was not the role he had been playing until now. He no longer looked like a man being held prisoner. Something about that glimpse of him, the way he was moving, the way he was talking, suggested authority. He was giving orders, telling people what to do.

She felt that same strange jump of fear in her heart that she had felt when Charlie had first made his claim about her father's real identity. Her whole being said it couldn't be true; yet, if it was true, it had to be faced, and faced now.

'All right, you take him,' she said, handing the dog over to Christopher. 'But make sure he doesn't get away again.'

'Okay!'

Christopher took the dog delightedly, holding him tight while Buzz licked his face.

'Take him back to your room and make sure he stays there. I'll be along in a minute.'

She watched until the boy and dog had disappeared into the house, then turned back to the barn. The fence had a gate that she opened carefully, keeping her eyes on the window where she had glimpsed her father. But she didn't see him again until she got much closer. Then she saw him further away, framed against the light from the big doors on the far side which were open. He was still talking, still giving orders to people she couldn't see. She ducked below the window to get past and headed for the corner. Her heart was beating now, and she realized she was biting her lower lip so hard she had almost drawn blood. It was something she'd done as a child when she felt under pressure or afraid of being found out over some small transgression.

But now she wasn't the one who was about to be found out. Her fear was of what she was about to discover. Her greatest fear of all was that she knew already.

She could hear his voice now. She stopped and listened.

'Remember – his reaction times are less than half yours. Once he's in the open, that's when he's most dangerous.'

Somebody else spoke, though she couldn't make out what they said, but it must have been a question because she heard her father's answer as clearly as before. 'No, you wait till I give the signal. Have you all got that clear?'

There were murmurs of assent from several voices.

Then her father's voice again, firm and confident, the man in command. 'All right, get to your places. They'll be landing in twenty minutes.'

She pulled back around the corner so that the men didn't see her as they filed out. She knew them all, had spoken to most of them at times. They did various jobs around the place – driving, looking after the horses, tending the pool and garden. Michael was among them. And Joe, the helicopter pilot. Seven of them in all. Each one of them carried a small, compact, lethal-looking machine-gun.

A moment later they had all dispersed. She heard a car start up. It sounded like the station wagon, but she couldn't see it. She couldn't see her father, either. After a while she wondered if he was still in the barn or if he'd left by some other door. Then she heard his footsteps. They were unmistakably his, and they were coming towards her. Any second now he would turn the corner and they would be face to face.

She wanted to run, to hide the fact that she had been spying on him. She felt guilty, as though the fault was entirely hers. She had spied and eavesdropped on her father, and had been punished by learning things that only caused her pain. That was what happened to naughty girls who thought they knew best. It always ended in tears, like now. She realized that her cheeks were wet, and she was sobbing.

When he saw her, he stopped dead. His face turned white and his mouth fell open in shock. She tried to say something, but all that came from her was a whining sound that made her hate herself for such weakness.

But the anger that followed on its heels, strengthened her determination to go on and get through this. She owed it to herself, above all to Christopher, and in a strange way she felt she owed it to her dead mother. They had all been betrayed by this man who stood before her, and she owed it to them to be the stronger of the two, the one who stood her ground and judged, not the one who backed off and became his victim.

'So,' she said, her voice shaking with emotion, 'it was true, what Charlie said.'

He didn't even try to deny it. His jaw worked a couple of times, and then he found the words by which he sought, she supposed, to excuse himself.

'I had no choice,' he said. His voice was hollow, lacking resonance, unrecognizable as the same voice she had heard issuing crisp orders to his men only moments earlier. 'Believe me, they would have killed you.'

She tried to say something, but all she managed was another wrenching sob. She passed her hand and part of her sleeve across her face, angrily wiping away the tears she so despised in herself.

'Like you killed John?' She got the words out in a rush, failing to suppress the howl of pain that came with them.

He shook his head. 'No, not me.' There was an urgency in his voice, as though he really believed that if he tried hard enough he could still convince her. 'I tried to save John, and failed. But I managed to save you.'

'You delivered me right into their hands. The Pilgrim Foundation!' She spat the words contemptuously at him. 'I suppose you put them up to approaching me in the first place.'

'Try to understand – your work was always going to be in *someone's* hands. That's inevitable when you need the kind of funding you needed.'

315

'Who's behind them? The government? The CIA? Who are you working for?'

'For people who make sure that what needs to be done *is* done.'

'My God . . .!'

She almost laughed at the pathetic attempt at self-justification that lay behind his words. She felt a sudden irrational elation. This man couldn't be her father. It wasn't possible, there was some mistake. It was just another lie that would be exposed and discarded in the end.

'If I'd known it would go this far,' he protested feebly. 'If I'd even suspected . . .'

'What would you have done? Changed your convictions? Or just made even more sure that I never found out the truth?' She paused, feeling stronger every second, more secure with each successive breath she took. 'You should have let them kill me.'

But no, she thought as soon as the words were out of her mouth, that wasn't what she wanted. That way her father would have got his hands on Christopher, remade him in his own image – or tried to. It would never have worked, of course. She believed profoundly that her son would have remained her own and John's child, never her father's. But the experiment would have caused him a lot of pain and trouble, and that was something she would give a great deal to avoid. No, Amery Hyde would never get his hands on Christopher.

'You disgust me,' she said, and her voice, though unsteady, had an icy edge to it. She saw the dismay in his eyes as the words cut into him.

Then his gaze shifted and focused on something over her shoulder. She turned.

Mrs Hathaway stood in the doorway through which Christopher had disappeared with his dog only moments ago. There was no sign of the dog now, but Christopher was there, standing in front of her, with the woman's strong hands resting with proprietorial firmness on his shoulders. He was watching the strange drama unfolding between his mother and his grandfather. He couldn't hear what they were saying, but he was troubled by what he saw and what he sensed. Something was wrong, though he didn't know what.

But Mrs Hathaway knew. A thin smile of triumph played around her lips as she met Susan's gaze. It was as though she'd read the younger woman's mind, 'Never get our hands on him?' she seemed to say. 'But we already have. He's ours. So are you. And there's nothing you can do about it.'

'Go back to your room, Susan,' Amery Hyde said. His voice was tired and drained of emotion and sounded to her as though it came from far away. 'It's better if you stay there till this is over. It won't take long.'

52

'We'll be ready to leave as soon as you land.'

Amery Hyde's voice came loud and clear over the cellphone that Latimer West held so that both he and Charlie could hear what was being said. There was a film of sweat on West's upper lip. His whole body felt clammy with fear. The main reason was that Charlie's right hand rested with apparent casualness on the back of West's neck. But West knew the strength in those fingers. His spine could be broken in an instant, or the life choked silently out of him, or he could simply be rendered unconscious. Whatever Charlie chose to do, he could. And if West made one mistake, made even the slightest attempt to warn Amery Hyde of what was heading his way, then Charlie would do it.

'That's good,' West said, managing to keep his voice steady only because Charlie's eyes burned a warning into his. 'We'll be on the ground in just over five minutes.'

'Look out the window – you'll see us when you fly over,' Hyde said.

'Will do.'

West signed off and slipped the phone back into his inside pocket. Charlie looked out of the cabin window as the small jet tilted and prepared to head for the narrow landing strip that wasn't yet visible beyond the trees. His eyes flickered briefly to the pilot, whose back was just visible through the open cockpit door. The pilot, so far as Charlie knew, was unaware of what was going on, but he kept an eye on him just in case, and he would be specially watchful once they touched down.

He looked out of the window again. They were passing over the highway that Susan had shown him in the VR demonstration, losing height rapidly, the small plane see-sawing one way then the other, throttling up and then back. Suddenly, sprawling out to one side, he could see the main buildings of the ranch, their layout just as he'd memorized it. Looking forward over the pilot's shoulder, he could see the landing strip. Something was moving on the ground. As they got closer, he saw it was a station wagon driving from the main house to meet them. Just as Amery Hyde had promised, they were going to be ready for an immediate departure. That was good.

They made a perfect touchdown, landing with scarcely a bump. The twin jets roared into reverse thrust and the plane braked with a sharpness that would have been impossible in a larger craft. Charlie glanced at West, warning him to stay silent as the pilot manoeuvred the plane through a tight circle in readiness for take-off, as West had instructed him earlier.

'Keep the engines running – right?' he said over his shoulder.

Charlie glanced at West and nodded.

'Right,' West answered. 'Open the door, we're going to board passengers immediately.'

'Any idea where we're headed from here?' the pilot asked, levering himself out of his seat and automatically putting on the grey cap that matched his uniform. 'Just thinking about fuel.'

Another warning glance from Charlie.

'We'll tell you in the air,' West said. 'Just open the door.' Then, in response to the slightest further lift of Charlie's eyebrow, he added, 'You board the woman and child first, then Mr Hyde. Is that clear?'

'Got it.'

The pilot threw a catch and was about to turn a lever that would open the door when Charlie's command exploded at him. 'Stop!'

The man froze, and looked towards Charlie to see what was wrong. Then he followed Charlie's gaze out of the cabin windows, and saw all four doors of the station wagon fly open and four men with machine-guns pile out. On the other side of the plane three more, also armed, had emerged from bushes and a storage tank. The fifth man out of the station wagon was Amery Hyde, unarmed, the general in command of his troops.

'Get over here,' Charlie ordered the pilot. 'Move!' he pointed to one of the empty passenger seats.

The pilot looked uncertain. He glanced at Latimer West, whose eyes had glazed over with terror. He wasn't even aware of the pilot's questioning look. Instead he was pleading with Charlie. 'I didn't know,' he kept repeating. 'I didn't know . . . I didn't warn them, I don't know how they . . .'

'Shut up,' Charlie said, getting to his feet. West obeyed, falling silent except for his breathing, which was hard and ragged, like a man out of condition who'd been running.

'You,' Charlie said, pointing again to the pilot, 'over here.'

A gun, the pilot now saw, had appeared in Charlie's hand. It wasn't pointed anywhere in particular, all the same the pilot held up his hands and moved to where Charlie had ordered. 'Look,' he said, 'I don't know what's going on here, I just fly this thing . . .'

'Sit down and keep your hands where I can see them,' Charlie snapped. The pilot obeyed.

Through the window Charlie could see Amery Hyde taking out a cellphone and dialling a number. The phone in West's pocket buzzed. Charlie nodded for him to answer. West's hands were shaking so hard he could barely manage. 'Hello?' he said, after clearing his throat a couple of times.

'Give me Charlie,' Amery Hyde said. 'And don't worry, we'll get you out of there safely.' Charlie could hear Hyde's voice faintly from the phone, synchronized with the movement of his lips outside.

'For God's sake be careful,' West said, his voice cracking. 'Don't get me killed. Tell him! Tell him it wasn't me who warned you!'

'I don't give a damn who warned them,' Charlie said, and snatched the phone impatiently. 'All right, I'm listening.'

'And I imagine you're looking at me, too, Charlie. So you know who I am.'

'I know who you are now – Mr Hyde.'

'I'm still Control, Charlie. I'm still giving the orders.'

'Not to me. Not any more.'

'Charlie, you're good. You and I both know how good. But even you can't win this one.'

Everything Charlie had been trained to do in a situation like this flashed through his mind. The first thing was to take his time, stretch things out and begin scoring points to unnerve his enemy. Then he recalled it was Control who had taught him most of those tricks, so they would be wasted here. He cut to the chase. 'Where are Dr Flemyng and her son?'

'That's none of your affair.'

'I've got two hostages here. I want Dr Flemyng and her son on this plane now. You'll get your hostages back when I'm through with them.'

Amery turned and coolly nodded to one of his men. There was a burst of automatic gunfire, aimed low. The plane rocked, then hunkered down like some ungainly bird settling on its nest.

'We've shot your tyres out, Charlie,' Amery said. 'This plane's going nowhere. Nor are you. Just come out with your hands up, and we'll get this whole misunderstanding sorted out.'

53

The sun came out from behind a cloud and hit Amery Hyde full in the face. He narrowed his eyes, which meant he had even less chance of seeing any movement inside the cabin. The windows were just opaque black spaces.

He knew Charlie had a gun. Along with two hostages, that was quite a hand he had to play. All Charlie's conditioning would make him fight this out and if necessary die in the attempt. Charlie was not programmed to quit. If he did, it would be an interesting development.

'Okay, while we're sitting here, let's talk.' Charlie's voice on the phone was laconic. Amery waited a moment, then was about to respond when a piercing scream of such force came over the phone that he jumped – only slightly, but he knew that Charlie would have noticed. He was annoyed about that; it would make Charlie think he was getting the upper hand, which wasn't true.

The scream had come from Latimer West. Now Amery could hear him whimpering in the background as Charlie said, 'What d'you say, Amery? Shall we talk?'

He wondered what Charlie had done to Latimer West, but quickly brought his concentration back to his own problems. What Charlie might be capable of didn't bear thinking about. Amery needed to handle this very carefully. It was the first time Charlie had ever been less than deferential to him in any situation, which made this a whole new ball game – for both of them.

'My daughter and grandson are safe, Charlie,' he said into the phone. 'They don't need your help, though I thank you for your concern on their behalf. No harm's going to come to anybody, including you, if you'll just step out of there now nice and quietly. The worst that'll happen is you'll go into a spell of retraining.'

'Don't you mean reconditioning?'

'You've got things out of proportion, Charlie. Tell me, what is it you really want?'

'I want Dr Flemyng and her son. And I want that helicopter I can see over there. And a pilot.'

'You already have a pilot, Charlie.'

Amery heard a muffled consultation over the phone, but couldn't make out what was being said. Then Charlie's voice came back. 'He says he can't fly helicopters, so I'm going to need your man.'

Smiling patiently, Amery shook his head, as though indulging Charlie's little joke. 'Okay, Charlie, we have lots of time. We can wait here till you change your mind.'

The jet engines, which had so far kept up a low rumble of white noise in the background, suddenly dropped to a whine and died out. The timing suggested that Charlie too was willing to dig in for as long as it took. This worried Amery. He had every advantage and all the firepower, but he didn't like the idea of a long stand-off. Charlie could remain alert and dangerous far longer than any human being. Also, Amery's men were in the sun, which would grow tiring in time, and he had no replacements for them.

'Just so you know I'm serious,' Charlie's voice came over the phone, sounding relaxed now, as though he had his feet up, 'I'm going to open this door – or, more exactly, have it opened, so hold your fire.'

Latimer West's panicky voice came over the phone. 'Don't shoot! He's making me open the door. Please don't shoot!'

Amery didn't say anything, just glanced around at his men to make sure they were ready for anything, though he was unsure if any of them could be ready for moves at the speed Charlie could make them.

The door swung out and back against the fuselage. Then a little staircase of metal steps unfolded automatically to the ground. Amery saw no more than the fingers of a pair of hands around the door frame, then they disappeared back into the darkness and there was no further movement. Amery realized he had been holding his breath when Charlie's voice came over the phone again.

'Now I'm sending you a message – like I say, just so you know I'm serious.'

There was a movement in the darkness, and the figure of the pilot, still wearing his uniform and cap, backed into the open door. He seemed to be holding out his hands, half in surrender, half in some futile effort to ward off whatever Charlie was threatening to do to him.

'I'm sending the message out with this guy,' Charlie's voice said over the phone. 'I want you to pay real good attention to it. Are you ready?'

A single shot rang out in the plane's interior. The pilot doubled over as though he'd been punched in the stomach. The force of the impact lifted him off his feet and threw him backwards into space. He landed face down in a lifeless heap several feet from the plane's steps. He looked dead, but it was hard to be sure. All the same,

Amery held up a warning hand to keep his men back and out of Charlie's line of fire. He waited a while before lifting the phone to his lips again, and spoke in tones of regret more than anger.

'You didn't have to do that, Charlie. It's done you no good. But I'm still giving you a chance to come out with your hands up.'

There was no reply at first, then another scream from Latimer West, oddly muffled this time, as though something – Charlie's hand perhaps – was over his mouth. The noise went on, and Amery could see it was beginning to affect his men, as Charlie no doubt meant it to. They were exchanging looks uneasily with one another, losing concentration.

'All right, Charlie, if that's how you want it,' Amery said into the phone, but loud enough for the men around him to hear, 'I'm sorry it had to end this way.'

He nodded to the man on his right, Michael, who recognized his cue and opened fire. The others joined in, raking both sides of the fuselage with a hail of bullets, ripping and tearing the gleaming shell of the plane with round after round of burning lead, making the plane jiggle and bounce in an almost comic parody of airborne turbulence.

Amery Hyde stepped back a little to observe his handiwork. The noise of gunfire was deafening but, as it continued, it took on a hypnotic quality that was almost soothing. It signified, to Amery Hyde, a problem solved. Charlie Monk had served his purpose but was now unmanageable. He had refused every chance to surrender in a reasonable way: that was something to which every man here would testify – assuming that anyone ever questioned Amery's decision, which was unlikely. The only grounds on which he might be criticized would be the deliberate sacrificing of Latimer West in this inferno of gunfire. However, it would quickly become clear that the danger posed by Charlie on the loose far outweighed West's future usefulness. He had done good work in the past, but no one was indispensable. All that mattered was the cause. That was what Hyde had to keep on telling himself. Even the loss of his daughter's love had to be set against the cause. He would have to live with that loss, just as he had always been prepared to live with the consequences of his decisions.

His mind must have wandered for a moment, dulled by the brain-numbing rattle of gunfire. It had gone on long enough, he decided. It must be over by now. But it was only as he raised his hand to signal ceasefire that he registered fully and consciously what was happening. Michael was down, not moving. A second man was writhing on the ground, his screams of agony thinly audible through the gunfire. And, as Amery watched, a third was hit by a bullet that turned his face into a crater of blood.

Amery's eyes darted this way and that, searching for an explanation. This couldn't be right. How was this possible? It was a mistake.

Then he saw him – the pilot, on his feet, firing a handgun and moving with a speed that defied the eye to follow him. But Amery didn't need to follow him to know that this was Charlie, and to understand the trick that he had played on them all. Amery watched, cursing himself helplessly for having underestimated this creature that he himself had, at least in part, created. He watched as Charlie, in lethally graceful movements, drop-kicked a fourth man, seized his weapon, and mowed down the remaining three in one swift burst of fire while simultaneously diving and rolling so fast that he was no more than a blur of motion.

A silence fell so abruptly that it felt unreal. The first thing that struck Amery was the sour smell of cordite that hung in the air. His men were all dead, not even a moan or a whimper from any of them now. The only sound at all was the sound of Charlie coming towards him, his soft footfalls on the earth as he came around the tail of the shattered plane, a metallic clink from the automatic weapon that hung loosely from his hand. There were stains on his clothes from the earth where he'd rolled and from other men's blood, but none of his own.

Charlie didn't take his eyes off Amery as he strolled almost casually to the door of the airplane. Only then did he turn his head to glance inside.

Latimer West, or what remained of him, was slumped in the seat where Charlie had tied and gagged him. The pilot, shivering in his underwear from fear more than cold, was crouched in the cockpit where Charlie had told him to stay. He seemed unhurt, which pleased Charlie. 'It's all right,' he said, 'the shooting's over. You can come out.'

Then he turned back to Amery Hyde, who hadn't moved, and who still didn't move as Charlie walked towards him. Amery knew that all that remained of his life now was its end. He didn't fear death; he never had. All he had ever feared was the domination of evil, and he did not think of Charlie as evil. Charlie was a tool of good who had spun out of control. Well, it would be up to someone else to solve that problem now. The man who had been Control faced Charlie squarely, his gaze level, his breathing steady.

Charlie stopped and contemplated the older man for some moments, then spoke as though understanding what was going through Amery's mind.

'I'm not going to kill you, Amery,' he said. 'You're not dangerous. Not any more. Not to anyone.'

Amery flushed. He felt a stab of indignation that took him off guard. He cleared his throat. 'All right, Charlie, what do you want?'

'I want what I came for. Where are they?'

Amery began to nod his head slowly, acknowledging some kind of understanding between himself and Charlie, a deal from which they could both emerge with dignity and decency intact. 'All right, Charlie, you win. Get my daughter and my grandson out of here, and do what you have to. Because that's what I did. What I had to. I tried to do my duty.'

As he finished speaking he bent down and reached for something on the ground. It was the pistol that Charlie had taken from one of the guards at Irvine, and which he had flung aside as he seized the heavier weapon he now held.

'Hey—!'

This time it was Charlie who was taken by surprise, unprepared for the calm defiance of the other man's action. Control, still stooping and with his hand on the pistol, looked up at Charlie. There was the hint of a smile on his face. He knew he had the advantage now and was enjoying it.

'What, Charlie? You think I'm going to try and shoot it out with you? Don't be absurd. There's nothing further from my mind.'

He straightened up unhurriedly, moving in his own time, back in control. He hefted the pistol in his hand. 'Still a couple of shots in it, I see. That's good.'

'Put that gun down!'

Charlie's body had tensed and his hand tightened on the trigger of the machine-gun.

Amery smiled openly, on the point almost of laughter. 'Oh, really, Charlie. And what are you going to do if I disobey? Shoot me?'

Slowly and deliberately he raised the pistol to his temple and held it there.

Charlie watched with a strange fascination. He knew he could have acted. He could have shot him in the leg, disarmed him in a dozen different ways if he'd really wanted to. The strange thing was he didn't want to. Not because he wanted Amery dead. The real reason was that, in some curious way that he didn't fully understand, he didn't feel he had the right. And Amery knew it.

'Tell my daughter I love her. I always have, and always will.'

He pulled the trigger.

54

Charlie gazed down at the body. He didn't have to check: there was no question that Amery Hyde was dead. He wondered what he would tell Susan. The truth, of course. But would she believe him?

Time enough to worry about that later. Before that he had to finish what he'd come here to do, what he'd promised her he would do.

He listened. There was no sound anywhere. If there was anybody up at the house, they would have heard the shooting. He couldn't believe there was nobody left. There must be somebody.

Quickly he collected a couple of machine-guns and some clips of ammo. He threw them in the station wagon, then drove it towards the house at speed. When he got close he spun the wheel and skirted around it, tyres squealing.

A shot rang out. It was what he'd been waiting for, what he'd put on this show for – to draw their fire, find out how many of them there were. It looked like there was only one, which was even better than he'd hoped.

He fixed in his mind an image of the house's interior, as shown to him by Susan on their VR tour of the place. He knew where the shots so far had come from. As he swung around a corner and started along the south side, the next shot came from where he had anticipated it. He could visualize the landing and the short flight of stairs that connected the two windows. Now he knew what to do. He swung around another corner, then hit the brakes and pulled into a small yard enclosed on three sides by different parts of the sprawling property. He tried the door he knew would be there. It was open, as Susan had said it usually was. He took both guns with him, one slung over his shoulder, the other in his hands. Both had been reloaded, and he had more ammunition in his pockets.

When the lone gunman, a huge young man with a weightlifter's body, came down the stairs in his singlet and jeans, barefoot and silent as a cat, Charlie was in a corner watching him. He was big all right, and strong as two ordinary men. The weapon in his hands looked like a toy against the size of his arms and the swell of his shoulders.

'Drop it,' Charlie said.

The young man froze. He didn't know where the voice had come from.

'I said drop it.'

The young man turned, and saw Charlie. He saw too that Charlie's gun was trained on him, and his own on nothing at all. So he let it drop obediently and raised his hands.

Charlie walked over to him, kicking the abandoned gun across the floor. He was shorter than the young man, so he had to look up to him when he spoke.

'Where are Dr Flemyng and the boy?' he demanded.

There was the hint of a smirk on the young man's face as he shook his head. Maybe Charlie had the gun, he told himself, but he was no match physically. He was also standing too close for his own safety. Any moment now, if the young man could just keep on lowering his hands imperceptibly, he would—

The next thing he knew was the impact of his own body hitting the floor. Then he realized what had happened. He had received a hammer blow to his stomach more powerful than any he had ever known. The massive armour-plate of muscle that he had spent countless hours in the gym developing had given way like a slab of butter, knocking every last ounce of breath out of his body.

Still using only one hand, Charlie pulled him roughly into a sitting position. He placed his fingers on the back of the young man's neck, and stretched his thumb around and placed it under his chin. He wasn't exerting any pressure, but the young man could feel the tensile strength in those fingers and knew that his spine could be snapped any second.

'I know you can't speak just now,' Charlie said, 'so just nod your head in agreement. You'll take me to where they are, won't you?'

The young man managed to nod.

Two minutes later they were standing outside a heavy wooden door that the young man said led down to the cellar. 'She's locked it from the inside,' he said, still short of breath. 'She's got them with her.'

'Break it open,' he said.

'But she's got a gun.'

'Then you'd better ask her not to use it, hadn't you?'

The young man was breaking out in a sweat now. This was more complicated than anything he'd signed on for. He rapped on the door with a knuckle, like a nervous fan at the star's dressing room. 'Mrs Hathaway?' he called out. 'Mrs Hathaway, this is Rod. I have to come down

333

there, Mrs Hathaway. I have to open this door. Don't shoot, please.'

He waited for an answer, but there was none. Charlie gestured for him to go ahead. The young man opened his mouth to protest, but no sound emerged. If ever he'd known how it felt to be caught between a rock and a hard place, this was it. On the whole, he decided he'd rather face Mrs Hathaway and a gun than Charlie. He shouldered the door open. It didn't offer much resistance, and there was no immediate blast of gunfire.

The young man breathed again, then, pushed firmly on by Charlie, started down the wooden steps into the dark basement. Charlie stayed right behind him, awaiting his moment to hit a light switch that he'd seen on the wall. When he did, he gave the young man a shove in the back that sent him hurtling down the last few steps to the cellar floor. If anybody had been there with a gun trained up towards the intruders, they would undoubtedly have shot the young man. But nobody was there.

'Okay, Rod, on your feet, you'll live,' Charlie ordered in a low whisper. Then added, 'So where is she?'

The answer came from an unexpected quarter. A dog barked – twice, before being muzzled with a shrill whine of protest. Charlie found himself looking at a second door, open just a crack. He lifted an interrogatory eyebrow in the young man's direction.

'Wine cellar,' he explained.

Charlie gestured for him to move forward. 'Get in there, put on the light,' he said.

Again the young man's faced creased with silent protest, but again he obeyed.

'Mrs Hathaway, it's me, Rod. If you're in there, please

don't shoot. I'm going to push open the door and switch on the light.'

Moving slowly, every muscle in his over-developed body so tense that he could barely move at all, he pushed the door back. It creaked on its hinges, but nothing happened. Then he reached around the wall. A single overhead bulb went on.

'I'm not going to shoot you, Rod,' Mrs Hathaway said. 'Everything's under control.'

Charlie moved into the open door and took the scene in. Mrs Hathaway stood with one hand over the terrified Christopher's mouth, while the other held a gun to his head. Susan stood nearby, distraught and holding the equally terrified dog, trying to keep him quiet.

Behind him, Charlie heard a stumbling clatter of feet. A couple of packing cases and a bucket went over noisily. The young man, Rod, was making a desperate dash for the stairs and safety. Charlie could have easily picked him off, but he didn't want to. He didn't think Rod was going to present any danger to him. The kid was out of his depth. They weren't paying him enough for this. Worst of all, they hadn't trained him for it.

He turned back to Mrs Hathaway. This one was tougher. She was intelligent, more involved in what was going on here, more dedicated. Charlie could see she didn't frighten easily. He was going to have to make this good.

'Look, lady,' he began, fixing her with an unblinking gaze, keeping his voice low but with an edge of barely contained menace, 'I'm three steps away from you, which means you might just get the chance to pull that trigger once. But you won't get to pull it twice. Now I don't know how much they've told you about me, but if you know anything at all, then you'll know how much you're going to regret not getting a chance to put that second bullet through your brain.'

He paused, letting his words hang in the air a while. Nobody, not even the dog, drew breath for several moments. He didn't take his eyes off Mrs Hathaway. She blinked, and there was a barely perceptible tremor at the corner of her mouth. That was good. She was scared and unable to hide it. He pressed home his advantage.

'Let the boy go, now.'

Mrs Hathaway felt a cold shiver of fear run down her spine. She hoped Charlie hadn't noticed, but felt sure he must have. There was something about his eyes that saw everything, as though his gaze penetrated to the back of her skull and scooped out her thoughts. She blinked involuntarily, trying to wipe away the ugly feeling that her mind was being somehow violated, but the gesture didn't help. She became aware, too, of a change in the way he held himself. He hadn't visibly moved since entering the room, but now she could see that every fibre in his body was ready to close the distance between them in a flash and carry out the hideous threat he'd made.

It was too much for her. Too much for anyone. Slowly she lowered the gun, and dropped it to the floor. Charlie stepped over, picked it up and slipped it into his pocket.

Christopher was already clinging to his mother, sobbing and trying to understand why 'Auntie May' had wanted to kill him. The dog ran whimpering around their feet.

Charlie looked around. Mrs Hathaway followed his every move, fearful of what was yet to come. She knew he was deciding what to do with her. She saw him start to usher Susan and Christopher out of the room, and felt suddenly afraid that he was going to come back and do something to her. But she heard Susan say, 'Don't hurt her, Charlie. She's been good to Christopher till now. Let's just get out of here.'

He came back, but only for a second. There was a key on the inside of the wine cellar door. He took it, gave her one last warning glance, then locked her in.

Christopher was still drying his eyes as they climbed the cellar steps. Susan put the dog in his arms, which seemed to comfort him. 'Hold on to him,' she said, 'we don't want him disappearing now.'

Charlie went first, making sure there was no trap, no sign of Rod or anyone else. But the house seemed deserted. He led the way to where he'd left the station wagon.

'My father . . .?' Susan asked as they walked.

'I'm sorry,' Charlie said. He was about to try to explain when she touched his arm and said, 'No, tell me later.'

Christopher was with them, and, whatever the details were, she didn't want him to hear them just now. The child had been through more than enough for one day.

55

They reached the station wagon, got in and drove off without incident. Only as the house was shrinking in the rear-view mirror did Charlie notice a movement that made him frown. It was the young man, Rod, sprinting from his hiding place in some outbuilding and heading for the main house. Charlie thought he would have been a mile away by now, running for his life.

Susan saw Charlie's expression. 'Something wrong?' she asked.

'Looks like muscle boy's going to free the woman,' he said.

She looked back just in time to see Rod go in the door they'd just come out of.

'Can they do anything?' she asked.

'Come after us, I guess,' he said, though he didn't seem concerned at the prospect – at least not until they'd travelled another mile or so. Then Susan saw his face darken again as he spotted something else in the rear-view mirror. 'Damn,' he said, barely audibly.

'What?'

Her question didn't need an answer. When she turned to look back, she saw the helicopter at once. It had risen just a few yards in the air, but was already tilting to come after them.

'I should have made sure,' he said grimly.

Susan wondered what he meant by making sure. Killing Mrs Hathaway, or the young man, or both? Or simply crippling the helicopter? Whichever, this wasn't the time to ask him.

'Christopher,' Charlie said, 'are you strapped in back there?'

'Sure.'

'Hold on to Buzz.'

He swung the wheel, taking the vehicle off the smooth surface and onto bumpy, dry ground. Susan found herself grabbing the dash to stop being uncomfortably shaken about. 'Where are we going?' she asked.

'Those trees,' he said.

She looked ahead. The nearest trees were about two hundred yards away. When she looked back at the helicopter she saw it was gaining on them fast. 'D'you suppose it's armed?' she asked.

The answer came in a burst of automatic gunfire that sent up little puffs of earth only a yard to the right of where she sat in the speeding vehicle.

They were still far from the trees when the chopper overtook them, swinging to the right and preparing to turn. As it passed, they saw the muscle-bound figure of young Rod hanging out of one side, gun blazing, living his fantasy of movie heroism.

Again the shots almost but didn't quite connect. They would have to get closer. Charlie watched the chopper arc around to do just that. He could see the woman at the controls. She flew well. He was impressed, and he cursed himself again for having let this happen.

'It's Auntie May!' Christopher shouted, not from excitement but alarm. He had trusted this woman, which made the fact that she was now trying to kill him all the more terrifying. He screamed as the helicopter's clatter became deafening overhead, as though it was going to crush them physically. Another spray of automatic fire exploded around them. This time at least one bullet hit the vehicle; they heard a dull thud somewhere in the bodywork, though it was impossible to say exactly where. Charlie held his breath, but there were no immediate consequences, not even a warning light on the dash.

He spun the wheel again, fish-tailing this way and that, making the vehicle as tough a target as possible. The woman flying that thing was good, but muscle boy was undisciplined and poorly trained. He missed totally on the next pass. Charlie had a glimpse of them as they came in low then banked away, screaming accusations at each other. Not exactly a dream team. All the same, he knew they'd get lucky in time. She was a good enough flyer to lock on to their vehicle just long enough for muscle boy to pump lead through the roof and get them all. Even he couldn't miss if all he had to do was shoot straight down and look out for his foot.

The chopper made another pass, there was another burst of gunfire, but no damage. Charlie was relieved to reach the trees before they could attack again. The trees were pretty sparse at first, but the important thing was they kept the helicopter high. Muscle boy kept shooting, but his shots went wide. After that, the chopper pulled up higher and raced ahead. Charlie wondered what this meant, and decided there must be another open space coming up, and the woman was planning to ambush them.

He slalomed left and right between the trees, but he

could tell from the movements of the chopper that the gap ahead was big and probably unavoidable. He tried to remember what he'd seen when he flew in, but couldn't recall enough detail.

Suddenly, as he'd feared, they were out in the open again. The chopper was ready for them, hovering low and to one side. It came at them at an angle, muscle boy giving it all the firepower he had. Several bullets hit the vehicle. A couple of times the dull thuds were sickeningly heavy and sounded more serious than before. A red warning light started blinking on the dash, then another. Charlie didn't have time to read what they were telling him before the window next to him shattered.

Susan spun around to check that Christopher was unhurt. He was all right, but wide-eyed with a shock that went beyond fear and probably insulated him from the worst of what was happening. The dog, still clasped in his arms, was emitting a series of long, mournful howls, as though calling to its lupine ancestors for help.

'Look out, Charlie—!'

Susan had turned forward just in time to see the perimeter fence of the ranch looming up at them. It looked like it was made of wood, horizontal slats with steel wire between, maybe electrified or just to reinforce. Every few yards there was a concrete upright. Charlie was aiming for the middle point between two of them.

'Get down!' he shouted.

'Oh, my God! Chris, get down—!'

She didn't think this was going to work. She *knew* it wasn't. These things couldn't happen like they did in movies, where people casually smashed their cars through gates and barriers of all kinds, splintering them like the matchwood they were in fact made of. It *couldn't* be the same in real life. They were going to die in a mangled pile of blazing wreckage any second.

Time froze as the front fender of the vehicle made contact with the fence. Froze, but didn't slow down. The next thing that happened was something smashed her in the face and the world disappeared.

But the sound of the impact didn't disappear. Or the roar of the engine. Or the clatter of the chopper overhead. Or the sense that they were still moving. It took her a moment to realize that her air bag had inflated. She looked over and saw that Charlie's had too, but he was already tearing his out of the way.

'You okay?'

'Yes,' she managed to say, trying to wriggle free of the thing in front of her. 'Chris?'

'Yeah, I'm okay. That was neat!'

She turned to look at him. A transformation had come over the child. Instead of being catatonic with fear, he was now smiling as though they were at the funfair. The dog seemed to have taken comfort from this change of mood and become silent.

Susan figured that the same thought had gone through Christopher's head as hers when they hit the fence – that it was just like the movies. But in his case the idea had reassured him. He knew where he was now – in a movie, it was all beginning to make sense. Susan said nothing. Whatever worked.

'Better cover here,' Charlie said. 'They can hardly see us now. I think I know where we'll come out if we carry straight on – there's a track down the mountain to the highway. The trouble is we'll be out in the open again.'

He paused a moment, thinking, then said, 'Can you drive this thing?'

'Sure.'

He found the densest cover he could, then stopped the vehicle but didn't cut the engine. He tore the remains of Susan's air bag out of the way, then got out while she slid across behind the wheel. He, meanwhile, went around to the back, opened it up and climbed in. He picked up one of the machine-guns he'd stashed there, checked its magazine was full, and told Susan to drive on. 'Keep straight ahead. When we're close to coming out of the trees, slow down while I figure out our next move.'

'Okay.'

She drove less fast than Charlie, but the passage was just as bumpy. Christopher swivelled in his safety harness to see what was happening behind him. Charlie was trying to arrange himself in the back, constantly ducking to the window and looking up to where he could see the chopper intermittently visible in patches of sky between the tree tops, weaving this way and that, searching for them.

'We're coming out from cover,' Susan called over her shoulder.

'Okay, slow down,' Charlie said. He was lying on his back now, feet wedged behind the rear seat and interior sides of the vehicle, the upper part of his body extending out the back with his gun ready to fire into the sky. 'Slow right down,' he said, 'but be ready to go when I say.'

'I'm ready.'

He could see the helicopter still circling above the trees and waited until it was as far away as it was likely to get from the point where they would emerge.

'Now – go!' he said. 'Fast!'

Susan floored the accelerator. They shot out into the sunlight and on to a dry, rocky track. The wheels threw up clouds of dust, blinding Charlie, which was something he hadn't bargained for. He could hear the helicopter, the note of its motor changing as it spotted them and turned, but he couldn't see it. Furiously he wiped his eyes with one hand. He could see something now. The plume of dust was thinning out a little and the chopper was gaining on them fast, coming in low. Muscle boy started shooting.

'Charlie? Are you all right?' Susan shouted.

'Yes. Keep going, don't slow down.'

Charlie fired back as best he could, still half blinded, lying horizontal and firing both up and backwards. His first shots went wild, but then a long burst connected with the bulbous perspex nose of the chopper. It was bullet proof, of course, but nothing would resist that kind of attack indefinitely. The woman at the controls pulled sharply back and up to get out of his range. He fired off a couple more rounds. He knew he'd hit the chopper more than once, but he didn't seem to have done any damage. He watched as it swung out to one side, keeping pace with them, deciding on its next move.

The track they were going down was growing steeper. On one side was a wall of rock, on the other a sheer drop that seemed paradoxically to be getting deeper the further down they travelled. Charlie knew he didn't have much time. If Susan made one mistake, or if the vehicle lost a tyre, they would all be killed. They still had miles to go before they could reach help. If they died now the only witnesses to their fate would be their murderers.

There was something in the way the helicopter shifted and adjusted its position in the sky that made him think of a cat bunching up in readiness to attack. In truth, this was a cat and mouse game they were playing now. The chopper came in from an angle that was hard for him to hit, muscle boy blazing away. Charlie sensed as much as heard the slam of more bullets hitting the vehicle. He lifted his head to check that Susan and Christopher were unhurt. They seemed to be all right. Then he waited for what he knew would be his one chance to get the chopper as it pulled up and back to avoid the rock face behind them. At precisely the right moment he got a long burst at the chopper's tail. He knew he'd hit it, but again there was no sign of real damage.

Susan was screaming something but he couldn't make out the words. 'Keep going,' he yelled back. 'Just keep going!'

The chopper was preparing to attack again, head on this time. That was bad. From that angle he had even less chance of hitting it. He cursed the fact that he hadn't anticipated being blinded by dust in those vital first few seconds. That was when he'd lost the only real advantage he was going to get. Now it was almost too late.

But it wasn't over yet, and he wasn't about to quit. He shifted and stretched his lower back, which was being painfully jolted by the bouncing vehicle, and braced himself for the next attack.

He saw the chopper start to move in. Muscle boy was hanging out ready to start shooting, and even at this distance Charlie could see his lips part and his white teeth flash in a grin of triumph, sure that he'd get them this time. But the next thing that happened wiped that grin off his face faster than Charlie could have done if they'd been in the same room.

Without warning, and for no apparent reason, the

helicopter began yawing wildly from side to side. Charlie saw muscle boy nearly lose his grip and fall, then he started screaming furiously at the woman, who was screaming back.

The yawing got wilder, then turned into a spin. Charlie knew what had happened. He'd got the tail, as he'd thought – maybe hit the rotor, or one of its controls. At any rate, it was out of control now. There was a strange and morbid fascination in watching the machine waltz slowly in the air, then faster, spinning with a fatal elegance, until suddenly it ceased to be a flying machine and fell like a stone.

From somewhere below and behind them now came the sound of an explosion, followed by a billowing fireball of smoke and flame. Charlie exhaled a sigh of relief, and levered himself upright. 'Okay, you can slow down. It's over,' he called forwards to Susan.

They were travelling faster than ever, and he could see her hunched forward, gripping the wheel, wrestling it this way and that.

'I can't,' she screamed back. 'They've shot the brakes! That's what I was trying to tell you.'

Somehow she was holding the vehicle on the road, but any moment an unexpected bump or a sharper than anticipated corner would fling them out by sheer centrifugal force into the abyss.

'Hold on, I'm coming!'

Charlie, scrambled over the back seat, over Christopher and the dog, grasped Susan's shoulder and pushed her to one side. His hand was on the wheel before hers left it, and almost before she was out of the way he was in the driver's seat with his feet on the pedals. It was as she'd said: there was no pressure in the brakes, and the handbrake was equally useless. They were in free fall, and still gathering speed. At least the steering worked. It was all he had.

'All right.' He kept shouting over the screaming motor and the crash of the suspension as the vehicle leapt into the air and hit the stony track again, 'it's all right . . . I've got it . . . I've got it . . .'

EPILOGUE

Charlie felt a pleasant drowsiness. It was what they had told him to expect. He had been reassured more times than he could remember that there was nothing to worry about. He did not understand the details, but the doctors had explained, with the help of X-rays and a lot of impenetrable jargon, that although it was a simple surgical procedure, a general anaesthetic would be necessary because of where the tiny implant was located in his chest.

'It doesn't *have* to be removed,' he'd been told. 'You can live with it. It won't do you any harm. It's completely inactive now.'

All the same, he preferred to be rid of it – just in case. He didn't want any repetition of those sudden blackouts ever again, and as long as that thing was in him he felt there must still be a risk, however slight. And anyway, as Susan had reminded him, the congressional committee looking into the whole affair needed to have the implant as evidence.

Where was Susan? She should be there by now. She knew he was nervous about the anaesthetic; the threat of loss of consciousness for whatever reason still troubled him, and probably always would. So she had arranged to be present throughout the operation, not performing the surgery but as a medically qualified observer. The thought that she would be with him greatly reassured Charlie.

Suddenly he saw her hurrying down the corridor towards him, already in green surgical gown and cap. She pushed her mask down to her chin and bent over him on the gurney where he lay. 'I thought you'd forgotten,' he said weakly, with a smile on his face that he knew must look pretty silly because of the way his head was going pleasantly around and around after that last injection.

'Of course I didn't forget,' she said, taking his hand in hers. 'I was on the phone with your lawyer. He says it's not official yet, but you're definitely going to get a presidential pardon for any criminal acts you may have committed. I thought you'd like to know that before you went in.'

'That's great,' he said, and saw her face light up with pleasure at the relief her news had brought him.

The gurney began to move. She walked alongside, still holding his hand as they turned sharply and went in through the doors of the operating theatre. She let go of him now and pulled up her mask so that it covered her face, like all the other faces around him. He could only tell who was who from the eyes. His surgeon – he recognized him. The anaesthetist, a pleasant woman he'd met once. The nurse . . . yes that was the nurse he remembered . . .

And there was Susan, her eyes on him, full of reassurance and encouragement . . . it was going to be all right . . . everything was going to be fine . . .

He was about to open his mouth when he felt another little jab in his arm. Whatever he'd wanted to say vanished from his mind as he fell almost at once into a deep, luxurious oblivion . . .

*

He awoke with no sense of time having passed. Of course it must have: at least several hours. He was alone now, staring at a white ceiling. Looking to his right and left he saw white walls, the lower halves of which were made of tiles, also white and slightly old-fashioned looking. There didn't seem to be any windows.

It was a good-sized room, plenty of space on both sides of his bed and between its foot and the far wall. But it was entirely bare. There wasn't a stick of furniture apart from the bed itself, but if he turned his head as far to the left as it would go he could see a white washbasin fixed to the wall with a mirror above it. Whether there was anything behind his bed, or even anybody, he couldn't see at all. He would need to sit up for that.

He tried, but found it strangely difficult. It wasn't pain or stiffness, it was just that his movements were somehow restricted. He tried to figure out what was wrong. He could move his legs a little, but the problem was his arms. In fact his whole upper body felt paralysed.

Had something gone terribly wrong? Why was nobody there to tell him what had happened? Where was Susan?

He experienced a moment's panic. How could he be paralysed? He felt as though his arms *should* move; they just didn't. He began to struggle, and only then did he realize that he was strapped into something that restrained his movements.

Why had they done that? Nobody had warned him that this would be necessary. Just a small incision, they said. Fairly deep, but it would leave only the tiniest scar. Nothing about having to be bandaged up like a mummy.

He had to fight to sit up. It was hard without the use of his arms, though his stomach muscles were in good shape, iron-hard. At least, they used to be. They felt a little soft now. Which was strange. How could they degenerate so quickly. They were fine yesterday. He'd worked out in the gym as usual.

It *was* yesterday, wasn't it? Or at most the day before. Before the operation.

How long could he have been here?

The pain of sitting up was agonizing, but he made it through sheer determination. He had to pause to get his breath back. He could feel his face red and hot, suffused with blood from the effort.

That wasn't like him. He never felt like this. What had they done to him?

Something moved to his left. He turned, and realized that his head was now level with the mirror above the small sink. He could see his reflection.

Except it wasn't him. He was looking at another man. Middle-aged, grey-haired, with staring, frightened eyes, slack-mouthed. He'd never seen this man before.

It wasn't a mirror. It couldn't be. It had to be some kind of trick.

He moved to the right. The reflection moved. He moved left. The reflection did the same.

How? Why?

He looked down at himself and saw he wasn't bandaged at all. He was strapped into a straitjacket, white like the rest of the room, his arms bound tight across his chest and the sleeves secured behind his back.

What in hell . . .?

There was a sound. He turned. A door had opened in the far wall. He hadn't noticed it before; there was no handle on the inside. But now – thank God, at last – Susan came in. She wore a long white coat and had a serious expression. She looked like a doctor. A silly thought, of course: she *was* a doctor.

'Hello, Brian,' she said, stopping just short of his bed. 'How are you feeling now?'

It took a moment for his brain to register what she'd said, and then to form the question.

'Brian? Did you call me Brian?'

'It's your name. You're Brian Kay.'

He stared at her, his brain too paralysed by shock to function. 'Susan, what have you . . . what have they . . .?'

His eyes returned to the mirror on the wall, to the reflection of that unknown, frightened man. He could see the image of Susan standing behind him. There was nothing wrong with *her* reflection. She was herself.

'Susan, what's happened to me? Why do I look like that . . .?'

Her reflection took a step closer to his in the mirror, then laid a hand on his shoulder. He felt its gentle pressure, reassuring, kind but strangely impersonal. There was no intimacy in the touch. It wasn't Susan's touch.

'It's all right, Brian,' she said. 'Try to stay calm.'

'Why do you keep calling me that?'

'Listen to me. You've been ill, Brian, but you're better now. However, the virus has affected your memory . . .'

He turned his head sharply to look up at her – at Susan, not her reflection.

'I'm Charlie Monk! I'm not . . . I'm not this man! Why do I look like . . .?'

'It's you. You're Brian Kay. We've partly cured your memory, but now you're suffering from some side effects that we hadn't anticipated. But don't worry, we'll take care of them in time.'

'Side effects? What side effects? I don't know what you . . .'

'Just listen to me, please. Try to trust me. These side effects of your treatment take the form of various fantasies, sometimes quite complex ones. They only last a split second in real time, but to you they seem to go on for hours, days, even months sometimes. You've just had one, actually quite a bad one. That's why you've had to be restrained. But you're all right now, back where you belong. The memory will fade in a few minutes, even though it still seems so real now.'

She paused a moment, then sat on the edge of his bed, bringing her eyes level with his.

'The most important thing, Brian, is that the memory we were trying to give you, and which we've now successfully implanted in your brain, has proved resistant to either fading or variation. And to show you how true that is, your wife's here to see you . . .'

She turned back towards the door. He followed her gaze. A woman had entered – middle-aged, with an anxious, care-worn face that must have been quite pretty once. He had no idea who she was or what she was doing there.

And yet, somehow – what was happening to him? – somehow he felt he should know who she was. Why was that? A name began playing on the tip of his tongue. *Her* name. What was it?

Then he remembered. It burst from him spontaneously.

'Dorothy!'

'What did you say, darling?'

He opened his eyes. He was breathing hard, perspiring. Then he heard her voice again, distantly.

'Darling? Are you all right?'

A shaft of electric light fell across the carpet from the bathroom where she was. The sky outside was almost dark. Was it dusk or dawn? A window was half-open and a curtain rippled in a light breeze.

'Charlie?'

'I'm fine.'

'You sounded strange.'

'I must have fallen asleep. What time is it?'

'Almost seven. You'd better get ready, we have to leave in half an hour.'

Of course – they were going to dinner with those people who wanted to make a film of his life. To that fashionable new restaurant in Tribeca. They'd been in New York for a week – he could hear the traffic now, far below – doing press and TV interviews about the book they'd written together. It had gone straight to number one, and looked set to stay there for some time.

He pushed himself up on his elbow, savouring the relief at being himself again, the nightmare over. The sheets were soft and clean against his skin. He wanted to enjoy the feeling a few moments more, remembering how he and Susan had come in around five after taping a TV show. They had made love and then fallen asleep in each other's arms. It had been perfect.

There was a long mirror on the wall. He rolled over to see himself in it. His reflection stared back at him, reassuringly familiar in every detail, right down to the tiny scar on his chest, which was the only sign that remained of the operation he'd had six months earlier to remove the implant.

Life had been good since then, better than he'd ever dreamed it could be. He thought back to how Susan had got to the hospital only moments before he lost consciousness, just in time to tell him about the presidential pardon.

But the best moment of all had been when he woke up after the operation to find Susan sitting by his bed. She was holding his hand, and as soon as he'd opened his eyes he'd told her that he loved her. He probably wouldn't have had the nerve except for the strange and agreeable feeling, left over no doubt from the anaesthetic, that everything was possible – even that she was telling the truth when she said she felt the same way about him. They'd kissed right there in his hospital room for the first time. After that she'd picked up the phone and, throwing him a mischievous glance, had told someone on the other end that he wasn't to be disturbed till further notice. Then they'd lain in each other's arms for what seemed like an eternity and yet somehow no time at all. They'd been together ever since, Susan, Charlie, Christopher and Buzz. And the baby they would eventually have if the tests said it was all right.

'Charlie – you're not even out of bed yet.'

She came from the bathroom wearing only a light robe and with her hair swept back the way she sometimes wore it in the evenings now. Sitting on the edge of the bed, she took his face in her hands and prepared to scold him gently.

'What's the matter, darling?' she said. 'Are you so rich and famous now you think you can show up as late as you like?'

'I'll be ready in five minutes. I just fell asleep and had that dream again.'

'What dream?'

'You know – where I think I'm Brian Kay. I'm in this hospital room, and you're my doctor, then this woman

356

comes in who's supposed to be my wife though I've never seen her before, and suddenly I say, "Dorothy!" '

A puzzled frown gathered on Susan's face. 'You've never told me about that dream before.'

He looked back at her disbelievingly. 'What d'you mean? Of course I've told you. I've been having it for the past six months.'

She took her hands from his face and sat back slightly, looking serious now and even worried. 'Charlie,' she said, 'not only have you never told me about this dream, but as far as I recall I've never even told you about Brian Kay. And I'm certain I've never told you his wife's name.'

Charlie looked at her for some time before saying anything, searching her face for a clue to what was going on.

'You're kidding – right?'

She didn't answer, and he went on waiting for that curious expression of hers to resolve itself into a smile, a burst of laughter, a confession that she was teasing him.

Why didn't she just lean over and kiss him on the lips? That was the way this was supposed to end.

Wasn't it?

AUTHOR'S NOTE

While researching the feasibility of creating Charlie Monk, I spoke with several geneticists and was startled by the casual way they accepted my premise. 'We can't do it yet,' was the general tenor of their response, 'but go ahead and tell your story, and the details will catch up with you soon enough.'

On the 21 February 1999, the *Sunday Times*, in its 'Chronicle of the Future' series for the new millennium, predicted that the first human–chimp hybrid would be created in a laboratory in 2012. 'All you'd have to do,' says their expert, 'would be to insert a gene sequence taken from a human embryo into a chimp embryo, and then implant the combination into a surrogate chimp mother.'

Whether we'll have to wait till then only time will tell, but I can't help remembering some play or film I saw a few years ago. At the start there was a statement of time and place. For 'time' we were simply told, 'Sooner than you think.'

When it came to virtual reality, I found a similar response from the experts I questioned. Although, so far as I am aware, nobody is yet capable of doing everything I describe in the novel, progress is accelerating daily and there is no obstacle in principle to our getting there. In his book *The Fabric of Reality* the Oxford physicist David Deutsch says: 'We realists take the view that reality is out there: objective, physical and independent of what we believe about it. But we never experience that reality directly. Every last scrap of our external experience is of virtual reality. And every last scrap of our knowledge – including our knowledge of the non-physical worlds of logic, mathematics and philosophy, and of imagination, fiction, art and fantasy – is encoded in the form of programs for the rendering of those worlds on our brain's own virtual generator.'

Other books which I found useful in research were Jared Diamond's *The Third Chimpanzee*, *The Lives to Come* by Philip Kitcher, *The Language of the Genes* and *In the Blood* by Steve Jones, who was also good enough to talk to me on the phone a couple of times.

Particularly useful in terms of chimpanzee behaviour were *Chimpanzee Politics* by Frans de Waal, *Next of Kin* by Roger Fouts with Stephen Mills, and *Through Our Eyes Only?* by Marian Stamp Dawkins. I am also indebted to Mick Carman, head keeper of monkeys and apes at London zoo, for taking time to talk to me at length and introduce me around to some of his charges.

I am especially indebted to Professor Ian Craig of the Social, Genetic and Developmental Psychiatry Research Centre at the Institute of Psychiatry, London, for his generously given time and help.

Finally, a special thanks to my good friend Serge Lentz for his invaluable help with the scenes set in Russia.

D.A.